The Author

Catherine Mercer studie
and, with a degree in French, ha
and the Middle East.

The Languedoc, in the foothills of the Pyrenees, has been a major influence in her life. As a child she was fascinated by stories of the French resistance and soon recognised the strategic importance of the events which took place there, which have often been overlooked in English accounts of the period.

Her understanding of this area, its culture, history and people, makes her novel a work of unique interest.

REVENGE AND REGRET

A novel by

Catherine Mercer

Published by Camdale Press

Camdale Press
4 Thorndale Bristol BS8 2HU

Copyright © Catherine Mercer

ISBN 0-9539616-0-5

All rights reserved. No part may be reproduced, stored in a retrieval system or transmitted, in any form or by any means, electronic, mechanical, photocopying, recording or otherwise without the prior written permission of the publisher.
This book is sold subject to the condition that it shall not by way of trade or otherwise be lent, resold, hired out or otherwise circulated without the publisher's prior consent in any form of binding or cover other than that in which it is published.

A catalogue record for this book is availlable from the British Library.

Printed and bound by Antony Rowe Ltd
Bumper's Way Bristol Road
Chippenham SN14 6LH

PROLOGUE
AUGUST 1994 The village fête

"Mon Dieu! Here he is again. Robert Peyrou! We just can't get away from the bastard, can we?"

The young man's complexion was sour, pitted with angry eruptions of acne. His speech was slurred with drink, thick with the nasal twang and dragging vowels of southern France. But the bitterness was unmistakeable.

"I don't even know him," Robert muttered, taking Helen by the arm and edging away, annoyed that this uncouth lout was spoiling their evening.

"Oh là, là! He's running away. A coward! Too afraid to stay!" The young man was shouting angrily. He swayed and then, frowning and concentrating his efforts, he lunged towards his victim with his fists bunched, ready for a fight.

The village fête was in full swing. A ten piece band, a healthy young vocalist and hefty amplifiers, ensured that the words were lost to most of the crowd. But a couple of his friends, who had laughed at the taunts earlier in the evening, were growing uneasy and moved to restrain him.

"Allez!" He shrugged them away. "Clear off!"

Helen was smart, blond, petite. "Let's go home," she said, her hand tight on Robert's arm. She felt threatened, disturbed by the young man's hostility and she was shaken by a further outburst as he realised she was English.

"Bloody foreigners!" he cried. "The English! Treacherous bastards, they are. Sank our fucking fleet, didn't you!"

"That's enough!" The voice was crisp and clear, the voice of a man used to authority. The mayor of La Bastide did not want to see his boys disgrace themselves at the Ste Agathe fête. "Behave yourself, Daniel. And if you can't behave properly, go home."

To their surprise the young man moved off. Their protector turned to them. "He's always been a problem, that lad. I taught him in junior school. Difficult then and no better now."

Robert greeted him gratefully. "Robert Peyrou. And Helen. She's from England." They shook hands. "I don't know the chap. Never met him in my life. Why he should pick on me, how he knows my name, I've no idea."

The mayor of La Bastide said nothing but some momentary hesitation might have suggested a sudden spark of understanding. "Robert," he repeated. "Robert Peyrou."

"You may know my father. He was brought up here. Joseph. Joseph Peyrou. He's retired now and moved back here six months ago. We're just visiting." Robert felt that he was talking too much. "Would you join us for a drink?"

The music was loud, the rhythm insistent. Coloured lights hung in the trees, flashing garishly, red, green, purple, yellow. Beyond the village was the darkness of the empty hills but the square was noisy and crowded, bustling with holiday activity.

It was hot and humid. A storm was circling, threatening the village but bringing no relief as yet. They needed something cool and refreshing.

For a moment the mayor hesitated. Then he seemed to accept their proffered friendship. "How kind. I'd love a drink." He smiled.

They made their way through the crowd and found a space on the parapet of the old bridge. Below them the river ran swift and dark, the sound of the tumbling water drowned by the music, the microphones, the happy clatter of the crowd. Robert went to order their drinks. He was a slim young man, erect and neatly dressed. He returned happily concentrating on the glasses he was carrying, moving slowly and politely through the throng of people going to and fro around the dancing and Le Fast Food stalls. He glanced up to check where he was heading.

He did not see the young man returning. Daniel, flushed and determined, was coming back across the bridge, at a lurching, alcohol-fuelled pace. Cheerful villagers moved aside to let him through, still chatting happily together, though some turned to look again as he passed, disturbed by his rough, single-minded progress and surprised to see a young man with his shot gun at a village fete. Surprised but not alarmed, for Ste Agathe is hunting country: 'la chasse' is a man's occupation and even those out gathering mushrooms will wisely arm themselves for the possibility of a rabbit or a bird.

Daniel's friends, a few paces behind, were less serene. As he moved to raise his gun, they surged forward. Daniel fired, twice, as they grabbed his arm.

The music throbbed and the singer still belted out her song. Robert fell. Glasses of wine crashed to the ground and shattered. A red stain spread over his designer jeans and his smart holiday shirt.

CHAPTER 1
September 1939: War is declared

Joseph Peyrou was a peasant boy, kitted out in clothes that had served many others before they reached him and had little more wear left in them now. His short trousers were baggy and dusty. He had outgrown his pullover which was unravelling at the hem and had a yellow scorch mark on the front. His legs were spindly, his knees monstrously bony. But he had a mop of dark brown hair and big brown eyes that glowed brightly and as he ran up the steps of the Hotel du Commerce his happiness was infectious.

It was his birthday. The second of September. Not just any birthday either. This was his tenth birthday. And it was a Saturday. Market day in La Bastide. And he was going to help Monsieur Monnier in the bar of the hotel.

Then he remembered Madame Monnier. The last thing he wanted was to meet her. A nasty woman, with a spiteful tongue, who always shouted at him. Nor did he want to meet Auguste. That would be just as bad, because Auguste would go straight to his mother and tell her Joseph was there and she would come out and make trouble..

So for a moment he hesitated, hovering in the doorway. Once he reached the bar he would be safe, but Madame Monnier sometimes stood at the bottom of the stairs, by the counter where the keys to the rooms were hung, waiting to see who might book into the hotel, watching the customers leaving the bar.

Joseph would have liked to slip in unnoticed behind a noisy crowd of farmers. They usually went to the hotel on market day, once they had delivered their produce and finished their business. But he was on his own to-day.

He peered round the door. The corridor, dim and dusty, was empty. There was no sign of Madame Monnier or Auguste. He scurried along to the bar and went in.

The place was packed. Every table was crowded with men talking and arguing in deep, serious voices. Cigarettes hung from their lips and the tables were littered with ash and crumpled packets of Gitanes and Gaulloises.

Joseph coughed and blinked, as the smoke caught at his lungs and stung his eyes. Before he could recover, Monsieur Monnier spotted him. He was a big man, not old but already going bald. His head glistened and, with a line of dark hair circling his bald pate, he looked like a tonsured, well-fed monk. He smiled at the boy, his big brown eyes warm with affection.

"Here, lad, we need you. Take this bottle to the table by the window."

Monsieur Monnier nodded towards the table and Joseph took the bottle and squeezed between the customers, happy to be helping.

There was little interest in cards to-day. Only one group had picked up a pack and most of the cards they had dealt were still lying on the table, gathering more stains of wine and ash. Everyone was shouting and arguing.

The Spanish refugees were particularly excited. They were gesticulating wildly and banging on the table. After theSpanish Civil War they had come over the Pyrenees when they lost to Franco. They had settled in France, on the northern slopes of the mountains rather than live on under a fascist government. They hated the fascists, all of them: Franco, Mussolini, Hitler and his Nazis.

"We've seen the bloody bastards in action."

"They bombed Guernica."

"They kill civilians. There were no troops in Guernica."

Nobody was talking about crops or the price of cattle. It was all politics to-day. War. Joseph sighed.

"This is it, now!"

"No. It'll be just like last year. Poland won't be any different from Czechoslovakia. They'll all travel to Munich and make friends, just like they did last time."

"No! This is different!"

"They didn't release the men who finished their army service in March, did they?"

"And they've called up a lot of the rest already. My son's had to go. Had to report to Nimes."

"Everyone'll have to go. It'll be General Mobilisation any day now."

"It's not just the men, either. They've taken donkeys from some of the villages round here, you know."

"Oxen?" an anxious voice asked.

"No. They seem alright for the moment."

There was a lull in the conversation as the men digested the news.

"You going for a soldier, Joseph?" someone asked him as he cleared the dirty glasses from the table.

"Me? No! Not me!" He wanted to tell them it was his birthday but they were too full of their soldiers.

Joseph thought about it. He moved up to Monsieur Monnier and put his hand out, touched him to attract his attention.

"Monsieur! Monsieur!"

Louis Monnier turned to the boy.

"You won't go, will you?" he asked.

10

" 'fraid so, lad." He ruffled Joseph's hair.

The boy was bewildered. "But ... the hotel? Who'll look after things here?"

"This place'll be like all the others, lad. Those left will have to take care of it."

"But, who?" Joseph insisted.

"Well, Madame Monnier. And Auguste. And my mother."

There was little confidence in Louis's tone. Joseph could not imagine Madame Monnier washing the glasses and wiping the tables and Auguste never showed his face in the bar, even on the busiest days.

All the sunshine had left the boy's heart. They both knew that without Louis, with Madame Monnier and Auguste in charge, there would be no place for Joseph in the Hotel du Commerce.

"Make the most of it to-day, lad," the men advised him.

"Come on, you give us a hand properly this morning and I'll give you something to take home," promised Louis, towering over the boy, the picture of genial protection.

"Another few weeks and you won't hardly get the chance to come in to La Bastide, anyway," they told him. "You'll be doing a man's work in Luxat. They'll all be going as soldiers from Luxat too, you know."

They went back to their talk about the war. Someone claimed to have heard on the wireless that France had was going to send an ultimatum to Hitler.

"No! That was England! "

"No, France as well. Germany is to clear out of Poland or we're at war."

"What about Italy?"

"Italy?"

11

Nobody seemed to know about Italy. They turned to the Spanish refugees.

"Italy? What's Italy doing?"

"Non-belligerent."

"What's that mean?"

They shrugged.

Joseph was kept busy. He had never seen the cafe so full and he was scurrying round, collecting dirty glasses and wiping the wet tables, emptying ashtrays, collecting orders for wine and absinthe and brandy.

"Here, Joseph!" came the constant call.

"Get us another bottle. My throat's so dry I can't think."

"It doesn't seem to stop you talking, though."

They laughed, without malice, and the discussion went on.

"Joseph!" Monsieur Monnier was holding an empty bucket. "Go and get me some water lad."

Joseph hesitated. He usually kept well away from the yard, where the tap was. It was too near the kitchen and Madame Monnier might see him. But Monsieur Monnier wanted water and Joseph was eager to help. He squared his shoulders and took the bucket.

Madame Monnier did see him, of course. She was sitting at the table shelling beans and the kitchen door was open.

"What are you doing here?" she asked, with obvious irritation.

Auguste, slouched at the table beside them, bit into a peach and glared at Joseph.

"Clear off, you," he shouted. His mouth was full and the juice was beginning to run down his chin.

Joseph looked round for refuge but there was nowhere to hide and anyway, Monsieur Monnier was waiting for the water. He stayed where he was, watching the water flowing into the bucket, impatient for it to fill up quickly, so that he could escape back to the friendly bar.

Auguste threw away his peach stone, wiped his mouth with the back of his hand and lumbered to his feet. He was a slob, Auguste, and might not have been a threat to a lad his own age, but he was heavily built, four years older than Joseph and on his own home territory. He had played rugby for the Colts and with several seasons of training behind him he could move surprisingly fast when he came in to tackle.

Joseph hardly saw him rise from the table. His hand was still on the tap when Auguste's fist crashed onto his head. The mouth of the tap, sharp, unpolished brass, cut his temple as he fell. The pail clattered onto the paving stones, emptying a flood of water over the yard. The tap streamed unchecked and the blood from Joseph's wound added to the mess.

Joseph doubled over as Auguste gave him a vicious kick, which caught him on the thigh.

One of the men coming out of the cafe saw what was happening. "Hey! Leave the lad alone," he shouted. "Stop that!"

It brought Louis Monnier to the door. "Auguste! Lay off!"

Louis Monnier, an easy-going man who liked to be surrounded by happy, smiling friends, could not understand why anyone should enjoy inflicting pain and was always puzzled when he found his son bullying smaller children.

Auguste looked very like his father. He was tall, overweight, with a round face and a ruddy complexion. But whereas Louis could be kind, even protective, to those weaker than himself, Auguste liked to watch them suffer.

He looked up as his father came into the yard. Joseph twisted out of reach and started to stumble to his feet, blood pouring from the cut on his brow.

Madame Monnier left her beans, wiping her hands on an overall that was none too clean. "You give him what for, Auguste," she urged.

Sensing that there was only one safe spot in the yard, Joseph pressed against the innkeeper's homely paunch. Louis put his hand on Joseph's shoulder.

Madame Monnier lost her temper. A scrawny hen squawking in defence of her chicken, she yelled at her husband. "And whose side are you on, then?" she shouted. "Auguste's your son. You never think of your family, do you? Why should this boy come in here, as if he owned the place?"

It was an old complaint. Louis's affection for Joseph infuriated his wife but the boy had only been trying to help, fetching water for the bar, and Louis felt responsible for sending him into the yard.

"Marie ... " he pleaded.

"Don't you Marie me!" She turned her attention to Joseph. "As for you, there's the door! And don't you ever let me see your face in this inn, ever again. We don't want you here."

It was no good. Louis never risked a confrontation with his wife and he did not want to provoke her now by defending Joseph. His hand dropped. He let the boy go.

Knowing that she had won, Madame Monnier grabbed Joseph roughly by the shirt. Louis watched as she pushed him through the kitchen, past the reception desk, along the dark corridor. Opening wide the front door she shoved him down the steps. He fell onto the pavement, his clothes wet and bloody, his face streaked with tears.

"I never want to see you here again!" she shouted. Her face twisted with anger, her lips were thin, sneering. She tossed her head and, arms akimbo, watched him struggle to his feet. He was hurt and humiliated, his trousers were torn, his knees grazed.

He was trying not to cry but his breath came in choking gulps. That morning he had run lightly up the steps of the inn, now he was hobbling, bruised by Auguste's blows, bent with pain, bleeding from the cut on his brow.

Joseph was frightened, too, overwhelmed by the strength of an animosity for which he could see no cause. It was frightening to be set upon so unexpectedly and punched like that without knowing why. There was a deeper trouble still, a distress that he hesitated to admit: Monsieur Monnier, whom he admired and served with unquestioning devotion, had failed to protect him, abandoning him instead, with little protest, to the fury of his wife and son.

Joseph limped back through the market. Usually he enjoyed the activity and darted around inspecting the goods for sale, watching the animals, savouring the smell of the cheeses and sausages or trying to grab a piece of fruit but today he slunk past without a second glance, anxious only to find Maman and get back home to Luxat.

Maman had brought in a couple of hens that morning, with the eggs, and he knew that she would still be there, sitting among the straw and the poultry, chatting to friends and customers. He found her seated on a packing case, catching up on news of La Bastide, telling the tale of Luxat.

Around her the dusty ground was littered with wooden crates. Chickens, crammed tightly together in their boxes, peered out suspiciously, with small, mean eyes.

Rabbits lay fat and sleek, with their ears flat along their backs and their flanks heaving with fear. They sniffed, their noses twitched, poking above the rim of the box. Nearby a woman stood idly chatting, holding casually by their legs three chickens which dangled unprotesting, their necks hanging endlessly long, their heads grazing the path.

Joseph crept up. Maman saw him and without a word she opened her arms and took him on her knee and held him tight. The tears welled up and safe in her embrace he let them flow. She stoked his hair and whispered words of comfort. "There now," she said, hugging him close. "It's alright now."

Maman knew Joseph had been to the inn. "What happened?" she asked. "Did Auguste pick a fight with you?"

Joseph nodded, his tears gradually subsiding.

"Just keep away from him," advised Maman. "He's a lot bigger and older than you and he's a bully." She turned his face towards her and saw the cut on his brow and the dirt and the tears. "We'd better get that cleared up, hadn't we." She sent him over to the fountain to wash his face.

Cool and dark, the fountain lay in the shade of the big, misshapen plane trees that lined the road. Thick green moss covered the pillar down which the water flowed and the pool below the pillar was still and deep. The surface of the water sparkled with flecks of silver where light filtered through the trees.

Joseph sat on the rim of the pool and let the water trickle through his fingers. The palms of his hands were grazed and he held them up to inspect the cuts and the bits of grit. He took his time. The water was cool. The gentle, regular plashing was slow and soft and soothing. The tumult and the pain began to ease.

He knelt down on the dusty roadside and, taking a deep breath, plunged his face into the water and came up spluttering, shaking his head and scattering a cloud of raindrops. Gingerly he touched his brow. He was going to have a terrible bruise. It would probably go yellow and purple and green and red. Everyone would see it and would ask him what had happened, so that he would have to recall his humiliation and explain. He sniffed determined not to cry.

The cuts had started bleeding again. Maman gave him a rag to dip in the water of the fountain and then, as he sat patiently on a packing case beside her, she folded the rag into a pad, laid it gently over the cut and tied it in place with a big red napkin.

"There," she said, patting the bandage and offering encouragement. "Now you look like a real pirate." Joseph tried to smile. "But before you get up to any more piracy, you'd better wash those knees. And then we'll find Marcel and be off home."

Marcel arrived while Joseph was still by the fountain and Maman sent him over to help his brother. He swished the water, swirling up waves and currents and flicked some over Joseph, observing the necessary rituals of brotherhood, though he had other, more important matters on his mind this morning.

"You heard about the war?" he asked, his voice thrilling with excitement.

"Yep!"

"Don't suppose we'll see anything of it down here." Marcel sounded wistful.

"No." Joseph paused. "Monsieur Monnier says all the men will go as soldiers."

"Well, I'll go when I leave school," said Marcel, chin up, full of martial pride.

"Auguste Monnier's left school now. Do you think he'll go?" There was hope in Joseph's voice.

"No." Marcel reconsidered, for though he knew nothing of recruitment regulations, he suspected that fourteen might be too young. "Don't know." The prospect of soldiering was perhaps not really imminent.

"So who did that to you then?" Marcel asked. "Auguste?"

Joseph nodded. Tears welled in his big brown eyes.

"Oh come on, silly. He's just a bully. You know that." Marcel gave Joseph a brotherly shove. Maman called. They helped her gather her baskets and they all crowded onto the bus back to Luxat.

That evening, after supper, Maman trickled water onto the cloth which had stuck to Joseph's wound.

"Sit still! Don't fidget!"

He tried to obey but it did hurt when she pulled at the cloth.

"There. That's off. We'll let it have some air now."

"Why does Auguste Monnier always pick on me?" he asked.

Maman looked at him, considering, but she said nothing.

"And why is Madame Monnier always so nasty?"

"Well, she always has been a bit sharp-tongued has Marie Monnier," Maman said. "I dare say she's had her disappointments in life and they've left her sour and miserable."

"Yes, but why me?"

Maman knew that Joseph brooded. While Marcel was quick to anger, quick to react, quick to forgive and forget, Joseph was tenacious and hugged his hurt.

Mathilde Barthez was bringing up the boys on her own. They were foster children, taken in because she was poor and the Public Assistance paid her to look after them but taken also because she was lonely, a widow with no children of her own.

There were a lot of Public Assistance children in Luxat. Some families took them for the money and made them work hard and did not feed them properly. Mathilde Barthez loved her boys. She worried about them and wanted to protect them.

She knew that there was no man in her house. Her husband, Jean, had died at Verdun in the Great War. She knew that Joseph had turned to Louis Monnier as a father figure and Louis had encouraged him and welcomed his devotion but maman thought he exploited the boy. Joseph would work for hours, helping in the bar, while Auguste, the son of the house, did nothing. It was not fair, she felt, to encourage such devotion without returning it.

Now Joseph had been hurt. It would do no good, however, for the boy to dwell on the disappointment and brood.

"I shouldn't worry about it, if I were you," she advised. "I shouldn't worry about any of those Monniers. We've got each other, haven't we?"
Joseph nodded.

She gave him a big hug and he snuggled up happily. When his anxietiy seemed to have retreated, she kissed the top of his head and pushed him gently away.
"Come on now. Time for bed!"

Maman dug her hands into the two deep pockets in the mattress, to plump up the corn husk filling. Joseph jumped onto the step beside the bed and climbed in, pulling the linen sheet up to his chin as maman smoothed the eiderdown around him and drew the curtains, enclosing him in his snug, dark world. The mattress rustled dryly and tickled as he turned over.

But as he drifted into sleep he was still wondering why Madame Monnier and Auguste were always so nasty to him.

CHAPTER 2
September 1939 - February 1940: The phoney war

The rumours in the bar at La Bastide had proved true. France, like England, had sent an ultimatum to Hitler and was now at war with Germany. Mobilisation orders were posted on government buildings: at the Town Hall at La Bastide, at the Mairie at Festes. Even at Luxat, where they had neither Town Hall nor Mairie, the noticeappeared, by the door of the school which was the only public building they had.

When lessons ended Joseph and Marcel solemnly read the official proclamation. Joseph thought it looked very splendid, this crisp white paper headed with the crossed flags of the tricolor, coloured blue, white and red. The population of Luxat was informed that men were to join the forces fighting on land and sea and in the air.

"How are they going to fight in the air?" Joseph asked.

"In aeroplanes, stupid. Aeroplanes with guns." Marcel wheeled round, his arms spread, puttering vigorously in imitation of machine gunfire.

"It's not only men they want. It says that animals, cars and carts may be requisitioned for military purposes. What do they want animals for?"

"What do you think? To feed the soldiers. And horses for the cavalry. And to pull the guns. And donkeys to carry the baggage."

Marcel seemed to know a lot about war.

It was not a war which stirred great patriotic fervour in Luxat. In 1914 the young men had volunteered eagerly but they knew now what war was like. It was a hell in which too

21

many men were killed. But they were called up and they went.

One of the first to go was Raoul Vidal, the schoolteacher at Luxat. Simone, his fiancée, went with him to Montpellier to say good-bye. She was a bright, vivacious girl, with her hair cut in a smart modern bob, but she was overwhelmed by the crowds of soldiers and by the noise and smell of the big railway station. And she was afraid of what might happen to Raoul, fearful of the danger and loneliness and uncertainty ahead. They stood together, trying to find the words they needed, inhibited by the strength of their emotions and by the anonymous crowds around them.

Other men soon followed. When Louis Monnier left, Madame Monnier and Auguste stayed at home but Janine, Auguste's little sister, thin and wan, was at the station at La Bastide, clutching her grandmother's hand. Old Madame Monnier, Louis's mother, stood grim-faced, remembering how her husband had gone to fight, leaving from this same railway station. Her husband had been killed in battle and with a terrible sense of panic she saw her son now leaving for another war and prayed that he would return safely, that this war would not add to her sorrows.

The carriage doors finally slammed shut. The guard's whistle shrilled its imperious command and the engine puffed into steam. Old Madame Monnier and Janine, left on the platform, waved until the train was lost to sight. As they turned away the acrid smoke brought tears to their eyes and caught at their throats, leaving a bitter taste.

Too many fit young men had gone off to war but work on the land could not stop because they had gone. The old men, the women and children left behind had to keep things going.

Already the first snows had fallen on the grassy slopes of the Frau, high up in the Pyrenees. Bells echoed round the hills and through the villages as Tomas the shepherd brought his flock down into Luxat, his dog trotting beside him, ready to dart off and circle the the sheep with bossy concern. In his arms he carried a lamb born during the night, too weak yet to walk. Its mother bleated anxiously at his heels.

Joseph now took charge of the village sheep. Many families kept a few sheep, for their wool and for the meat and the milk of the ewes and they were happy for Joseph to look after them for the last few weeks of good weather and they paid him in hay that could be used to feed the animals during the winter.

He would get up early in the morning, feed the pigs and collect the eggs and then, gathering up his food for the day, he would set off for the pasture land, taking his dog with him. Picart, a mass of thick woolly fur from head to tail, looked like part of the flock but when Joseph saw one of the sheep straying to forbidden pasture, a quiet word would send Picart bounding after it, racing from side to side, to usher it back into the fold.

When the sun rose high in the sky they would sit in the shade of a tree and stop to eat. Joseph came from a poor home and his clothes were old and worn, but they were country people and ate well. He would have a hunk of bread, a chicken leg, a length of sausage, an apple or some nuts. And Picart would stretch out beside him, with one eye on the sheep but making sure that Joseph did not forget to give him his share, the last morsel of chicken or sausage or cheese and a good slice of bread.

As they roamed the countryside Joseph would gather milkcaps and hazel nuts and the strange funnel shaped chanterelle mushrooms. At dusk they would return to the village and Joseph would fill a bucket with sloppy swill and rouse the pig from its slumber and chastise it gently for its greedy, snuffling guzzling. "You'll only get fat and you know where that will lead you," he warned, drawing a finger solemly across his throat.

Joseph loved the animals and tended them with affection. He would pick up a big wooden rake and scratch the pig's back, enjoying the regular rhythm and the rough sensuousness of the wood grating on its bristly hide.

The rabbits would press twitching pink noses against the netting of their cages and Joseph would stroke their ears and talk to them gently. He loved to find one morning that the straw in their cage was heaving and he could see the little noses of frightened baby rabbits risking their first sniff of the outside world.

He would watch enthralled as eggs cracked and a little head emerged and a pretty chick. He would put the chicks gently in a basket lined with a soft duvet and carry them to the fireside and prepare for them a dish of bread and milk.

On a Sunday morning he would stand a wooden trough on a couple of old chairs out in the yard and as a special treat for the sheep he would fill the trough with a mixture of oats and salt. He would treat their ailments too, when he could. If one of the sheep suffered from scabies he would clean the wound, boil up a mixture of gorse and belladonna, then add salt and soot and apply this poultice to the sore.

Joseph loved the animals and gave them names and knew them individually. When the moment came to kill them Marcel or Maman would sharpen the knife while Joseph ran away to find work elsewhere. But when he smelt the stew cooking in the pot on the fire, he would sniff happily. They ate at a thick old-fashioned wooden table, with bowls hollowed into the surface. Maman would ladle out the stew and Joseph would eat with relish, rubbing his bread round the bowl to mop up the last drop of juice.

The animals were reared to be slaughtered and sold or eaten. One of the most important annual events came early in February when Achille Cambon arrived to kill the pig. He set up a trestle table near the pump, took his bag, opened it and, lifting out his tools, laid them carefully on the table. He tested a big, long knife, worn thin with age and use. Rubbing his thumb across the blade he frowned and cogitated, then picked up his sharpening steel and stroked the blade of the knife across the steel, increasing speed until it was flashing back and forth, the metal ringing with hypnotic rhythm.

Small children gathered round, holding their breath, watching, entranced. When his audience was fully prepared, Monsieur Cambon straightened up and tested the blade once more, slowly drawing it across the thick, leathery skin of his thumb. He nodded, satisfied, thrust his knife firmly into the pig's belly and with one clean cut killed the beast.

Blood poured from the severed arteries. Joseph turned to leave. But someone thrust a bowl into his hand and gestured for him to collect the blood. The pig had not been kept as a pet. It had not been killed for fun. They needed this pig to feed them through the cold, barren months before the Spring and they could not afford to be squeamish.

So they collected the blood. The women of the village were all there, with huge pots of water and they filled the manger with boiling water and scraped the skin, hung the carcass from the beams of the stable, carved up the joints and carefully cleaned and washed the intestines. For the rest of the week they would be boiling and salting ham, filling sausages and preparing their meat for the winter.

But that night, the night of the pig killing, they had a feast. They cooked the best joints of pork and made a stuffing of cabbage and potatoes and herbs and bread and chestnuts and they ate their fill.

They banked up the fire so that the warmth spread out to the furthest corner of the kitchen and when they had finished eating they put out the lamps and sat in the flickering light of the fire, their shadows dancing on the walls as they sang and told stories and the children listened, wide-eyed and sleepy as Maman told the story of Jules and the wolves.

"Jules was a young wood cutter who lived up in the forest above the village. One day he had come down to the village, with his little girl, for an evening's feasting. He was climbing back up the cliff that night, with the child strapped on his back and a few scraps of food in his pocket to take home to his wife, when he thought he heard footsteps behind him. He was being followed!"

Maman paused, for dramatic effect. The children stared at her, their hearts in their mouths, not sure if they wanted her to go on.

"Then he saw their eyes. It was a pack of wolves."

The boys on the bed giggled and punched each other, to show they were not afraid.

"Jules was just coming up to the steep part, near the top." They knew the spot. Little children could go no further, it was too steep for them after that. Small children would stop there and wait, sheltering in a natural hollow in the rocks. "You know the cave?" Maman asked. They nodded. It was their cave, their secret spot. "Jules stopped there. He slipped the sleeping child from his back and hid her there, covering the mouth of the cave with twigs and branches."

They knew a child would be safe there. It was never too cold in the cave, or too hot, and you could play inside or look out and watch the birds and wait and hope to see a rabbit or a deer or even a wild boar. Only they knew about the cave. Nobody else knew about it. Even Monsieur Vidal would not know about the cave. Even wolves would not find you in the cave.

Maman continued. "The wolves were close upon him, now. Panting, he set off up the steep part. To keep the wolves following him, he threw them scraps from the food in his pockets. The path is long and steep and he had very little food to give them. The poor man scrambled, panting, up the cliff." Maman paused once more.

"They found Jules, next morning. Or bits of him, what the wolves had left." She looked round at her audience, wide-eyed with hope and fear. "But the child was safe."

They sighed as Maman reached the end of her tale. It was a sad and bloody end, but heroic and satisfying.

On the stroke of midnight they sang their last song. The neighbours collected their chairs and ushered home their sleepy children, the dogs barking because they had been disturbed by this unexpected night-time activity.

Pig Day ended happily as it always did, with well fed villagers returning home, after hard work and pleasant company. Their men were away in the army, waiting at the front, but it was a funny sort of war, a 'drôle de guerre' as they said, with no battles. In the village, life went on as usual, as it always had and always would, no doubt. They said good night, happily unaware that this was the last Pig Day they would ever celebrate, the end of a tradition that would never be revived.

Winter was hard in Luxat. The houses sheltered at the end of a narrow valley, pressed against steep wooded cliffs. Snow and freezing cold kept the people huddled indoors. Maman slept in the kitchen, where the fire never really died but the boys' beds were in the room next door, where there was no fire. In the morning there would be ice on the narrow window panes and at night they would race across the cold space to reach the warmth of their beds. For their beds were warm.

An hour or so before bedtime they would fill a brass pan with glowing embers and ash from the fire and put it in the middle of the bed , protected by a wicker cage they called the 'monk', which held the warming pan and lifted the bedding to prevent it from scorching. So Marcel and Joseph could snuggle down, pull up the covers and draw the curtains round the bed, well protected from the cold.

This year, as winter moved into spring Luxat woke slowly from its long hibernation, with no sense of impending change. In the early months of 1940 only the absence of its men seemed to have disturbed the regular rhythm of the seasons.

Luxat was isolated. Buses went daily in to La Bastide. Every year Tomas the shepherd came in early summer to take the sheep up into the mountains and he would return in the autumn to bring them home. He would pass on news of the hills and valleys round about. He told them tales of weddings and funerals, of unexpected deaths and mraculous conceptions. Occasionally a young lad from a village nearby would cycle in to see a girl he had met at a local fête or wedding but pedlars rarely called at Luxat and no travellers passed through the village.

Who could have guessed then that this isolation was about to end? The first of many strangers was about to come to the village and events in the world outside would transform their lives and change, irrevocably, their hidden home.

CHAPTER 3
March 1940 - June 1940: The defeat of France

So far the war had barely touched Luxat. In Paris one might have expected it to have had more impact but even in Paris they were reassured by the long, calm months of a winter spent preparing for battle rather than fighting. There was so little military activity that soldiers were allowed home on leave. In March, Jacques Fournier joined his wife, Gabrielle, in Paris.

Gabrielle Fournier, née Peyrou, had been brought up in the south of France, in the foothills of the Pyrenees, on an isolated farm near La Bastide. It was a period of her life which she preferred to forget. She now lived much more comfortably in Paris, in an elegant apartment in the 16e arrondissement where her life had changed so much since those early days that she now felt justified in complaining because her children's nanny had left to work in a factory.

She was exasperated one evening when her little girl wandered snivelling into the dining room while she and her husband were at dinner, wailing that she could not sleep.

"Well, I'm sure it won't help to wander round like this. Go back to bed," Gabrielle told her sharply.

A few days later she was woken by shrill voices as the children played noisy games far too early in the morning. She did not want to spend her time looking after the children and for a moment she wondered whether life might be easier with her family in the south, where Monique, her brother's wife, might be happy to look after the children.

"A few weeks on the farm would do them good," she declared, though she was thinking of herself more than of them.

Her husband had seen the farm. Once. Shortly after they married. He considered their spacious Paris apartment, the drawing room, where intricately carved chairs and expensively upholstered sofas were arranged on a fine Nain carpet, pale blue and beige, and he contrasted this with that farm, a hovel, where he had been sent to wade through inches of oily mud to fetch water from a pump. He shuddered as he remembered the nauseous smell of cabbage soup and cows and the overpowering stench of the heap of dung by the entrance.

"It is perhaps rather primitive," he reminded her.

Gabrielle pouted. Her lips formed a charming, rose-tinted moue. The elegant line of her eyebrows rose in gentle protest, but she reflected more carefully.

She remembered escaping from the farm to go and work in La Bastide, a town with shops, with a market and factories, and a railway station with trains to Lavelanet, Mirepoix and Bram. She had been so excited, she had met so many people and enjoyed so many new experiences. Then she had got pregnant and had returned to the farm, to weeks of claustrophobia as she waited for the baby to be born, made all the more unbearable because she now knew of a world beyond the farm which she could no longer reach. Gabrielle reconsidered. Perhaps she was not quite so keen to go back to that farm.

There was after all no real reason to leave Paris. It was not as if they were in any possible danger, as they might be if they were near the frontier. In any case they had the defences of the Maginot line to keep out enemy troops and they knew that France had the best army in the world.

Jacques Fournier, though, was not impressed by the military leaders and mocked General Gamelin mercilessly.

"He's far too old. Quite gaga. They call him Gagaman." He laughed, with patronising disdain. It did not occur to him that such weak leadership might impair the performance of the French troops. "If the French army has to fight, they'll beat the Germans easily," he confidently assured Gabrielle. "Paris itself will be in no danger. You and the children will be safe here."

So when Jacques returned to the front Gabrielle reflected that life in Paris was more comfortable than anything the farm could offer. She stayed where she was.

Important events which were to affect the outcome of the war did not impinge on Gabrielle and her neighbours. They were not concerned when things went badly wrong in Norway and were barely aware that Churchill had replaced Chamberlain in Great Britain.

Then, at daybreak on Friday 10th May, Holland and Belgium were invaded.

In her flat in Paris, Gabrielle was woken by the shrill wail of an air-raid siren. She stumbled from her bed and snatched up a silk peignoir, which she was still tying at the waist as she felt her way round the furniture in the drawing room and fumbled with the catch on the shutter. She could hear the rattle of guns and her hand was shaking.

Philippe, only three years old, was upset by the commotion. He had woken and begun to whimper. Gabrielle picked him up and took him to the window. Jacqueline, his sister, slipped from her bed to join them.

All round the square shutters and windows were open and sleepy heads peered up into the sky, trying to identify the danger, though all they could see were the birds which had flown up from the trees and were circling nervously above the square.

Then, high up in the sky, they saw a tiny toy plane. For a moment everything was still. There was no movement. There seemed to be no sound. They stood at their windows watching, their eyes following this tiny, deadly speck as it crossed the sky and turned and wheeled, master of all that space.

A German aeroplane had flown, unchecked, across the frontier, across the north of France. It had reached Paris and was flying now over the city. Why had it not been stopped? What was it doing here? Had it come to drop bombs? How many more planes would come? It was frightening.

A man on the sixth floor opposite raised his fist and shouted, "Down with the Boche!" They turned towards him, grateful for this gesture of defiance, and laughed and cheered.

Their confidence had been shaken, though. There was no French plane up there fighting off this intruder. Gabrielle was once more aware of the guns hammering but could those guns reach that speck in the sky?

She shivered, felt the chill of the early morning air, clutched her peignoir more closely to her and closed the window.

'This is it,' she thought. 'This is war.'
She tried to remember what she had heard about the last war. Paris had been threatened then, but the Germans had been turned back. They would be safe in Paris, surely, Jacques had told her there would be no danger for them in Paris. But what about Jacques himself, at the front? War seemed suddenly real and frightening.

33

In the days which followed, Gabrielle tried to carry on as usual. She went shopping and met her friends for tea. She even spent one afternoon at the races, at Auteuil.

She worried, though, when she heard that German troops had crossed into France.

Refugees began to arrive. When Gabrielle and her friends met for tea, they would see big, luxurious limousines which came from Belgium. Poorer people, who had come by train and bus, were camping at the Gare du Nord.

The Dutch surrendered. The King of the Belgians capitulated without letting his allies know.

The news was relentlessly bad. Paris no longer seemed so safe. The refugees were leaving the city, moving south.

Early morning sirens became part of daily life. When Gabrielle heard the siren she no longer bothered to get up and open the shutters and the children would sleep on undisturbed. The concierge's husband would go out and, shielding his eyes with his hands, would peer up into the sky, searching for planes. If there were none to see he would shrug his shoulders and call to people round the square,

"Don't worry! They aren't coming here to-day."
They all knew, though, that the planes would be back.

It was on the first Sunday in June, in the Tuileries gardens, that Gabrielle heard about the bombing. German planes had dropped leaflets, warning that they were going to bomb Paris the next day. Jacqueline had found one and showed it to her mother.

That night Gabrielle slept fitfully, worrying whether they should stay in Paris or go south, away from danger. When morning came it was a gloriously clear and sunny day. She was glad to get up and move about the house, instead of lying in bed, awake and anxious.

There was no alarm that morning. They waited.

Still not sure what she intended to do, Gabrielle began to go through her jewellery. She cleaned some of her favourite pieces and wrapped them in tissue paper. She found little boxes in which to pack them.

They were finishing luncheon when the siren sounded. Would the Germans drop bombs on the city? They could hear the roar of planes, the angry puttering of guns. This time they could hear, too, bombs thudding and exploding. They were frightened. Gabrielle thought the windows might shatter and closed the shutters. They cowered, stifling, in the airless room.

Gabrielle was tired and frightened. She did not want any more morning raids and bombs and fear. However mean and miserable that farm near La Bastide, it suddenly seemed blessedly safe and free of bombs.

"I don't have to stay here," she declared.

She did not hesitate. She gathered up her jewellery and swept through the apartment, snatching up her favourite coats and dresses, tossing them into suitcases, flinging in hats and shoes and handbags. Money! She dashed to the bank and waited, fretting impatiently, in a long queue of customers urgently withdrawing cash.

The next morning she loaded the car, a smart green six horse power Renault Juvaquatre.

"You're lucky it's not a great big, thirsty thing," the concierge's husband told her, as he stowed away a couple of petrol containers.

The sleekest car on earth could not have moved fast that day. The roads were choked with traffic. Cars and buses, cycles and wheelbarrows, carts and tractors, vehicles of every sort clogged the highways. When they could move they managed little more than a walking pace and for minutes, sometimes for an hour at a time, they simply waited, not moving at all. Occasionally they met soldiers driving north, columns of motorcycles, lines of trucks carrying troops who were going to fight the German invaders. Once they were overtaken by a big official limousine, taking an important government minister away from danger.

The children, hot and tired and crammed together with suitcases and boxes on the back seat of the car, frightened and fractious, whined and quarrelled all the way, irritating Gabrielle immeasurably. By evening they had travelled just over thirty miles. They needed food and sleep. There were no rooms to be had and even the benches in the square were full of sleeping refugees. They washed that night at a public fountain and slept, fitfully, in the car.

In the morning Gabrielle gave Jacqueline a fistful of money and told her to join the queue for bread. Then, outside the Town Hall, she saw a picture, a photograph of a child who was lost. A boy with sad eyes and tight lips, trying hard not to cry, had been discovered on his own, separated from his family. Gabrielle could understand only too easily that on a trek like this a family might lose sight of one of their children. Admitting wryly to herself that the journey would be so much easier if she were on her own, she shrugged her shoulders, overcame her unmaternal impulse, collected Philippe and joined Jacqueline in the dreadful queue.

Traffic lessened as they moved further south. Stoppages grew less frequent. But there was still a constant stream of vehicles. They avoided the mountains of the Dordogne and took the coastal route round Bordeaux and Toulouse.

After a week of travelling they reached La Bastide. Doubtful of their reception at the farm, Gabrielle glanced at the Hotel du Commerce, wondering whether to break the journey and spend the night there, but the past flooded back, full of conflicting emotions, and she knew that she could not stop at the hotel in La Bastide.

She drove on, along the narrow, winding road to Festes. Past the village they carried on, taking the main road towards Quillan, then turned up into the hills, to the farm, to Laurac.

The rough track was not made for cars and they bumped and jolted uncomfortably, aware of the dogs ahead barking ferociously to warn of their approach. As they turned into the farm the dogs barked and the chickens, geese and turkeys scattered wildly, honking and hooting and snorting. In the car Jacqueline and Philippe sat rigid with fear, staring out with wide eyes, waiting for the animals to attack. At the door of the stable a woman stood, alerted by the clamour.

Gabrielle got out of the car. In Paris she had seemed casually dressed. In Bordeaux she had been ashamed of her scruffy, dirty clothes. Here, faced with Monique's drab overall and unkempt hair, she felt obtrusively elegant. Quickly she removed her hat and shook out her hair and was embarrassed to notice the varnish on her nails, even though it was chipped.

"Oh my God! What do you want?" Monique did not like her sister-in-law. And life was hard enough, trying to manage on the farm while her hasband Paul was away with the army. She really did not need to have this idle parasite and her two children added to her burdens.

Gabrielle noted the lack of enthusiasm and stepped forward with her warmest greeting. "Monique! How lovely to see you. You remember me, surely. Gabrielle. I came down with Jacques shortly after we were married."

"Humph!"

Gabrielle accepted the greeting. "And this is Jacqueline. Come on Jacqui, come and meet your aunt."

From round the corner came a boy, carrying a pail of pig swill.

"This must be Marius!"

Marius stared at the elegant apparition, at the car, at the two children dressed like dolls at a fair.

"I do hope we're not disturbing you," Gabrielle continued, with desperation. "Only Paris was ... Paris was ..." Faced with stolid, unspoken hostility, Gabrielle, exhausted by the journey, could feel tears threatening to overflow, but recognising that tears would not impress Monique, she regained her control. "Paris has been very difficult. We wondered if you might be able to find somewhere for us to stay." Delicately, Gabrielle fingered the leather handbag which held her papers and her purse. It was a smart, burgundy coloured bag and seemed to revive her sister in law.

"You'd better come in," Monique said.

Gabrielle went into the dark, cramped house, nearly tripping on the uneven tiles of the floor. The children were reluctant to follow and stood silently by the door, tired and grubby, close to tears, holding hands to comfort each other.

Monique's mother, crouched by the hearth preparing the evening meal, looked up at the visitors. "It's you, is it," she said by way of greeting.

Gabrielle looked round for somewhere to sit and drew out a bench that was tucked under the table.

"Have you heard from Paul?" she asked. Paul was her brother, Monique's husband.

The old woman sniffed. Monique wiped her hands on her overall and stared at Gabrielle.

"We're hardly likely to hear from him are we? He's not exactly a scholar, is Paul, writing letters every day. Anyway, everything's a mess right now. No letters would get through, would they."

Gabrielle murmured that news from Jacques had also been sparse recently.

"I suppose he's in the north, somewhere?"

Monique was contemptuous. "Well, he would be, wouldn't he? That's where the fighting is."

There was no point in trying to exchange civilities.

"Do you think we could stay here for a while?" Gabrielle asked.

To her surprise they responded more pleasantly to this practical question. They found her a bed and brought mattresses for the children. It was even worse than she had expected but at least she was safe from the bombs and the German soldiers.

A peasant's life is hard. Since she married, Gabrielle had not been used to long hours of physical labour. Here, though she had only one room, she had to clean it herself, with the two children constantly underfoot. She had to wash their clothes herself, in the cold water of the stream, kneeling on the muddy bank. She had to help prepare the meals: cabbage soups and sausage and beans and potatoes, endlessly stodgy and boring.

The children loved it. Jacqueline followed Marius with devotion, gathering eggs, straining to bring water from the stream, feeding the livestock, undertaking with joy the tasks that fall to a peasant's child. Philippe was happy to totter in their wake.

Gabrielle was pleased that she did not have to bother about the children.

She would get away whenever she could. There was no petrol for the car but she would go for long walks, or take the bus to Festes or on to La Bastide or beyond. The others were happy for Gabrielle to wander. They did not want her with them and when she went out she usually came back with a welcome treat, a rabbit, or some sausage or some cheese.

Gabrielle paid monstrous prices for the treats she brought back to the farm.

"Someone's doing well out of this war," she said sharply as she passed over a fistful of money for a tray of peaches at the market at Foix.

"Well, it's not me," came the swift reply. "Smart people from Paris have been through my orchards and taken everything they could lay their hands on. And not one centime have they paid me, the thieving swine. Refugees! I'd let them all rot!"

There were refugees everywhere. Gabrielle recognised that she was lucky to be at the farm at Laurac. In Foix whole families were sleeping on the streets and she heard that it was worse in Toulouse.

She picked up news on her excursions. She would listen to the gossip on the bus and the train and she would buy a newspaper to find out how the war was going. That was how she knew when the Germans occupied Paris in the middle of June and learnt that they were sweeping on south, beyond Lyons, towards Bordeaux and Grenoble.

Monique heard from Paul at last. A grey postcard arrived, printed in German script, its message short and impersonal: 'I am a prisoner in Germany. I am well.' It gave his address.

"Not much, is it?" said Monique, turning the card this way and that, as if she might discover something more, something more personal. "It's been so long, waiting for news. I wanted a letter. Real news. I want to know where he is, what it's like. Is he warm enough? Does he get enough food? Does he have any friends with him?"

She wanted, too, a personal message, some word of love. She wanted to feel some contact with her husband beyond this dry official card.

"He's alive, isn't he?" said her mother. "That's the main thing."

Monique nodded. She even smiled and hugged Marius who stood beside her, anxious for news of his father.

"Is he coming back?" the boy asked.

"Not yet. But he's all right."

They wanted him home. They needed him working with them on the farm but, for the moment, they were simply glad that he was safe.

"Marshal Pétain says we should make peace," Gabrielle told them.

"So we should," they agreed.

"Then our Paul can come back home."

Without actually saying so Monique seemed to imply that they would be glad to get rid of Gabrielle, too, however welcome her treats might be.

When Pétain signed an armistice with Hitler on 22nd June Gabrielle told them the news. "The German army will still occupy Paris, though, and the north."

"What about Marshal Pétain then?" asked Monique, interested for once in the news from Gabrielle's paper.

"It says here that the French government won't go back to Paris. They'll stay in Vichy. They'll control the south of France but not the north."

"And what about the prisoners?" Monique asked.

"They'll have to stay in prison camps, in Germany," Gabrielle told her.

Monique frowned. "That's not fair!" she declared and she turned angrily from them, her hopes dashed. She had thought the prisoners would come home once the armistice was signed.

Gabrielle did not argue. She wanted the war over, however the end came. When she heard that Jacques was back in Paris, she was relieved. She was ready to go back to Paris and he was looking forward to seeing his family again.

There was one thing, though, that Gabrielle wanted to do while she was here in Laurac without her husband. She wanted to see her son.

She had been fourteen years old when, bursting with excitement, she had left school and gone to work in La Bastide. She had been young and naive and within a year she was expecting a baby, had lost her job and had to return to the farm at Laurac.

Once the baby was born she had to find another job. She might have gone to Biarritz or one of the spa towns, to work as a wet nurse, feeding someone else's baby, that was how girls usually earned money when they had a baby. But Gabrielle set her sights on something better than that. She packed a cardboard suitcase and took the train to Paris. She left the baby, a boy named Joseph, at Laurac with her mother. Old Madame Peyrou did her best to look after him, but her health had been failing for some time and she died when the child was scarcely more than a year old.

At their mother's funeral, her brother Paul announced that he would be getting married.

"And I can't look after Joseph as well as everything else," Monique told them. "In any case he should be with his mother. Gabrielle should look after him. It's not natural, to abandon a child like that."

"And how do you expect me to look after him?" Gabrielle asked. "I work in a hotel. He can't live with me there."

"Well then, it will have to be the Public Assistance," Monique declared. But she liked the child and felt that it was not right. "Poor little mite," she added, still hoping that Gabrielle might relent.

In Paris Gabrielle prospered. She had found work in a grand hotel and one reason why she could not cope with Joseph was that she was being courted by a clever, rather shy man, some ten years older than herself, who was doing well in his work at one of the ministries and knew that it was time to find a wife and start a family.

When Gabrielle married Jacques she meant to tell him about Joseph but it was not easy to find the right moment. He was very correct, very conscious of his position in society. As the years went by she felt it would do more harm than good to tell him about the child she had almost managed to forget.

Coming back to Laurac now, though, she remembered Joseph and hoped he was being well cared for.

"He's at Luxat," Monique told her when she asked. "With a widow who looks after him well." There was an edge to her tone. "I'm surprised you don't want to see him. Your own child."

Gabrielle decided that perhaps she ought to show some interest. It might help soften Monique's hostility. Jacques was not there and need never know about the visit. Besides she did wonder what the boy was like. It might be only selfish curiosity but she would like to see him. Once, at least.

So she wrote to Mathilde Barthez and arranged to go to Luxat. She borrowed a bike. She did not want to go on the bus, with the other passengers wondering where she was going and why. So she jolted along the rutted track that led down to the main road and sped, free-wheeling, down to the valley and on, past Festes with its medieval castle, along the final spur of green valley, to Luxat, nestling beneath wooded cliffs.

Mathilde was expecting her, sitting on the rough wooden bench beside the door, sorting through their winter clothes, patching and darning. Joseph was weeding.

Gabrielle arrived, tanned and fit, glowing with health and with the exertion of bicycling. Her eyes shone, her lips were cherry red. Her hair was piled high at the front and fell to her shoulders in rippling waves.

Like Marius before him, Joseph gazed in wonder. He propped his hoe against the wall and marvelled at such a rare and beautiful creature.

Maman's response was less enthusiastic. She had no time for Gabrielle, a woman who had abandoned her child.

'What a painted fashion plate!' she thought contemptuously. Perhaps, as she watched Joseph succumb to his mother's charm, she even felt a twinge of jealousy.

Her voice was gruff as she told him to fetch a chair for the lady. He ran inside and brought a chair and placed it carefully next to Maman's bench, gently rocking it, to test that it was standing firm and steady. He watched with admiration as the lady gracefully took the proffered seat, her legs folded elegantly to one side. It was a hot day and, with unexpected thoughtfulness, Joseph ran back into the house and brought out an earthenware pitcher, which he filled at the pump, offering, wordlessly, a beaker of cool water. A ring on her finger caught the light and sparkled as she took the drink from him.

Maman told the lady how well Joseph was doing at school but she did not chatter away as she did when one of the nieghbourscame over and sat beside her.

Joseph examined her bicycle. "My friend Lucien has a bicycle," he explained. "His father gave it to him before he went as a soldier." Joseph paused. He did not want to boast. But he had to tell her. "I can ride a bicycle," he said proudly.

"I borrowed this one to come here," she told him.

"Where do you live?" he asked.

"In Paris. But I'm staying near here at the moment, at a farm near Festes." She had not considered her words.

Joseph's eyes shone. "I come from there," he exclaimed. "From Festes."

Maman sniffed, wiped her hands on her apron and stared at the lady with what Joseph thought was a very unfriendly look, apparently not sharing his delight at this news.

The lady stood up. "I'd better be going," she said. "It's a long way back. And uphill, too." She laughed, nervously. She was embarrassed. Joseph was delightful, she thought, but his life now was here in Luxat. She might have told him that she was his mother but he could not possibly join her in Paris. It was better not to tell him.

Perhaps she did feel slightly guilty, though. As she left, she gave Maman some money. "For the boy," she murmured. "You might use some of it to buy a bicycle." Joseph's eyes were wide with excitement. Maman took the money but she showed no gratitude.

Joseph was puzzled. He did not know what to make of the strange lady. Perhaps he would see her again one day?

He thought about her after she had gone, telling everyone how wonderful she was.

It was Marcel who finally tired of his innocent prattling. "She's your mother," he told Joseph. "Must be. Why else would she come out to Luxat? She came to see you. Wanted to know what you'd turned out like, I expect. What she must have thought when she met you, God knows."

Joseph knew that Maman had fostered him, but to him she was simply Maman, his mother. He had admired the lady who visited them but she did not feel like his mother.

"Is she my mother?" he asked Maman.

Mathilde had no sympathy for Gabrielle. She had had a child herself, once, a boy, Claude, who had died while still a baby. She had not forgotten him and still grieved for him. She could not imagine how any mother could abandon her child and go away and leave him alone in the world and then turn up with great drama, dressed like a picture from a fashion magazine, condescending to speak to the boy for an hour or so before disappearing again. She would have liked to tell Joseph that his mother was a selfish bitch, not worth a minute's thought, but she knew that children needed to think well of their parents, so she answered him as kindly as she could.

"Well, yes. When you were born she was only a young girl and she had no money and had to get a job and she couldn't take you with her. So she left you with her mother. But her mother died. So they brought you here, to join Marcel and me, because we needed you and wanted you."

Joseph found it hard to understand. The lady was not poor. He had never seen such a vision of sophisticated elegance, an elegance far beyond the means of anyone in Luxat or La Bastide or Festes. He tried to explain this to Maman.

"She's not poor now, my love, but she was poor when you were born. And anyway, if she is rich now, it's not really her money. She's married a rich man. It's his money really."

Joseph gathered that this rich husband would not be spending his money on a young boy from Luxat. He would have liked to know more about this woman who was his mother. He wondered why she had come to see him and whether one day, she would want him to go and live with her in Paris. It seemed unlikely. The other children on Public Assistance, and there were plenty of them in Luxat, did not go off to Paris. Most of them had no idea who their mothers were, of course. He liked the idea that he had a mother and that she was rich and glamorous and lived in Paris but he decided that he was better off in Luxat with Maman and Marcel.

He wondered, though, if perhaps one day another stranger would come to the village. As he was going to bed one night, he asked Maman. "If that lady was my mother perhaps one day a gentleman will come. My father."

He was not sure, but he thought he would like that. But Maman told him to go to sleep.

CHAPTER 4
July 1940 - February 1941: Vichy France

Everywhere you looked there were pictures of Marshal Pétain, the man who had brought the war to an end. By working with the Germans, by what his Prime Minister, Laval, called 'collaborating' with them, he had saved the French government and even if the north of France was still occupied, the south was free.

Pétain, the hero who had rescued France from the horrors of Verdun in 1917, the military leader who had ended the mutiny of French soldiers and brought peace to his country then, had returned now to take charge once more. From the posters his benign features gazed down upon his flock.

It was foolish to doubt what the great man decided because, as the caption asked, "Do you know more than him about to-day's problems?"

Marcel was one of the few who was not impressed. Fourteen years old, he had just left school and started working at the saw mills in La Bastide. Earning money and paying for his keep he was proud of his new status and only too ready to question authority. He glanced round. The lunch hour was coming to an end. Nobody was watching. He had a red crayon.

"Yes," he wrote across the bottom of the poster. The silly old fool was almost bald. And far too carefully groomed, with a crisp white collar, a dark suit, a carefully knotted tie. Marcel coloured his neatly trimmed moustache a good, bright red. He was considering whether to give him red eyebrows or a pair of spectacles when he was interrupted.

"Hey! You!"

It was Auguste Monnier, the bully from the Hotel du Commerce. Marcel turned, all innocence.

"Me?"

"Yes, you, with the red crayon."

Marcel looked down and saw that the wax had stained his hand. "So what?"

"You could get into trouble for doing that," Auguste told him, smugly.

Marcel began to wonder if improving posters was, perhaps, not as clever as it had seemed.

"You want a fight then?" he growled, clenching his fists and glaring at Auguste.

Fortunately the foreman from the factory had finished his lunch and was on his way back to work when he spotted them. No good having one of his boys fighting in town during the lunch hour.

"Marcel! You should be at work by now. On your way!" he called.

Auguste disappeared. Marcel set off, walking self-consciously two steps in front of authority. As they passed through the gate Monsieur Bouladou had a word with him.

"Take care, lad. The war may be over but this isn't the time to go looking for trouble."

Marcel did not argue.

That evening, though, he tried to question Mathilde. "Do you like Marshal Pétain, Maman?" he asked.

"Well, I don't know," she said. "They used to call him the army doctor, you know, because he was good to ordinary soldiers. After they'd had a couple of months at Verdun, he'd send them home on leave. And said they shouldn't have to go back there afterwards.

"He saw what was really happening at the front. He didn't live like a lord, like the other generals did, in some nice chateau, miles from where the fighting was. When he was at Verdun, he was up near the front and knew how the men were suffering and he did what he could for them. In the end he stopped all that terrible killing.

"And he's brought us peace now. And he's said he'll try to get our prisoners back home. We shall have to wait and see. There's nothing we can do about it, anyway."

"He's the father of the nation," Joseph told them, reciting a phrase he had heard.

Marcel rolled his eyes in despair. "The grandfather, more like."

Joseph smiled, assimilating a new and pleasing concept. Grandfathers had not, so far, figured in his picture of happy families. Marcel groaned. "Sometimes, you are so stupid ...!"

Marcel thought about Monsieur Bouladou. Somehow he felt that the foreman had not been angry when he had seen he had seen him scribbling on the poster, but had simply been trying to help him keep out of trouble. "You know, I don't think Monsieur Bouladou likes Marshal Pétain," he declared.

"Did he say that?" Joseph asked, awed and slightly frightened that anyone should judge the marshal and that a man as important as Monsieur Bouladou should show any lack of respect.

"Well, not exactly," Marcel admitted, with a gallic pout and a shrug of his shoulders that was already proving attractive to the local girls.

"If Monsieur Bouladou kept his mouth shut, there's no call for you to tell everyone what he thinks," warned Maman.

Marcel shuffled his feet and frowned.

"Just keep quiet, Marcel, and keep out of trouble," she told him.

Which was just about what Monsieur Bouladou had said.

Once the armistice was signed the war was over. Great Britain had not yet made peace but it was obvious that they could not hold out much longer.

The soldiers were coming back home. Jacques Fournier, already back in Paris, was impatient for his family to join him and Gabrielle, sweltering in the cramped farmhouse, in temperatures that rose every day to 35 degrees, was eager to return and increasingly frustrated because a demarcation line had been set up, separating Vichy France from the German-occupied north, and she could not get the pass that was needed for her and the children to cross the line.

Her family, hoping daily for news that their man was on his way home, shared her irritation.

"We need Paul here, not a painted clotheshorse with two small children," Monique's mother grumbled.

"At least the children are willing to help," Monique sniggered. "Well, the girl is. Boy's still a bit young, yet."

Fortunately, Monsieur Fournier was rich and important so it was not long before he was able to get a pass and bring his family back home. Jacqueline, torn from a blissful life with ducks and geese and fluffy, yellow chickens, was devastated. She missed Marius, too, and he missed his faithful follower.

Gabrielle's brother, Paul, was still in prison in Germany. The two women left behind to run the farm, found themselves overwhelmed with work but happier to make their way without the visitors from Paris.

The summer that year was blazingly hot. Day after day the temperature rose to 35 degrees and beyond and they welcomed the evening storms that sometimes relieved the heat.

Joseph, working in the fields, was scorched The sweat poured off him and was dried by the sun so that his skin was dry and salty, tanned to a leathery brown.

He was up before dawn to scythe the hay in the meadows and worked until the light failed, when his last task was to bundle into bales the swathes cut the previous day. And if a storm was threatening he had to rescue that day's cutting and load it all onto a wooden sledge and harness one of the cows to bring the hay back to the store above the stable.

When June ended and the hay was in, there were the oats to harvest and the wheat, cutting close to the ground with his sickle, chasing the nesting quail from their shelter among the stalks. And there was still the vegetable garden to tend, hoeing along the neat rows, gathering the herbs and the leeks and onions, lifting the potatoes and carrots, picking the beans and the peas, as they ripened. And there were peaches and apples to gather from the orchard, nuts from the hedgerows.

At night Joseph would drop into exhausted sleep and not stir until he had to set out for work next day. But on Saturday he would go into market with Maman. He no longer went anywhere near the inn, but stayed with Maman, helping her sell their produce for unbelievable prices.

"Look at that!" Maman said, patting her pocket with satisfaction. "Everything sold in a flash before we've even had a chance to settle down and say hello to our friends. And top prices, too. Though there's no need for anyone to know that."

Joseph grinned back at her, heaved a sigh and blew out his cheeks, impressed by this good fortune.

The soldiers were beginning to return to La Bastide. Monsieur Monnier was one of the first to come back. His wife and Auguste, even his mother, had done their best while he was away, but trade had been slack. The young men had been in the army, the old men were overwhelmed with work and most of the customers in the bar had been refugees, who stayed a long time but did not spend much money. When Louis turned up, though, everyone crowded in to greet him.

The bald patch on the top of his head was bigger, the encircling tonsure was thinner and greyer. He had lost weight too. His trousers no longer dipped low at the front to make room for the overhanging paunch, his shirt buttons no longer strained to contain loose flesh. The loss of weight had done him good. He was fitter now. He moved more quickly and decisively.

Joseph soon knew that he was back. He saw him chatting with a couple of customers who were sitting at a table on the pavement outside the Hotel du Commerce. Joseph had avoided the hotel since Auguste and Madame Monnier had kicked him out but seeing Monsieur Monnier he was drawn, as by a magnet, up the road towards the inn.

He dawdled in front of the hotel, inspecting the stall opposite, which sold cycle accessories. He was going to have a bike soon, Maman had told him, so he wanted to know what parts would be needed. He fingered pumps and tyres. He looked at puncture kits. He seemed to consider the price of a saddle. He tested one or two bells. Then, scuffing his feet in the dust of the road, he veered towards the hotel. Monsieur Monnier called to him.

"So, you alright then?" he asked, ruffling Joseph's hair. Joseph nodded, happily.

"Look, brought this back for you," said Louis, handing Joseph a bright new coin. "Reckon you deserve a bit of my demob money."

Joseph was overwhelmed. He smiled as he put the money in his pocket, feeling first with his fingers to make sure there was no hole.

"Yes, well," said Louis. "Better go and see what's happening in the café." He glanced at Joseph with a flash of embarrassment, picked up a dirty ashtray and left.

Joseph made no move to follow. He sat on the stone bench underneath the window, listening to the hum of voices in the bar, remembering the days when he used to be part of the activity, helping Monsieur Monnier.

He got into the habit of sitting there on market day. He would wander up to the cycle stall and hang around the hotel, sitting on the bench, kicking his heels, looking forward to having a bicycle so that he might be more independent.

Sometimes Monsieur Monnier would come out and have a word. With his easy going good-nature, he was well-liked in La Bastide. When he went over to collect the bread at the baker's opposite, people would stop to congratulate him on his safe return and he would regale them with stories of his adventures in the army. If she had no customers to serve young Alice Chauvet, whose husband was a prisoner of war, would stand at the top of her steps and listen to his tales, full of admiration for this local hero.

They all heard stories about what Monsieur Monnier had been doing as a soldier. Auguste boasted that his father was such a wonderful shot that he had successfully fought off a German artillery unit with nothing but a rifle.

Marcel was not impressed. "A likely story!" he scoffed. "Fat Louis defeats the German army with a conscript's pea shooter! Some hope!"

Maman's judgement, too, was surprisingly sharp. "Well, he got back home fast enough! Probably led the retreat to Toulouse! First in line to leave the front!" She saw Joseph's face crumple. "Don't be silly, Joseph," she chided. "We can't all be heroes. For some of us, it's just too difficult. Anyway," she added, with a touch of asperity, "Louis Monnier was born with no backbone. Or had it surgically removed by his mother in childhood."

Joseph would have liked to think that Monsieur Monnier was a hero but it was not easy to cast him in that role. His friends in La Bastide enjoyed his stories without believing every word he said.

It was different with Raoul Vidal, the schoolmaster at Luxat. He could well qualify as a hero. Slim, upstanding, always trim and neat, he was not as tall as Louis Monnier but he was a man of commanding presence. He came back from the front with the Croix de Guerre and wore, discreetly, on his lapel, the ribbon of the Légion d'Honneur, a civilian honour, spoken of with awe and admiration by the highest authorities in La Bastide.

"Monsieur, Monsieur," the children asked him, "how did you get your medal?"

Monsieur Vidal would not tell them. "Funny things happen in war," he said. "You find yourself on your own. You do what you can."

"Yes, but what did you do, monsieur?" they persisted, crowding round him, jumping up and down, pulling at his sleeve, begging for answers. "Did you kill a lot of Germans?"

Sharply, modestly, he rebuked them. "There's nothing to be proud of, killing someone. If you're a soldier, you may have to kill other soldiers in battle, but it's not something to boast about. Soldiers are only ordinary people, you know. Doing what they've been told to do. How many of your fathers were out there fighting? You wouldn't want somebody going round boasting about killing them, would you?"

The military fervour of the children subsided as Monsieur Vidal ushered them back to their desks and told them to get on with their work.

At home, as he fed the livestock and watched the baby rabbits scrabbling round their bowl of water, Joseph thought about Monsieur Vidal and tried to make sense of his words. There was Monsieur Monnier, boasting about being a hero when nobody believed he'd done anything in the least bit brave, and all the time Monsieur Vidal, who had got himself decorated, was saying that was just perfectly normal and ordinary.

Maman approved of Monsieur Vidal. "A good, kind man," she called him. "And a scholar. You listen to what he tells you, Joseph."

Joseph did listen to his teacher. Eleven years old now, he was in the top set, with boys and girls of thirteen and fourteen. He was doing well, too. In Luxat they spoke mostly patois. At school they spoke French. Joseph enjoyed learning the complicated grammar. At dictation Monsieur Vidal would give him more difficult work than the others, and Joseph still made very few mistakes. He read books, too. In the autumn, when the hard work of the harvest was over, Maman would sometimes ask him to read to her in the evening while she would get on with her knitting or mending or preparing preserves. They read 'Jim, The Rebel Peasant' They liked tales of rebellion and uprising or stories by Alphonse Daudet about village priests and country folk.

One Saturday when he was sitting outside the inn, Joseph heard the men in the bar congratulating a young soldier who had just been demobbed. Jean-Paul was the name on everyone's lips. He had been at Dunkirk it seemed and they all thought he was lucky to have survived.

"And not been captured by the Germans."

"Mind you, the English might have given him a hand and taken him with them when they ran," someone declared.

"Oh, he's better off at home."

The conversation faded and Joseph was surprised, a few minutes later, to hear individual voices, as if someone had moved to a table by the window.

"So, Jean-Paul, you're back." Joseph recogtnised the voice. It was Monsieur Vidal, his schoolteacher.

"Yes. I'm glad to be home. Too many lads are shut away in German prison camps. The Germans got you didn't they?"

"Yes."

The voices faded for a moment, drowned by a busy clatter of glasses. When Joseph could hear them again the two men seemed to be discussing their journey home. Monsieur Vidal was explaining that his papers had stood up to examination at a check point. "Though they must have thought I was a very good linguist for an Italian. I seemed to understand everything they said to me in French."

"And I had no excitement at all! Just had to wait for my demob papers and travel warrants." Jean-Paul paused for a moment. "Mind you I'm not sure I like the way things are going here."

"Well, the war isn't over yet," said Monsieur Vidal.

"You think things might change?" asked Jean-Paul. His question sounded serious. There was even a hint of hope in his voice.

"The Germans are very strong. Their industrial output is in a different class from ours. But Great Britain isn't quite finished yet. And if they can hold out for a bit, America might come in on their side one day. They entered the last war late and their intervention made all the difference."

Jean-Paul took up the theme with enthusiasm. "Exactly. And the Germans may have a treaty with Russia at the moment, but Stalin isn't a natural ally for Hitler."
"Which is what Charles de Gaulle is saying. He's made a speech on the wireless, in London. He thinks the Germans are going to be defeated in the end. And he wants France to carry on fighting. He wants us to be right there, on the winning side, when the Germans lose."

"Which is exactly what I want," said Jean-Paul.
"And so do I," said his friend.

Joseph had heard every word. They would not have known that he was sitting under the open window, listening to them. He had not understood everything but it seemed that some people were not happy with Marshal Pétain's peace and wanted to carry on fighting. It didn't make sense. The war was over, the armistice had been signed, they couldn't carry on, could they?

So life seemed to return to normal. While the weather in August had been unbearably hot as autumn turned to winter that year it grew bitterly cold. Instead of letting the fire burn low at the end of the evening, they would build it up. Marcel would rake the fire and pile glowing embers into the warming pan. Then he would add twigs and sticks to the remnants of the fire, until new flames leapt brightly up the chimney. He and Joseph would heave out the heaviest logs, ones that would burn throughout the night, keeping the kitchen warm and in their beds next door they would set the warming pan in its cage so that when they climbed in, they could stretch out straight away in beautiful warmth and savour the delicious scent of wood smoke.

During the evening, after Marcel got back from the saw mill and Joseph came home from school, they stayed in the kitchen or worked in the stable where the livestock lived together in a warm, rich-smelling twilight, insulated by the hay stored in the loft above.

But they had to go outside sometimes. When the pile of logs in the stable dipped too low the boys had to bring in more wood. They had to clean out the dirty straw. And outside the cold was piercing. Wet snow froze in their clothes. Their chapped hands cracked with chilblains, their boots were never properly dry.

It was dark when they got up in the morning and dark when they came home in the evening. The road up into the hills was impassable for weeks and, that winter, even the valley road was closed for days on end, so that often Marcel had to stay with a friend in La Bastide and Monsieur Vidal had to stay in Luxat because he could not get back to Festes, where he lived with his new wife, Simone.

The village closed in on itself. They used the provisions that they had stored during the summer: bottled fruits, pickled eggs, potatoes, beans, lentils and sausage, though they were frugal, taking care not to dip too deeply into these reserves before the bad weather ended.

They tried to keep warm and dry and to feed themselves and their animals. They were not much concerned about the war. Most of them thought it was over. France had been defeated and they just had to accept it and get on with their lives. The north of France was occupied by German soldiers but that was all far away from them. Or so it seemed.

Joseph rarely thought about the war, but he did sometimes remember Gabrielle, his mother, a vision of the summer. He still wondered if, perhaps, one day another stranger would come to the village, a man, his father perhaps. It was a distant hope, a dream.

And then, one day, a man did come.

CHAPTER 5
February 1941: Living with defeat: resistance

Maman called. It was time to get up. Marcel kept his eyes shut, hoping that the morning would go away and he could stay in his warm bed. Joseph took one brave leap into the icy morning chill, grabbed his clothes and ran into the kitchen, pulling them on as he went.

Good. The fire was still red. He crouched on a stool in front of the hearth, jabbed the poker at the half-burnt logs, prodding and twisting till they split, then arranged the wood carefully to encourage it to rekindle. He picked up the bellows and pumped life into the fire and was going to add a big, new log when he heard the dog barking and the sound of someone moving in the stable below. He stopped, still holding the wood in his arms, and looked at Maman, frowning. Who would be coming to see them at this time in the morning? And why had they not called out? Maman nodded and Joseph stepped carefully down the open-tread stairs.

There was someone there, stumbling round, disturbing the livestock who were grunting and munching and mumbling. Picart, having brought his master to investigate, had stopped barking but was growling, pinning the intruder to the wall beside the door, where he was propped uncertainly, his knees beginning to buckle beneath him.

"All right, Picart. Good boy!" said Joseph.

The man swayed and put out his hand. "Raoul Vidal!" he croaked. "Do you know Raoul Vidal?"

If the stranger had said nothing they would still have given him food and shelter. They would not refuse a poor man who came to their door asking for help and if he knew Monsieur Vidal he was more than welcome. Joseph took his arm and led him, stumbling, up the stairs, to a chair beside the fire. He leaned back, easing his shoulders, taking the weight off his feet. His boots were worn and sodden. Joseph knelt and tried to untie the laces but they had been broken and reknotted too many times, so he sat on the stool and gently lifting a swollen foot, placed it on his knee. He took out his knife, sliced through the tangled lace and, as he pulled the boot away, he could sense the tingling agony of circulation beginning to return.

Maman looked at them and shook her head. "He's too tired to know his own name," she declared. "Put him in the bed here and we'll sort out later what to do."

So they settled him, still fully dressed, in Maman's bed and drew up the blankets and the eiderdown and he was asleep before they had closed the curtains round the bed.

At school that morning Joseph kept fidgeting. He could not concentrate on his work, his thoughts kept wandering to that strange visitor. Who was he? Why was he asking for Monsieur Vidal? When morning lessons ended Joseph walked home, dawdling so that he could catch Monsieur Vidal, his head full of wild imaginings.

He wondered if the stranger was someone who owed his life to Monsieur Vidal. Someone Monsieur Vidal had saved from death in battle. After all their teacher was a brave man, with medals and commendations. Perhaps this man had come to bring a reward. Perhaps Monsieur Vidal was to be honoured for saving civilians, dragging children out of a burning building just before it collapsed. Perhaps he had attacked a German soldier, when he was standing there ready to kill a poor old peasant. Joseph did not hesitate to embroider the drama. He could see the peasant, in his imagination, bent low, crippled and blind.

It was too far for Monsieur Vidal to cycle back to Festes for his dinner and on school days he ate with Madame Coste. He came up now and saw Joseph dawdling along with Lucien Coste.

"You two are going to miss your lunch. Your mother won't be pleased if you're late, Lucien."

"We were waiting for your monsieur," Joseph told him. "Maman says would you please call in before afternoon school. It's important."

"I'll call in later," Monsieur Vidal promised and Joseph ran off, with a sudden fear that the stranger might have gone.

"Is he still here?" he asked as he burst into the kitchen.

"He was asleep when I looked," Maman said. "Best leave him for the moment. Come on. Eat."

"I told Monsieur Vidal that you wanted to see him."

"Yes. Well, I went over to Madame Coste and said something to her."

They were clearing away after their meal when Monsieur Vidal arrived. Joseph was preparing scraps for the pig. They opened the curtains round the bed and when he saw the sleeping man, Joseph thought he looked terrible, gaunt and unshaven, his lips dry and cracked.

"Mon pauvre ami!" cried Monsieur Vidal. "Oh, Robert, my poor friend!"

Their voices woke him and he started, as if afraid, then saw them standing by his bed and sighed with relief and closed his eyes again, drifting off to sleep once more as he murmured his friend's name: "Raoul!"

"Don't worry. You're safe here. And I'll be back."

Monsieur Vidal thanked them. "He's a soldier, from Scotland," he told them. "We were together at Dunkirk. We were captured by the Germans and he helped me escape. We were on our way home when we got separated. At Brives." His voice shook as he remembered. "I just lost him."

That night Joseph tended the animals and then went to look after the friend who had helped Monsieur Vidal escape from the Germans. He warmed some milk and added a thick slice of bread and raided their precious store of sugar and carried the dish to the bedside and watched with pride as his patient scraped the bowl clean.

"All right?" he asked.

"Thank you. Yes."

"Do you want to get up?" Joseph was eager for him to join them at the fireside and tell them the story of his adventures and how he had fought at Dunkirk and been captured and escaped. But he was too tired. He smiled and shook his head and slid down once more under the quilt.

Next day Monsieur Vidal returned, bringing clothes for Robert. Joseph helped unpack them, inspecting everything with interest. There were trousers, a couple of shirts, a thick pullover and several pairs of socks. There were long woollen underpants. There were a couple of towels, embroidered with the initials S A. "Simone Alvitre," Monsieur Vidal explained. "My wife's initials before we were married."

"She sewed these for her wedding." Joseph was happy to show that he understood and thought Madame Vidal must be a nice lady to let Robert have her towels.

There was some soap, too, which was hard to get in the shops. Maman was saving theirs for the spring, when she would do all the winter washing.

On Thursday afternoon, when there were no lessons, Monsieur Vidal set up a tub and they heated lots of water, like they did for the pig killing, and put the tub by the hearth and Robert got in and soaped himself and put on clean clothes.

"That's better!" He had washed his head and was towelling his hair.

Joseph was impressed. His own washing was much less thorough. There was a bucket by the hearth and sometimes he would dip the corner of a cloth in the water and wipe it quickly round his hands and face. Obviously they did things differently in Scotland.

"Do you wash like that at home?" Joseph asked him.

Robert grinned. "I do," he said. "But at home I can't wash by a nice fire, like I can here. At home we have a bath fixed to the floor. In a special big, cold bath room."

Joseph frowned and shuddered. No wonder Robert was enjoying his bath here.

There was more to come. Monsieur Vidal had brought shaving things. Joseph, fascinated, helped to prepare the ritual. They put a mirror on the mantlepiece and there was a leather strop that they hung from a hook on the wall and a razor with the blade hidden inside a horn handle.

Like Achille Cambon sharpening a knife at the pig killing, Robert sharpened his razor. Then he picked up the brush with a thick skirt of badger hair and he worked the soap and lathered his face and slowly shaved one clear, soapless line. Silent and absorbed Joseph watched as, stretching the skin this way and that, Robert shaved away all trace of whisker and stubble.

He was a new man. Smart and less hollow-eyed. He was tall and handsome, with slightly sandy hair and bright blue eyes.

"Thank you," he said, astonishing Maman by putting his arm round her waist and giving her a big kiss. Smiling happily she pushed him gently away.

"Go on with you. I'm too old for that."

"Madame you are youth personified," he said and Joseph stared in amazement as Maman blushed and giggled. "I could live the rest of my life here with you in perfect happiness. But alas, I must be on my way."

"Yes. But not yet," Maman declared. "You've no more strength than a baby. Time enough to be off when you're fitter and the weather's better."

Robert shook his head. "It's too dangerous. For you. There's no mercy for those who shelter enemy soldiers and your lives are at risk while I'm here."

"As far as I'm concerned you're a friend of Monsieur Vidal and no friend of Monsieur Vidal is an enemy for me." Maman was going to stand for no argument.

"That's not how the Vichy government sees it though."

Marcel snorted. "Fuck the bloody Vichy government."

Joseph's big brown eyes were round with amazement. "Is it against the law for Robert to stay here with us?" he asked.

They laughed at his innocent bewilderment. "It is indeed."

"But we can't turn him out, can we?" Joseph protested.

"'Course not," said Marcel.

"No we can't," said Maman. "Right's right, whatever the law says. We'll just have to be careful, that's all."

So Robert stayed. If anyone in Luxat was daft enough to ask questions, Monsieur Vidal told them to say that Robert was his cousin from Alsace. "My mother comes from Alsace, so I do have cousins there. And lots of people from Alsace have come down south to escape the Germans. And if he's from Alsace that explains why he's tall and northern looking and speaks funny French."

As the days passed Robert grew stronger. His cheeks filled out, his skin lost its pallor, the blisters and chilblains healed. He was soon doing jobs around the farm, even helping Achille Cambon in the forest.

Joseph would follow Robert, helping him, listening, chattering, admiring. They talked together all the time. Robert spoke French easily but it pleased them both to talk in English and Joseph was soon surprisingly fluent.

Robert enjoyed the boy's company. "I've a wee lad of my own at home," he told him. "James, his name is. He'll be three years old now."

"Will you go back to Scotland to see him when the war's over?" Joseph asked. He knew what the answer would be.

"Of course. I hope I won't even have to wait that long. But you shall come and see us there when the war is over. I promise."

That was something, Joseph supposed. Though he would have to share Robert then with James and James was Robert's son.

There were better things to talk about than Scotland and James. "What was Dunkirk like?" Joseph asked.

"Scary. And crowded. Packed with troops. They were like flies on the beach. Masses and masses of men, with no space between them. The boats were off shore, waiting, and the men were wading out into the water. They tried to organise things but it was a mess, really."

"What did you do there?"

"Kept out the Germans. If the Germans had reached the beach they could have mown us down and wiped out the British army."

"So how did you keep them away?" Joseph asked, imagining Robert with a machine gun, camped behind one of the dunes on the beach.

"We had to blow up the bridges. It's called securing the perimeter, making sure they can't get in to the area where your men are."

Joseph was persistent. "How do you blow up bridges?" he asked.

"Well, you need explosive. And a detonator to set off the explosive. We had those. You need fuses, too and wire. And we didn't have anything like enough of those." Robert remembered and shook his head. "We were lucky that we managed to do the job. Alan Brooke, our commander, worked miracles."

"Monsieur Vidal was at Dunkirk, wasn't he?"

"He was indeed. He and his men got separated from their unit and they helped us. And they helped the civilians. Monsieur Vidal saved a lot of lives at Dunkirk."

For some time after he heard this story, Joseph and his friends would practise blowing up the old log that served as a bridge over their little river and securing the perimeter round the area where the women did their washing. Sometimes the 'Germans' broke through and the women would get cross because the boys were crashing about among the washing.

Joseph still sometimes read to Maman in the evenings, but as they sat by the fire Robert would often tell them stories of his life in Scotland and of his time in the army. Joseph would listen, enraptured, drinking in every word and Maman, getting on with her sewing and mending, or making a rag rug for the floor, found that her work went more swiftly and she smiled and patted her hair and remembered the days when she sat by the fire with Jean, her husband. Robert was a fine, manly fellow and it was good to have him in the house, keeping an eye on Marcel, entertaining Joseph and flattering her, telling her how good her soup was and slipping his arm round her waist and making her feel ten years younger.

One evening Joseph asked him how he had managed to escape from a prisoner of war camp in Germany.

"I forged a pass," he said. "Made a paper saying I was an Italian worker returning home on leave. It was fairly easy to get out of the camp. Travelling through France was the problem. But the pass worked."

"Did you make a pass for Monsieur Vidal? Was that how he escaped?"

"Yes."

"Did you make a pass for anyone else?"

"No." Robert thought for a moment. "No, I didn't."

"Could you, though?" Joseph had understood what was passing through Robert's mind.

"Well, I could make a pass. But I couldn't get it in to anyone in the prison camp, could I?"

"Madame Coste sends parcels to her husband. He's in a German camp."

Even Joseph could see that they could not simply send a parcel with a letter saying 'I've put a forged pass in the socks I've sent you, dear.' He thought about it, though, and discussed the problem with Lucien. Robert talked to Monsieur Vidal. Madame Coste used to send tins of food to her husband: cassoulet, prepared by Achille

69

Cambon's brother. Achille thought they could fit a false bottom to one of those tins and if Robert could prepare a pass, they could put it in the bottom of a tin of cassoulet.

Monsieur Coste still had to know about it, though, or he would eat the contents and throw the tin away. It was Achille Cambon who came up with the idea. Monsieur Coste would expect his wife to write to him and to mention the food she was sending. But if Monsieur Vidal wrote and talked about the food in the parcel and made some silly comment about hoping that they would get to the bottom of all their troubles and come home to more cassoulet, or something like that, well, Monsieur Coste would think about it and might realise what they had done.

"It may not work, but it's worth trying," Madame Coste decided.

So Monsieur Vidal wrote his letter and they sent off the parcel and waited. Madame Coste hoped they had done the right thing. She wanted her husband home but what if he escaped from the prison camp and was then caught, later, travelling through Germany or through occupied France? She dared not think what the punishment for that might be. So she waited, not quite sharing the optimism of the others and Joseph, who had enjoyed the excitement of planning the escape, was awed to realise how easily they were now breaking the law.

Robert was happy at Luxat and there was no doubt that he was useful but preparing the pass for Monsieur Coste had reminded him that he, too, must escape. Winter was coming to an end, the weather would no longer keep him imprisoned and after a month in Luxat he had regained his strength. "I'd better start making a pass for myself, too. I can't stay here much longer," he warned Raoul Vidal.

Joseph, never far from Robert, heard what he said. His heart sank.

"Why can't you stay? Don't you like being here with us?"

His voice was so plaintive, his disappointment so obvious, Robert sat down beside Joseph and put his hand on his shoulder. "Come on. I've already promised, haven't I? Really promised, that when the war is over, you shall come to Scotland. And stay with me and meet my family."

Joseph nodded, though the promise for the future did not console him for the present loss.

"You see, I have to go home. You wouldn't want to leave Maman and Marcel and Luxat, would you?"

Joseph shook his head.

"Well, I have to go back home and see my family. And I'm a soldier, I have to get back to my unit." Robert's voice changed. "Anyway, I can't stay here, it's too dangerous."

"Dangerous?"

"Yes. They'll catch me in the end. Monsieur Vidal's all right, he's French, but I'm a foreigner. An enemy soldier."

Monsieur Vidal gave him no time to think. "So, we've got to help Robert escape, haven't we?" he urged, hoping that to involve Joseph on his friend's behalf, would help him to accept his loss more easily.

Joseph would not have known where to start but apparently it was quite easy. All Robert had to do was cross the frontier into Spain. He could take the train from Foix one Sunday, get off at the Spanish frontier and mingle with the crowd and then, at the end of the afternoon, simply walk down the hillside on the Spanish side.

"Achille Cambon will take you into Foix on his cart, I'm sure," Raoul told his friend.

So that was settled and Joseph could make the most of his remaining time with Robert. They were happy days. Robert's deep voice would rumble and echo round the kitchen and he filled the room with a wonderful manliness.

He encouraged Joseph to be less timid. He would run across the tree trunk over the river and Joseph, who used to shuffle timidly along the rough bridge, would step out more boldly and confidently to join his friend. While Maman would warn him to be careful and not go too fast when he came down the hill on his bicycle, Robert would laugh and show him how to fall off into soft earth if he had to.

Joseph was growing up. He was even beginning to realise that, as Monsieur Vidal and his friend in the bar had said, the war was not yet over, though it had not crossed his mind that, quietly in Luxat, he was helping to carry on the fight.

For Joseph those weeks with Robert were idyllic. When he remembered them afterwards he always saw them bathed in brilliance, with the sun gleaming on ice-white snow or with logs flaming in the hearth, the room flickering in a rosy glow. Then there was the darkness of Robert's departure and he remembered not only the loss of his friend but the heartbreak of an unforgiveable betrayal.

CHAPTER 6
March 1941: Living with defeat: collaboration

Marie Monnier was a disappointed woman, as Maman had told Joseph. Her biggest disappointment was her marriage.

She had gone to work as a maid at the Hotel du Commerce, when she left school. It was hard work, scrubbing floors, making beds, preparing vegetables. The hours were long and the wages were not generous.

The only chance she could see of improving her lot, was to marry Louis, whose mother had run the hotel since her husband was killed in the trenches in 1916. She doted on Louis, who grew up tall and handsome but weak. He also grew up as an only child, who had no brothers and sisters to share his inheritance. Marie, the maid, thought that his wife would be able to employ staff, maids, to do the rough work. She would have money and status.

So she giggled and simpered and pouted, with all the art she could muster. She kissed Louis, then withheld her kisses, permitted his hand to wander, then refused permission. She allowed him into her bed at last because she feared he might lose interest if rejected any longer and because she believed that if she were carrying his child he would marry her.

She had reckoned without his mother. Old Madame Monnier would not have welcomed any wife for her son and she certainly did not want him to marry the hotel maid. "A brazen hussy, who's got pregnant so that she can trap you into marriage," she told her son.

Louis was miserable. He hated such tension and hostility in his home. But Marie would not let go easily. She wheedled and sulked and threatened and almost despaired until finally, three weeks before Auguste was born, Louis's mother reluctantly gave her permission and he married her.

The old lady did not like her son's wife. Marie might think she would run the hotel now, but the widow thought otherwise. There was room for only one mistress in the Hotel du Commerce. Louis might have been daft enough to marry the girl but his mother had been in charge of the hotel since his father went off to the Great War and while there was breath in her body, in charge of the hotel she would remain.

"You can have it after I'm gone," she told Louis. "Not before."

So his new wife found that after her marriage her life had not changed. She was still working in the hotel. Old Madame Monnier still ordered her around and complained about everything she did. Indeed, as she got older she got more peevish and difficult to satisfy.

The old lady always got up early. Since she went to bed early and slept for a couple of hours in the afternoon it was hardly surprising that she got up early in the morning. But she chose to regard it as a virtue and to criticise her daughter-in-law if she was not downstairs and already working before half past six.

"So here you are at last," she proclaimed one morning, looking pointedly at the clock. "About time too."

Marie Monnier sighed. "Plenty early enough, I'd have thought," she muttered.

"I've been round those bedrooms upstairs," the old lady continued. "This is a hotel, you know. People pay to come and stay here. I've seen under those beds. Filthy!

Balls of dust. Bits of paper. You need to get down on your knees my girl and clean under those beds."

Marie looked at her mother-in-law with silent fury.

"To-day! You see you clean under those beds to-day!"

Seething with anger, Marie longed to tell the old bag just what she thought of her! If only they were not financially dependent on her! She served the breakfasts that morning with a great clatter and prepared the vegetables for lunch as if she was a rabid republican guillotining aristocrats for the French Revolution.

While she was chopping up the vegetables with such vigour, Auguste, slouched over his bowl of coffee, was dunking his bread and slurping up the soggy mess that only too often dripped down his chin or dropped back into the bowl. His grandmother had said all she wanted to say and was quietly enjoying Marie's fury. Marie herself knew that if she said one word she would be shouting and yelling at everyone and, for the moment, she was getting on with her work, silently raging and wondering how she could get her own back.

"Do you know what?" Auguste mumbled through a mouthful of bread.

Nobody responded.

"There's a British soldier out at Luxat."

Nobody seemed to be listening.

"Well, that's what I heard, anyway." Auguste shrugged.

"Where?" his father asked, with fleeting interest, remembering that Joseph lived in Luxat.

"Luxat," Auguste repeated, irritated that nobody cared what he was saying. "Well, I heard that he's working in the forest above the village. But living with one of the families there."

Louis grunted. Joseph had nothing to do with the woodsmen in the forest and, apart from Joseph, he really had no interest in what might be happening in Luxat.

The hot coffee had affected Auguste's sinuses. He snorted and wiped his nose on the sleeve of his pullover.

"Anyway, if anyone reported them to the authorities they'd be in real trouble. They'd probably get sent to Le Vernet."

The idea of someone suffering in one of these camps appealed to Auguste. Spanish refugees, socialists, trades unionists and anyone else who might not support the Vichy government, was being sent to a prison camp at places like Le Vernet. They were generally believed to be very nasty places.

There was no obvious response from his family but they had heard what he said. His father dismissed the news, since it did not concern Joseph. Madame Monnier was not very interested, either. She wanted to get her own back on her husband's mother, she would like to see her suffer. If Joseph had been involved she would have been happy to make trouble for him because she resented her husband's kindness to the boy but, like Louis, she could see no connection with Joseph and she shrugged off Auguste's news about a British soldier at Luxat.

Louis kept his head down and swallowed the foul, wartime coffee as quickly as he could. It was a cold morning, one of those early spring days when winter rallies for a moment, before it finally succumbs to sunshine. Snow had fallen during the night and it was still freezing but the chill in the hotel kitchen came from the people as much as the weather and Louis felt no inclination to linger. He decided to go out and find a bit of warmth over the road, with Alice, the baker's wife, who was young and pretty, and had a seductive smile.

Louis had always been an incurable flirt and there were not many girls in La Bastide who had been able to resist his charms. When Marie went to work in the hotel she had been skinny and tight-lipped, a plain, unattractive girl, but Louis had put his arm round her waist and stolen a kiss and made her feel quite feminine.

At one time, after their marriage, they had employed a girl to help in the hotel. She was very young and easily seduced. When Marie Monnier learnt that the girl was pregnant she was furious. There had been no more young maids at the Hotel du Commerce and, though it was sometimes difficult, Madame Monnier tried to keep an eye on her husband now.

She had seen him lingering in the bakery opposite. When he came home after his army service he had found Alice Chauvet eager to listen to stories of his soldiering. He had told her about going into a farmyard and snatching a chicken and she had laughed at his description of how he ran after the squawking bird. She had held her breath when he told her how he had to wring its neck and she had listened, wide-eyed with admiration, as he explained how they had built a fire and cooked a delicious stew. Louis enjoyed talking to her.

She was young and hesitant. He felt that she appreciated his maturity. "Distinguished," she called it, how his hair grew round a bald patch on the top of his head. She was so grateful, too, for any little job he could do for her, round the house.

"It's difficult for me, on my own," she confessed. "I can't do these things."

Her husband was a prisoner in Germany and, though she rarely spoke of him, Louis thought she must be lonely on her own. He looked forward to providing the consolation she needed.

He came out of the hotel that morning and could see her on the steps of the bakery opposite, attacking the snow with youthful energy. Scattered by the onslaught of the broom, the soft snow flew up, and she scratched at the hard residue of impacted ice. Her eyes were bright, her cheeks rosy with the effort and the cold as she banged her broom on the pavement to shake out the slush. Louis Monnier slipped and nearly fell trying to step out of the way and she looked up, pouting but with a smile already twitching at the corner of her lips.

"Breaking hearts not enough for you, Alice? Trying to break a few legs now?"

She tossed her head and flicked away a dark curl, pretending to take offence. She began to punish the broom once more.

"Here, give me that. Can't have a pretty girl like you wearing yourself out sweeping up all this snow." Louis held out his hand. Alice, yielding easily to a few kind words, handed him her weapon. "What we need, of course, is a spade. Have you got a spade?" he asked.

The dark eyes smiled at him through the curls that had fallen again across her face. "Might have a spade." She pouted. "I suppose there might be one, out at the back."

Louis put his arm round her waist and gave a light squeeze. She was warm and soft. His hand slid down, patted her bottom and stayed, feeling the young body under the layers of cloth. "Don't you worry, ma chérie. Let's get that spade."

Alice smiled and shook her curls and ran up the steps, with Louis following, succombing to the charms of Alice as he had succombed to the maids at the hotel.

From the window of the restaurant, Marie Monnier was watching now, her cheeks pinched, her thin lips tight with anger.

Auguste glanced in, caught sight of his mother's face and withdrew. He would do better to go and see what was happening in town. Find out a bit more about that British soldier in Luxat, perhaps.

Joseph and Maman had come into market that morning with no premonition of disaster.

They had brought in a sack of potatoes.

"I know we meant to give them to monsieur le curé," Maman said, "but he doesn't know that, so he won't miss them, will he?" She looked doubtfully at the potatoes, the symbol of her lack of charity. "The trouble is, with bread being rationed, people are buying potatoes. We'd get a very good price for these in the market." She was still uncertain, justifying herself to Joseph who was already dragging them out of the stable.

They did get a good price. It was a cold morning and their customers did not want to hang around chatting and haggling for a better bargain.

Alice Chauvet was sweeping the snow from the steps of the bakery.

"She must have sold all the bread she had," Maman said. "There was a big queue this morning and some people are going to be disappointed."

They saw Louis Monnier follow Alice into the bakery and Maman turned to the woman at the next stall.

"So that's where he's setting his sights now, is it?" her neighbour said.

"I don't like Marie Monnier, but you can't help feeling sorry for her sometimes." Maman shook her head.

"And there's Albert Chauvet, too, poor chap. Sitting there in a prisoner of war camp in Germany while his wife's gadding about with Louis Monnier."

They clucked their tongues and shook their heads but their condemnation was not harshly unforgiving.

"She's only young, though," they agreed. "And she's got that bakery to run."

"Yes. She's lonely, overworked. Wants a bit of fun, I dare say."

Mathilde Barthez who was perfectly prepared to admit that her own life had been brighter since Robert appeared on the doorstep, could sympathise with Alice Chauvet.

"And I don't think it's much fun for Louis Monnier, married to that dried up grape, Marie."

"No. The fruit's much lusher on the other side of the road."

The two women laughed.

Joseph had wandered off. There was no point in hanging around the hotel. He turned the other way, towards the river.

Auguste had been looking for him. "So, what's happening out at Luxat then?"

Joseph shrugged. He did not want to talk to Auguste. "I hear you've got a British soldier out there."

Joseph's heart missed a beat. He remembered how Robert had explained that he could be in danger because he was an enemy soldier. He knew he had to be careful. He kicked a pile of snow, while he decided what to say.

"Oh, yes?" he jeered. "And Santa Claus too, I suppose?"

Auguste was not so easily diverted. Perhaps he had sensed the sudden tension.

"Where's he hiding?"

Thank goodness, Joseph thought, if he has to ask, it means he doesn't know where Robert is. He felt more confident.

"Oh, clear off!" he snapped.

It might have worked. Auguste was disconcerted when Joseph rounded on him. But he had bullied the younger boy for years and watched him cringe. So, as Joseph turned to leave, Auguste stuck out his foot and brought him crashing to the ground.

"So, where's the British soldier staying then?" He repeated his question.

Joseph did not bother to reply. Winded by the fall, he lay still for a moment then started to crawl to his feet. Auguste stamped on his hand and Joseph fell back.

"I asked you a question, little worm."

Auguste was standing on Joseph's hand, rocking backwards and forwards. The pain was excruciating. Joseph concentrated on trying not to cry.

"I think he's hiding with you," Auguste speculated. He intended to frighten Joseph, he did not really believe that they were sheltering the British soldier but he caught the alarm in his eyes and realised that he had made a lucky guess.

"Well, well!" Auguste said, removing his foot and letting Joseph struggle to his feet. "This time you really are in trouble, aren't you!"

Louis and Alice had cleared the bakery steps.

"If you need anything else, just let me know. I'm only over the road," Louis told her as he prepared to return home.

The steps up to the door of the Hotel du Commerce had not been swept. Inside, it was cold. Like everything else in wartime, wood was difficult to get though there were enough forests all round La Bastide Louis thought. Perhaps it was hard to get men to do the work. He shivered. The rooms were too big. They were cold and impersonal.

Gloomily, he went into the bar, where a couple of customers were already waiting for their aperitif. He saw Auguste come in and go down the corridor towards the kitchen and knew that he was unlikely to come and help in the bar. Not for the first time, Louis regretted that he had lost Joseph and was stuck with Auguste.

In the restaurant, Marie Monnier had begun to take the first orders. It was the start of the midday rush, when they had to take orders, serve meals, carry them into the restaurant and clear away again. Old Madame Monnier served out the food and Janine, Auguste's sister, was beginning to be useful, washing up, but there was still more than enough work for Marie.

Auguste was in the way.

"Go into the bar and help your father," his mother told him. "Or, better still, go into the restaurant and clear some of the tables."

Auguste stayed where he was.

"I know where the British soldier is hiding," he announced.

His mother took a dish of runner beans in one hand and a dish of swedes in the other, noted, without interest, how unappetising they looked and carried them through to the restaurant. She brought back a pile of dirty dishes and dumped them by the sink where Janine was already up to her elbows in greasy water.

"That soldier in Luxat. He's staying with Joseph Peyrou."

Auguste had his mother's attention now. They both knew that she hated the boy. "With that little bastard," she muttered.

"Well, don't just stand there struck by lightning. There's food to be served," the old woman interrupted, indicating the dishes filled with a pale, uncertain stew. Marie took them, thoughtfully.

"If the police catch him, they'll be in real trouble," Auguste reminded her.

"Yes, but ... "

There was no time to think. Marie knew that she would dearly like to cause trouble for Joseph, a nasty little brat. Louis was far too fond of him, far too ready to talk to him and welcome him around the hotel, even if he no longer came inside. She did not want to see him. Ever. Anywhere. This just might be a way of getting rid of him.

She had had enough that morning, anyway. Too much work and her mother-in-law ordering her about, telling her to dust under the beds, and Louis flirting with Alice, blatantly, in front of the hotel, with the whole town looking on.

How were the police going to find out about this enemy soldier, though. Then it came to her. Monsieur Delpech! The senior policeman in La Bastide would be here in the hotel. "Monsieur le Commissaire Delpech! Is he in the bar?" she asked Auguste.

He was not just a police man. He was the man in charge and a vociferous supporter of Marshal Pétain, too. He would deal with an enemy soldier and with anyone hiding him.

So Marie Monnier, having found her solution, served the lunches in the restaurant with a lighter step and when Monsieur le Commissaire Delpech finished his drink and left the bar, Madame Monnier had a word with him.

"There's an English soldier hiding out at Luxat," she told him. "He's with Madame Barthez and the two boys."

Monsieur Delpech responded with an air of official solemnity. "Don't you worry, Madame," he said. "We'll get him." He followed her into the kitchen, to hear what Auguste could tell him about the soldier. As he left he shook his head and thanked them. "I wish there were more people like you in La Bastide. There's not enough patriotism in the country these days."

CHAPTER 7
March 1941   Betrayal

Joseph had returned to Maman, almost incoherent.
"Robert," he stammered. "They know about Robert."
"Who does?" Maman asked.
"Auguste Monnier!"

Mathilde had no illusions about Auguste. He would cause trouble. She had known that it was dangerous for them to shelter a British soldier. Now that they were on the verge of discovery she was frightened.

"What are we going to do?" Joseph was close to tears.

The woman at the next stall was an old friend. "Oh do shut up!" she told Joseph. "I don't know what you've been up to but it doesn't sound like something you want to tell the whole town about." She began to help Maman pack up her things. "Just act normal," she advised as she saw them off to the bus.

Never had the journey back to Luxat seemed so slow. At every farm they came to they stopped. The driver slid from his seat, stood at the roadside easing the stiffness from his legs, then rummaged among the packages on the roof. The departing passengers collected their belongings, called good-bye and added reminders for the coming week. The driver climbed back onto the bus and set off once more, slowly negotiating the narrow roads. All the way, Mathilde was thinking and planning, praying that they would not be too late.

"Robert," she called, as soon as they entered the house. He came, smiling, from the stable, unsuspecting.

"They know you're here," she told him.

Hurriedly, Robert packed his things. Maman put together some food for the journey. Joseph offered his bicycle. "Leave it behind the cemetery at Foix," he told Robert as he handed it over.

Marcel advised him not to take the main road. "Don't go into the centre of town when you get to Lavelanet, go straight across the road and through Raissac and Ilhat. There's a lane along the ridge that comes down into Foix just before the railway station."

There was no time to say good-bye. Robert tied his case onto the carrier of the bicycle and was off, pushing the bike up the steeply twisting lane, towards the forest above. Joseph watched him leave. As he came to the corner, Robert turned and waved and Joseph half raised a hand in reply.

Maman scurried round, trying to make sure there was nothing left to betray them but when the police arrived she was still breathless from the exertion and shaking with fear.

"It's my heart," she lied, trying to offer a reason for her agitation.

The two young policemen were sympathetic. "That's all right, madame. My mother gets breathless, too," one of them confessed. He introduced himself. "Laurent Barde, madame. I think my mother is a cousin of your late husband."

Maman relaxed a bit. The young policeman seemed to be suggesting that he was a friend.

They asked her questions and they questioned Joseph, too. He had resolved to give nothing away but though he was frightened to begin with their questions were not probing and were kindly put.

"Have you seen any stranger in the village?"

"Has there been anyone around with a foreign accent?"

"Has anyone called at the house?"

"Have you had anyone staying here?"

"Someone has told us that you've been sheltering an enemy soldier. Now, why would they say that, if it's not true?"

"They say he's been helping up in the forest. Do you have a plot in the forest? A cabin?"

"Have you ever worked in the forest?"

Gradually Joseph began to answer their questions more confidently.

The two policemen went round the village asking their questions but nobody had seen a foreigner or any strange man in Luxat though some of them remembered Gabrielle. "In the summer. A lady. A very smart lady on a bicycle."

They searched the house but could find no sign of an enemy soldier.

"Monsieur le Commissaire Delpech won't be happy, I'm afraid," Laurent said. "He's very patriotic, Monsieur Delpech. Can't stand the English. He says Marshal Pétain's right. We've got to collaborate with the Germans, work together to make a stronger Europe." The words came out like a recitation with just a faint hint of mockery.

His friend agreed. "A shame we couldn't find any evidence for him."

They shook hands as they left.

"If you ever need any help let us know," Laurent told them.

Maman could scarcely believe their luck. "Those two would have had difficulty in seeing him if Robert had been sitting at the kitchen table," she declared, grateful that the interrogation had been so painless.

87

For Robert it was hard work, zigzagging up the steep cliff path, but once he could get on the bicycle it was faster and easier. He came to the main road at the Col de la Babourade and turned left towards Bélesta and Lavelanet. There were more people here, other bicycles, a few carts, even a couple of gazogenes, cars which the owners had kept running despite the lack of petrol, by fitting gas containers.

The ride was unforgettable. At first his way ran through the forest, through dark green branches which at this altitude were still burdened with snow, like decorated Christmas trees. Then began the long, steep descent into Bélesta with the valley gradually opening out, overlooked by snowy peaks glistening in the evening sun. The way down was steep and more than once he nearly spun over the handlebars or came tumbling off as he took a bend too fast but after weeks in the narrow confines of Luxat and the forest, the open road gave him a glorious sense of space and freedom.

After Bélesta the hills were less dramatic. How far was it to Foix? Twenty kilometers, just over ten miles, to Lavelanet and the same again to Foix? Robert tried to work out how long it would take him. Soon the road began to climb and he had to get off and push his bike. The rise into Lavelanet took him well over an hour and he was exhausted when he got there.

It did not seem safe to stop though and he went on his way on a country lane which ran along the top of a ridge. It was dark now, the lane was rough and stony, the light from his bicycle lamp was not enough and more than once Robert had to dismount and walk, pushing his bike. There was no traffic here, there were not even any people, though from time to time he came to a little cluster of houses or an isolated farmhouse where the dogs barked and he cringed into the shadows, and hurried past, afraid that he might be seen.

Then the moon came out as he began the descent into Foix. The road was very narrow, twisting constantly. There were no houses or farms now and with the light of the moon he could see where he was going and was able to get on his bike again.

At last the neat hedge of a cemetery suggested that he must be near the town. He walked round to the back and left the bicycle, lying on the ground, half hidden by the bushes, where he hoped Joseph would get it back safely. If it had been warmer he would have stopped to rest but the sun had not yet broken through the early morning chill and he carried on.

He walked down the hill for a mile or more, then the lane turned sharply and he found himself on the main road beside the river. He could see the castle, rising above the town, perched on a steep hill like an illustration in a medieval prayer book and almost immediately he saw the approach to the station, on the right.

He had to be careful now. He was no longer out in the empty countryside. He could not go straight to the station, it was too early, he would be too conspicuous waiting on an empty platform so he went past and walked across the bridge over the river. He looked down at the racing torrent far below and saw the water, an icy brown full of the snow melting in the mountains which reminded him of the streams of Scotland, and he told himself that he would soon be back home.

On the other side of the river he wandered through the narrow streets of the old town, found a café in the square opposite the church and went inside hoping to escape from the cold. The room was unheated but at least he was protected from the wind and the cup of coffee that he ordered, though it tasted terrible, was hot.

Robert lingered, tired and reluctant to move from the shelter of the café. He felt conspicuous. Tall, his face freckled, his hair too brightly blond, he was out of place among these short, dark-haired, swarthy men of Foix. A young woman who had followed him into the café was watching him. He shivered. He could not stay here.

The young woman smiled at him. "It's cold this morning, isn't it?"

Robert grunted in reply. His French was fluent but not good enough for him to risk a long conversation.

"We used to live in Foix. But my brother was killed in the fighting and we moved then, my mother and me," the young woman told him. "My father was killed in the last war." She sipped her coffee. "I hate ... war," she said.

Robert looked at her more closely. She was young, in her twenties perhaps. Well-dressed. She spoke good French.

"Are you a teacher?" he asked. Raoul had told him that village schoolteachers were nearly all radical, secular and anti-Vichy.

She nodded. "I teach in a village up the valley. Near Ax-les-Thermes."

"Are you going there now?"

She nodded.

"Perhaps we could go to the station together?"

She smiled.

They got up and he paid for the coffee and stepped out into the world once more. They went back across the bridge and up the hill towards the station. This was the dangerous moment. If the police had gone to Luxat they would know that he was already on his way. The Sunday train up to the frontier was a well-known route into Spain. The police would be checking on the passengers.

There were more people about now and Robert felt less isolated and exposed and much safer with the girl beside him. But he knew that he could not relax.

"Do you have papers?" she asked him. "An identity card?"

"Yes."

"Good."

He took her arm and walked with her down the station drive.

The train was already waiting. He could get his ticket and take his seat but he knew that he must not seem agitated. He tried to relax and smiled at the girl beside him as they approached the ticket office.

"Could you get the tickets?" he asked. "To Latour de Carol?"

They joined the queue. A policeman was inspecting their papers as the passengers moved towards the train. When it came to their turn he glanced without much interest at the girl's papers.

Robert was ready. This was the part he had always hated, when travelling with Raoul Vidal. He was so close to the enemy authorities. He felt close to discovery. He held out his papers for inspection, papers copied from Raoul Vidal's, in the name of Robert Boulanger, a teacher from Limoux. They were as good as he had been able to make them.

The policeman read them, slowly, taking in the details. He looked at the photograph and looked up at Robert, checking that it was his picture. Robert tried to seem unconcerned but he could feel the tension in every muscle.

The policeman handed back the papers. As they moved away he tried not to give any sign of the relief he felt. The girl glanced at him and seemed to appreciate his anxiety.

"It's all right," she said.

He gave her a hand up the steps of the train and followed her into the compartment. "Thanks."

"Don't worry," she said. "You can sit with me. We'll travel together. I've got tickets for Ax for both of us. It might be dangerous for you to go right up to the frontier by train."

When the inspector came round later, checking tickets and identity papers, she took his papers from him. "Go to sleep," she whispered. So he shut his eyes and she handed over his papers with her own.

At Ax-les-Thermes they got down from the train and walked up into the hills, to the village and to the teacher's flat above the schoolroom. Her mother was there. She shared out the lunch between them, showing no surprise to see the stranger her daughter had brought home and he soon realised how lucky he had been to meet this girl in the café. He was not the first British soldier she had helped on his way.

They showed him where to sleep and warned him to keep quiet during the day. "It doesn't matter now, it's Sunday, but when the children are at school you must be careful."

The next day a man came to see him and asked how he had reached Foix and he explained how he had been at Dunkirk and had escaped through France and spent the winter in a small village but had to move quickly when the authorities learned he was there. He was careful not to give details that might incriminate his friends but his story was accepted.

The young teacher's name was Marthe and she and her mother gave him food and shelter for a week or more. Then one evening she told him that it was time to leave.

"Tomorrow you will go higher up into the hills. If anyone aks why you're travelling, tell them that you're visiting your brother at the sanatorium. You'll go by train to Porta, then on by road, to the church at Dorres."

And so Robert joined a small group of British soldiers and airmen who left Dorres one night and took the long, arduous walk across the mountains into Spain, guided by Tomas the shepherd who had spent his life among those peaks and valleys.

At the Hotel du Commerce Monsieur le Commissaire Delpech had to tell them the results of his search for the British soldier. He always took his family to the Hotel for lunch on Sunday. He was an impressive man: his grey hair was receding with dignity, his eyebrows bristled with vitality. He swept importantly up the road and ushered his wife and daughter into the restaurant and then went into the bar for a few minutes, to enjoy an aperitif with his friends and colleagues. As he entered the bar on that Sunday when Robert left, conversation faltered for a moment. Monsieur le Commissaire smiled and nodded, accepting this as a natural tribute to his authority.

The law was not popular in La Bastide. Local people were, by tradition, radical and suspicious of government. For them smuggling was a popular and respectable way of life. It was natural to evade the law.

Louis Monnier, serving the busy Sunday morning throng, looked up and waited for the news Monsieur Delpech had brought. Auguste, who had to help when the bar was busy like this, was also waiting to hear what had happened to the British soldier. But where Auguste hoped that he had been caught and that Joseph's family was in deep trouble, Louis had been furious that his wife and son had betrayed the boy and was praying that no sign of the soldier had been found.

He poured a pastis and handed it to the policeman. Monsieur Delpech smiled. "We sent two men out to Luxat," he said. Silence fell. Some of the men in the bar had heard rumours of a British soldier hiding there.

"They questioned the old woman and the boys. One of them's Joseph, isn't he, the boy who used to help here?"

Louis nodded. His throat was dry. He wanted to know if Joseph was all right. Auguste smirked.

"They didn't find anything. They asked around the village but nobody could tell them anything."

Louis, who had been holding his breath, half smiled. Auguste looked sour.

"I should hope they didn't find anything," one of the customers muttered to his neighbour.

"At least they can keep their mouths shut in Luxat, even if some people here have too much to say!"

Monsieur Delpech had not finished. "We've had a word with our colleagues at Foix. They're checking on the trains in case he tries to escape that way." He looked round the bar. He was not happy with the response to his news. The men had their heads down. He could not hear any criticism but he felt they were not with him. It was the moment to make the position plain. "We can't have enemy soldiers running around the country. Marshal Pétain is determined to put an end to this dreadful socialism and see that we collaborate with our German friends. Then we'll get French soldiers coming back from the prisoner of war camps and we can get on with our lives."

The words were stirring but the men in the bar were unenthusiastic. Some of them seemed to be talking among themselves, not listening to Monsieur Delpech. He raised his voice. "So, thank you Louis."

They seemed interested now.

"Very grateful, we are, that you told us what you had heard. We need patriotic Frenchmen to support Marshal Pétain and your family has been most helpful."

Louis was caught unawares. It was his wife and son who had spoken to the policeman but Monsieur Delpech seemed to assume that he was responsible for calling in the police. What could he say, though? He could hardly announce in public that his wife and son might have told the authorities about a British soldier hiding in Luxat but it was nothing to do with him. There might be some advantage, anyway, in being on good terms with Monsieur Delpech, if he got into difficulties with his papers or with black market supplies. In any case, Joseph was safe and surely that was all that really mattered. No harm had been done, he decided, complacently. Perhaps, after all, he might gain something by it.

So, casually, with no agonising, with no long, painful consideration, Louis slid into the role in which others had cast him. He became a man who supported the Vichy government, a collaborator. How could he have known that he had taken a step which would give him some brief advantage but would lead eventually to a terrible tragedy?

The men in the bar picked up their glasses and started talking once more, though the mood was quiet. There were some who seemed distracted, reflecting on the policeman's words.

Bernard Bouladou, for one, the foreman at Marcel's factory, had never liked the British. They were treacherous bastards who had left France in the lurch at Dunkirk and then sunk the French fleet at Mers-el-Kebir. Still, he would not have betrayed a British soldier. England would be defeated by Germany, of course. The Germans had stormed through the rest of Europe and Great Britain was not likely to survive on her own. The papers were full of the news of London being flattened by bombs. But, for the moment, they were out there fighting and Bernard Bouladou was surprised to discover that he wished them well. As he drained his glass he decided that wine drunk in a café run by a man who could betray a British soldier, turned sour on the tongue. He would take his custom elsewhere in future.

Jean-Paul Ramel, who had been so warmly welcomed in the bar when he returned from serving with the army, sipped his wine and glanced at the friend beside him. He would have liked to stand up and argue against this craven acceptance of German authority. Instead he had to mutter so quietly that his friend could hardly hear him.

"Pétain's got a lot to answer for! We have to sit here and be told, by a French police officer, that a rat like Louis Monnier is a patriotic Frenchman!"

His friend was as angry as he was but clung to a distant hope. "Remember de Gaulle! The war isn't over yet. There's another round still to come and America could well change everything if she sides with Great Britain."

But at that moment, in the bar in La Bastide, it seemed almost impossible. They felt powerless. They were angry and humiliated. "O.K. maybe there's nothing we can do. Maybe there's no way we can fight for France. But at least we don't have to fight for Germany. At least we don't have to betray our friends!"

"I don't think I can stand this place any longer," Jean-Paul said. "The Café Terminus at the railway station may be a bit basic but I think I'd prefer the company there."

When Mathilde and the boys heard the news that Robert had not been caught on the way to Spain, they offered up a prayer of thanksgiving for his escape and another, a petition for the future safety of their friend.

They missed Robert. In a village where too many men had died in the last war or been taken prisoner in this one, they had enjoyed their moment of privilege, as a house where an able bodied man was living.

Joseph was inconsolable. There were other boys in the village who had no man in the house, some of the other boys on Public Assistance were living with widows and unmarried women, but Joseph had thrived under Robert's care and he missed him now. Monsieur Vidal complained that he was distracted in class, Maman constantly had to remind him to get on with his work at home, Marcel was irritated by his moaning and sulking.

"If your Englishman was so wonderful, for goodness sake, learn English and go to England and leave us in peace," Marcel urged.

"He's from Scotland, not England," Joseph pointed out.

"Wherever. Just go! You're no good to us, moping around here."

Joseph liked the idea. He began to prepare for Scotland. He wandered round muttering mysteriously in this foreign tongue.

There was jubilation in the village when Monsieur Coste returned and Joseph was overwhelmed with pride when he declared that, as long as he lived, he would never forget the British soldier who had brought him home and that when the war was over he would go to Scotland to thank him and take Joseph with him because he could speak the language.

It was Maman, though, who understood Joseph's deep hurt at Louis Monnier's betrayal.

Jean-Paul Ramel, a teacher at La Bastide, had complained to Monsieur Vidal. "I'm not going back to the Hotel du Commerce. Delpech, that pompous policeman, is full of praise for Louis Monnier, because he betrayed a British soldier. They say he was sheltering with young Joseph, too, the boy who used to help in the bar." Jean-Paul was disgusted. "I call that really disgraceful. If they'd caught the soldier there God knows what they would have done to Madame Barthez and the boys!"

Monsieur Vidal felt he had to warn his friends at Luxat. "Don't trust the Monniers," he told them. Joseph had hoped that Louis was not involved but Monsieur Vidal could offer no consolation. "I think he was. Monsieur Delpech thanked him, personally."

Joseph could understand that Monsieur Monnier had to obey the law. He wouldn't want to risk getting into trouble with the police. But he remembered how Louis Monnier had watched him being thrown out of the hotel. When he came back from the war he had smiled at him and given him a few francs. It didn't mean anything.

"It was silly. I really thought he was my friend," he confessed to Maman. "He never cared!"

Marcel, carefully slicking his hair into a dashing quiff, was getting ready to meet a girl in Festes. He had high hopes for the evening. "Forget it! Robert got away, didn't he?"

"I'll never forgive him! Never!" Joseph promised. "I'll get him one day. You'll see."

Maman shook her head and sighed. Marcel would have forgotten, or forgiven. Not Joseph. And his bitterness was all the greater because he was an affectionate boy and needed love and Louis Monnier had let him down, yet again.

CHAPTER 8
April 1941 - March 1942   Mocking the authorities

Joseph got on with his work. There was no sparkle in his eye. Picart pricked up his ears and swished his tail when Joseph came home, trotted at his heels, sat beside him looking up hopefully, tapped Joseph's leg with his paw, came and rested his head on Joseph's knee, but for weeks Joseph ignored his appeals.

The meadows were covered in flowers, blue and yellow and purple. Orchids and gentians blossomed richly on the hillsides. The summer came and the weather grew warmer and haymaking began. The hard physical labour gave him little time to think and the fresh air and exercise led to a good night's sleep and brought a sense of well-being. One day as he sat taking his midday break in the shade of a cherry tree, munching on a length of sausage, he held out a piece to Picart and commanded him to wait as he teased, jiggling the promised titbit in front of his nose. When he finally relented and gave Picart his treat, they rolled together in the newly scythed hay, laughing and gambolling like a pair of puppies.

There was a lighter tone to his voice when he got home that night. There was a sparkle once more in his big brown eyes, a cheeky grin on his face. His hair was tousled, he was dirty and sweaty and his clothes, covered in dust and bits of straw, looked even grubbier and more tattered than usual but Maman thanked God that at last there seemed to be some relief for Joseph's distress.

As the harvest ended and the village turned to threshing they had good news. Monsieur Vidal called to see them. "How about that?" he demanded, holding out a postcard.

Joseph peered doubtfully at the rather grubby card with its dull sepia picture of a town square surrounded by trees. "Monsieur?"

"Well, have a look at it. See what is says," he urged.

So Joseph, hope dawning, stretched out his hand and gently picked up the card.

"Who's it from?" asked Monsieur Vidal.

Joseph whooped and stamped his feet with glee and Picart raced round them barking wildly. "It's from Robert!" he crowed. "He got there! He's free!"

"In England?" asked Maman.

"Scotland!" Joseph muttered automatically. "No. Not Scotland but he's in Spain."

"What does he say?"

Joseph read out the message. "I've been for a long walk in the hills but am now returning to my family. Remember me to all my friends and tell them I shall come and see them as soon as I can. Roberto." Joseph turned to Monsieur Vidal. "Oh, when will he come and see us?"

"Not until the war's over I'm afraid."

Joseph blew out his cheeks in an exaggerated pout and trumpeted his disappointment but he was not truly sad: Robert had escaped and one day he would come back to Luxat. And take Joseph to Scotland.

The summer ended with Joseph altogether happier and more confident. He was in no sense reconciled to the Monniers though and when Auguste swaggered up to him one morning when he and Lucien Coste were kicking around an old football, Joseph was not prepared to be bullied.

"Well, if it isn't the bastard from Luxat," jeered Auguste.

"Don't you call me names." Joseph glared and kicked the ball viciously towards Lucien.

"Names?" Auguste was haughtily supercilious. "I'm just telling the truth. Your mother was no better than she should be and you're a little bastard!"

A year earlier, Joseph would have rushed in, fists flailing, and gone home bruised and beaten, his cheeks streaked with tears. This time he gazed coolly at Auguste.

"Perhaps you have not met my mother," he suggested. "She lives in Paris now." Joseph paused. He wanted his words to wound. "Of course your mother is a good woman. Solid. But she lacks the elegance of a Parisienne, wouldn't you say?" He turned to Lucien, who nodded wisely, in judicious agreement. Joseph was beginning to enjoy the exchange. "It's the clothes, of course." He paused again. Timing is important. "Partly, the clothes," he added on reflection. "There's also the face, the features. The hair. The figure." He was warming to the description. "After all your mother's got a face like the backside of an ox and hair like the tail of a mangy dog. The voice of a screech owl ..."

Auguste lunged. "You little bastard," he shouted. But Joseph had skipped away, whooping with delight.

"Next time," he vowed, "I'll knock him down and beat him into pulp."

Lucien was startled. Joseph had always seemed so timid and sensitive. Now he sounded bloodthirsty. And so determined.

Joseph was no longer that naïve law-abiding little boy he had been. When he and Marcel found themselves in La Bastide late one evening, his brother reminded him how shocked he'd been when Marcel had scribbled all over Marshal Pétain's poster.

"Oh mon dieu! How innocent you were!" marvelled Marcel.

"A long time ago," sighed Joseph like a veteran of many years suffering.

"The BBC's now telling people on the wireless to paint signs up. V for Victory. To show that we're not beaten and we'll win one day."

They were passing a house which was being repaired. The builders had left a pot of tar lying with their wood and their ladders. Joseph pointed. "Come on! Let's do a V for Victory!"

They looked round. The street was dark and empty. They picked up the bucket of tar and a couple of pieces of wood and traced a big, ragged V on the wall of the bakery.

"Isn't there some morse code too?" asked Joseph. "You know, dots and dashes."

"What dots and dashes?" asked Marcel, holding his stick ready, dripping tar all over the pavement..

"I don't know. Just put a line of dots and dashes."

Marcel had a better idea. "The cross of Lorraine," he suggested, painting a cross '†' and adding a second, wider horizontal bar below the first.

"What's that?" Joseph asked.

"Symbol of resistance. Charles de Gaulle comes from Lorraine and so people're using this cross to show they support him."

Joseph was satisfied.

If he could have known the trouble this protest would cause the Monniers, Joseph would have been delighted.

When Alice Chauvet came out the next morning she was not pleased to find the wall of her shop disfigured with black tar. Every customer had some comment to make and none of them seemed to support these symbols of resistance.

"It looks terrible, doesn't it!"
"I don't know what the world is coming to, with people painting on walls like that."
"Hooligans, that's what they are, youngsters to-day."
"How are you going to get rid of that mess?"

That was the trouble, of course. Alice had no idea how to remove tar from her wall. Her pale grey eyes opened wide in anxious perplexity. She looked at Louis, standing with the others in front of the bakery, shaking his head in sympathy. Perhaps he could help her?

"Do you know what to do to get rid of this stuff?" she asked.

He smiled and squared his shoulders. "Well, I'll try. Give it a go," he said. "You might have something in that storeroom of yous that would do the job."

So, tossing her head and lifting her arm to shake the dark curls out of her eyes, Alice led the way up the steps and through the bakery and Louis followed.

He was happy to help clear up the tar and he was hoping that his help might be rewarded. They could discuss the problem of the wall, Louis could offer warm sympathy and they could, if all went well, end up in bed together. Alice too was hoping that they might spend their time doing something more interesting than just washing a dirty wall.

Marie Monnier, from the restaurant opposite, saw Louis following Alice into the bakery. She had a very good idea where Louis and Alice were heading and she knew exactly what they were thinking of and what she was going to do about it. She walked out of the hotel, over the road, up the steps and into the bakery. "Louis," she called, going through the door into the big family kitchen behind the shop.

Alice and Louis were standing by the table. There were two glasses out and Louis was opening a bottle of

Muscat from Rivesaltes. They looked up, startled, as Marie came in.

"You haven't got time for that, Louis," she said. "You're needed, urgently, at the hotel. I'm afraid we shall have to go."

Marie moved round the table, took the bottle from her husband's hand, put it down and gently, but firmly, propelled him towards the door. She turned to Alice. "I'm afraid my husband won't be coming here any more, madame," she told her. "He has too much work to do at the hotel."

Alice was left speechless. Louis was over the road and inside the hotel before he could decide what to say.

His wife faced him. "Right. I've told you before, Louis Monnier, I won't have you chasing after every woman in La Bastide. This time it's all been nice and quiet and friendly. But if you go into that shop again and start chatting up Alice Chauvet and thinking you're going to sleep with her, you'd better think again, because I just might leave you to it and if I do, then you'd better check the tills very carefully because I'm not working here for nothing."

She paused. Louis was weak and lazy but he had been brought up to know the value of a profitable business and he looked horrified at the idea of his wife taking his money. Marie spelt it out. "I'm your wife. I share your life and your work. Or you take what you can get outside and I take what I can get here." She nodded, closing the discussion.

After that Marie herself, or one of the children, went to collect the bread and Louis saw very little of Alice Chauvet.

As the war went on shortages and restrictions were felt more keenly and the opponents of the Vichy government grew increasingly irritated. The teachers at La Bastide and Luxat were not out daubing the streets with tar but they made their own quiet protest.

A splendid poster was distributed to every school in the country. It was a portrait of Pétain, white haired, avuncular, wise, inscribed with the words of the Minister himself, comparing the old man with the vigorous young heroine of French history. Flowing across the side of the poster the words ran: "Like Jeanne d'Arc, his eyes are blue ...Like Jeanne d'Arc, he has saved France ..."

Teachers were told to display this poster prominently, within reach of the children, so that they could read the text and appreciate the heroism of their president.

Monsieur Vidal was the only teacher at the school at Luxat. He had no intention of encouraging his pupils to admire Pétain. "Another poster!" he complained to his wife. "Just look at the size of it. And the quality of the paper! They can find good paper for rubbish like this and every school in the country is short of paper for the children's work!" He tugged open a drawer in the dresser and slammed this poster on top of the growing pile he was keeping 'for the archives'.

Simone, his wife, taught at Festes. The school there had two teachers but Simone and her colleague did not put up the poster. There was no discussion, no decision to disobey the Ministry instructions. They simply left the poster on a table where it was soon buried under a pile of books and eventually, dirty and dog eared, it fell on the floor and was thrown out with the rubbish.

At La Bastide the headmistress distributed the posters and told the teachers to put them up. Jean-Paul Ramel put the poster for his class in the drawer of his desk. The headmistress was not happy.

"I want that poster up on the classroom wall tomorrow morning," she told him. "And not hidden away but somewhere within reach, where the children can appreciate it."

Jean-Paul thought it was his duty to see that the children were protected from the sight of a man like Pétain. He pinned up the poster by the side of the youngest children, well within their reach. He had just been writing in his markbook and there was ink on his fingers.

"Oh dear!" he said mildly as a nasty black blot appeared on the poster. He scrubbed at it, with a fairly clean handkerchief. The surface of the paper was damaged and the stain spread. During the morning some of the children tried to cover the damage by scribbling over it with white chalk. Others spat on their fingers and tried to wash away the ink. By the end of morning lessons Monsieur Ramel was pleased to see a very grubby, tattered poster.

When the headmistress returned to make sure that he had put it up, he was enthusiastic.

"The children really love it," he assured her. "They were fascinated. Kept on returning to it all morning."

"Well, they haven't looked after it very well, have they? You'd better take it down," the headmistress decided.

Jean-Paul nodded, trying to look as if he thought the headmistress was a wise woman who had just made a sensible decision.

He told Simone Vidal about it later, grinning with delight. "She'd only just told me to put it up and I'd done as she said and made sure it was within reach of the children. It looked awful and she really didn't know whether it was deliberate or not."

It might not be much but Jean-Paul had made his protest and felt better for it.

Jean-Paul felt better, too, for the news the BBC which brought hope from the world outside France. When his mother asked him why he bothered to listen to 'that foreign stuff' and reminded him that he'd go to jail if he was caught listening, he simply shook his head. "I can't live on the diet of German propaganda that we get from Radio France and from the newspapers. I need to know that there are Frenchmen out there, in London, who are still fighting. It helps to know that we're not alone."

In the café Terminus they were anti-Vichy to a man and every evening someone kept watch outside and they switched on the wireless and twiddled the tuning knob and strained to catch what was said, with the sound low and the voices distorted with static. When Germany invaded Russia they were encouraged to remember Napoleon and how he had been defeated by the terrible Russian winter. And they welcomed the American defeat at Pearl Harbour because now the power of the United States would be ranged against the Germans.

They wanted others to get this message too. There were newsletters to let people know what was happening and encourage them to see that the war was not over yet and the Germans might not be as powerful as they seemed.

Monsieur Bouladou was one of those who went round delivering news sheets and Marcel, young and twice as fast, was helping him. They would go up through the town, their pockets stuffed with papers and walk back down again, dropping the leaflets into letter boxes, pushing them under doors or propping them behind window boxes and pots of flowers. Marcel would zip into the narrow alleys that hid behind the shops and would run up and down the steps that led to the houses on the river bank below the bridge and though they shared the work, taking one side of the road each, Marcel usually finished his side first and came back to help Bernard.

Marcel did not mind these deliveries. It was exciting, dangerous, knowing that they would be in real trouble if they were caught. And someone would usually buy him a drink at the Terminus when they had finished.

For Bernard Bouladou it was different. He believed that they were doing important work, telling people that there were Frenchmen still fighting the enemy, even here in La Bastide, and encouraging others not to collaborate with Germany. He was not a young hothead though and his heart sank every time he got the message to pick up another bundle. It was not just that he found it tiring, going out after a day's work at the factory to tramp the streets at night, bending and stooping, straining his eyes trying to see in the dark. He knew that what he was doing was dangerous. He knew that if he was caught he would be sent to prison. How could he cope with that at his age? He might be used as a hostage. He might be shot. He was scared. Scared for himself and for his family.

They did not deliver the papers in the main streets, around the market place where there were open spaces and a police patrol might easily see them. They kept to the narrow alleys, round the old church and down by the river and the railway station.

Monsieur le Commissaire Delpech had no sympathy for protestors and his officers were out at night patrolling the streets, checking papers, following up 'information received'. There had been denunciations in La Bastide. A young woman had reported her neighbour for listening to the BBC. Bernard and Marcel knew that they could be denounced. Someone looking out of a window, peering through the shutters, might see them and write a letter to the Town Hall or to the police.

It was early in the Autumn. Summer had ended but the cold winter weather was still weeks away. Marcel was wearing his blue denim overalls but Bernard Bouladou was wearing a big winter jacket because it had good pockets, useful for holding papers and felt uncomfortably warm as he trudged through the streets.

They had been up to the top of the town and come down again. They had already delivered most of the papers. They had turned into one of the roads that led down towards the river. It was a narrow street of old houses, ancient wood frame houses, roughly plastered, where the first floor hung out over the road and the pavement had built up in the course of time, leaving the front door down below at the old level. Marcel had slipped into the dark, damp passage way beside the church.

Bernard's hearing was no longer very good. Perhaps that was why he had heard nothing, or perhaps he was simply not concentrating. Suddenly, in front of him, two policemen stepped out from the shadow of the houses. He walked straight into them.

"Your papers, monsieur."

"Steady!" he told himself. He had his papers ready, in his trouser pocket, and he handed them over. He tried to look unworried but his throat was dry, his hands were shaking and he could feel the strength drain from his legs.

"Pockets!" they said.

He responded with a vague, short-sighted smile and prayed for a miracle.

"Here!" The younger policeman grabbed his coat and felt in one of the pockets. God had granted a miracle. It was empty. All the papers had gone from his right hand pocket.

Then the policeman tapped the other pocket. There was something there. He drew out a dozen copies of the Franc Tireur.

"So now we know who's been sending this rubbish round the town. And you're in trouble, mon ami."

Marcel, ready to step out breezily from the passage, heard the voices and froze, every muscle tense. Carefully, he edged back, shrinking into the dark recess of the church door. It offered thin, narrow protection. Gently he twisted the iron ring of the door handle, his heart pounding as the rusty metal creaked. He released his grip. A creaking door could alert the police. Could he stay there, unseen? If they shone a light into the passage, would it catch him, pick out his white, terror-stricken face? He turned up the collar of his jacket and forced himself to face away from the street, hoping that his dark clothes would merge into the shadows.

Standing absolutely still, rigid now with fear, Marcel could hear very little. What was happening to Monsieur Bouladou?

One of the policemen shone his torch down the road, into the alley where Marcel was hiding. They did not see him.

Marcel stayed where he was, hardly daring to breath, until all sound of activity had subsided and when at last he edged out from his shelter, Monsieur Bouladou and the police had gone.

Maman knew something was wrong as soon as she saw him. "So what have you been up to?"

He was shaking as he told her what had happened and she was horrified.

"If the police catch you delivering papers like that Marcel they'll arrest you and you'll go to prison. And it may not be just an ordinary prison either. They could send you to a camp for political prisoners, like the one at Rivel. Carcassonne jail may be bad enough but Rivel is worse, believe me."

"They could use you as a hostage, you know," Maman went on. "Madame Coste told me that a German officer was killed in Bordeaux and they took a hundred hostages and shot fifty of them." She crossed herself. "And only God knows what's going to happen to the others."

Joseph looked up from his homework, the flickering light of the candle on the table beside him giving his face a pale, uncertain brightness. He stared at his brother as if expecting him to drop dead before his eyes.

"You can't go on with these deliveries Marcel," Maman warned. "It's too dangerous, it's got to stop."

Marcel shrugged carelessly and grinned at his brother but promised that he would deliver no more papers, though Maman had no illusions and wondered what trouble he would find next.

CHAPTER 9
April 1942 - December 1942 Demonstrations

There was gloom in the café Terminus.

Jean-Paul Ramel, a naturally cheerful young man, had stepped in for a drink and was looking forward to a chat and a laugh and even a game of cards, possibly. He groaned at the icy atmosphere.

"So? What's bitten everyone?" He clapped a hand dramatically to his brow, assuming an expression of deep tragedy. "Don't tell me! Ste Agathe have beaten La Bastide! We're out of the Languedoc Rugby League!" He pulled up a chair and sat down.

"Not quite as bad as that, mon vieux!"

"Laval's back."

"Merde ..." It was enough to dampen even Jean-Paul's good humour. "In charge of rationing? Internal security? Propaganda?" he suggested hopefully.

"Prime Minister. In charge of home affairs, foreign affairs, information. The lot."

"Mon Dieu! We've got Pétain who no longer knows what day of the week it is and goes round chucking little girls under the chin in a very suspect fashion and now we've got this German puppet brought back to run the government."

"We've got to do something."

""We've got to make some sort of protest."

"We can't just sit back and let them go on sucking up to the Germans."

"At least the boys painted slogans on the bakery wall."

"And Bouladou ..."

They faltered. They admired Monsieur Bouladou but he had been arrested and his friends shifted uncomfortably and scratched their heads because they were ashamed that they were not as brave as he had been.

It was Jean-Paul a few days later who told them about the idea for a demonstration which he'd heard about when he went to Toulouse University for a lecture.

"The anniversary of the Battle of Valmy. We can celebrate that."

The Spanish refugees had never heard of Valmy.

"The Battle of Valmy?" asked Juan.

Jean-Paul laughed. "20th September 1792. So 1942, it's the one hundred and fiftieth anniversary this year."

Juan did not actually ask 'So what?' but he raised an eyebrow and shook his head and had obviously no idea why it was important. Not all the Frenchmen could have said what it was about either.

"Every French child learns about it in school. In the French Revolution, the Prussians were threatening to invade France and the French army fought them off."

"They sang the Ca Ira! And shouted 'Vive la Nation'."

"What about the Marseillaise?"

"I don't know. They'd only just written that. Perhaps they didn't know the words."

"Goethe went to watch the fighting," Raoul Vidal told them.

"All very interesting, no doubt," said Jean-Paul, "but what are we going to do to celebrate this anniversary?"

The battle of Valmy did not stir the hearts of the Spanish refugees or even the socialist workers of La Bastide but it was a chance to demonstrate their patriotism and it was not obviously illegal or dangerous.

"A minute's silence. Terribly formal and solemn."

"Where?"

La Bastide did not have many national monuments. They considered the War Memorial but it was down by the railway, not in the centre of town.

"By the general's house."

A general of the Foreign Legion, killed fighting in Mexico, had once lived in La Bastide. His house was round the corner from the hotel, on the road to Festes.

On Sunday 20th September they gathered at midday, by the bridge over the river Blair, at the bottom of the main street. Monsieur Vidal was there in the front row. With his hair neatly trimmed, his shoes shining with polish, he marched smartly, a proud officer of the French army. Jean-Paul Ramel was there too, with a shadow of dark stubble round his chin because he had tumbled out of bed late that morning and not had time to shave.

The congregation, leaving the church after morning mass, was heading home or on the way to lunch at the hotel. The men marching up the centre of the road might have been confused with the throng of church goers except that the demonstrators had decorated their hats with a modest tricolor and looked painfully self-conscious.

Monsieur Delpech was on his way to the hotel, with his wife and daughter. "What's all this about?" he asked.

"It's the anniversary of the Battle of Valmy," they told him.

Monsieur Delpech had learnt about the Battle of Valmy at school. He knew it was an important battle but that was about all he did know. The men celebrating this anniversary were mostly middle-aged, well-dressed and respectable so, with barely a moment's hesitation, he went on his way, ushering his wife and daughter into the hotel restaurant.

Maman and the boys were in La Bastide for a family lunch and they joined the little crowd of curious onlookers. The demonstrators went past the hotel. In front of the general's house, with its commemorative plaque, they stopped.

A lecturer from the college in Quillan was leading the group.

"Mesdames, mesdemoiselles, messieurs," he began. "It is an honour to be here to-day, on the anniversary of a glorious moment in the history of France."

An ox cart lumbered past, bringing a family from Festes for a birthday celebration in La Bastide. The crowd pressed forward to allow it to pass.

"May I ask you all now to stand for a minute in respectful silence, in memory of our brave compatriots at Valmy who withstood the Prussian attack and saved our beloved country, one hundred and fifty years ago."

They took off their hats and bowed their heads and stood in respectful silence.

Taken by surprise, the crowd of onlookers was unsure how to respond. A few left and went on their way home. Others joined the silent tribute, shushing their children. They realised now that this was a demonstration against the power of the Germans in their country but it was a quiet, well-mannered demonstration and it was very satisfying to defy the authorities with such innocence.

Marcel had raised his cap with a flourish and was standing to attention. Joseph had taken off his cap too and was trying not to giggle.

Monsieur Delpech had not wanted any disturbance and had expected a quiet, restrained ceremony. He was going to enjoy his usual Sunday lunch. But Auguste Monnier had invited a group of young Legionnaires to the hotel that day.

These were not the staid veterans of the 1914-18 war, who joined the Legion for the companionship of other soldiers and because they wanted to show their support for Marshal Pétain. These were swaggering young men who enjoyed wearing military uniforms and marching through the streets with flags and banners because it gave them a sense of power.

When the demonstrators passed the hotel, the Legionnaires were drinking in the bar, laughing, talking loudly, preening themselves, to the obvious admiration of Auguste. The demonstration was an irresistable provocation.

"Right lads, let's show them."

They tumbled out into the road, formed up, tugging at their shirts, straightening their berets. "Left, right! Left, right!" The sound of their boots rang out and the street echoed to young voices singing the Chant des Cohortes: "We shall make France strong!"

They turned into the route de Festes and cut through the crowd, attacking the demonstrators, tearing off their tricolor cockades and lashing out with their fists and feet. Some of the onlookers protested but caught unprepared they were no match for hefty and determined Legionnaires beating up demonstrators who were, for the most part, mild-mannered and elderly.

This was no longer a quiet, innocent protest. Husbands called to their wives to get out of the way, mothers snatched up their children and ran screaming from the scene. Maman stood rooted to the spot, her arms clutched across her breast, her mouth open in speechless horror. She saw Joseph kicked to the ground. Marcel started fighting but picked an opponent who was a lot bigger and stronger than him and he was soon sitting propped against a wall, blood streaming from a cut on his head. For ten minutes there was chaos as blows rained and the citizens of La Bastide ran, stumbling, to escape the Legionnaires at their heels.

From the steps of the hotel, Auguste watched, enjoying the sight of respectable citizens scurrying away, chased by the young thugs in uniform. Some tried to shelter inside but Auguste blocked the door and refused to let them in, until his father shouted at him to get out of the way and they scuttled in confusion into the bar and the restaurant or hovered anxiously on the stairs that led to the bedrooms, relaxing only when they realised that the trouble had passed and the Legionnaires were chasing their prey down the road towards the river.

Two of the more elderly demonstrators were pushed into the water and were cut and bruised as they fell on the stones of the river bed. A young doctor left his table at the hotel and went to help the wounded.

When it was over the Legionnaires lined up once more and tramped back into the hotel, singing lustily.

Louis Monnier did not like the way they behaved but the Legionnaires had powerful connections. He was not going to quarrel with them and lose business. So he fed them well and served them with friendly courtesy while their loud voices and the arrogant way they boasted of their morning's work annoyed some of those eating at neighbouring tables.

Joseph and Marcel and Maman limped away to their party, to the sympathetic care of the family where the girls particularly tended Marcel with loving attention.

"Young louts, that's what they are, those Legionnaires," one of their uncles declared. "And I can't think why the government encourages them."

Joseph had little to say. He had seen Auguste sneering from the doorway of the hotel. He was a big bully He and his family and the thugs in uniform had the upper hand at the moment. But he'd vowed not to forgive Monsieur Monnier and he wouldn't. One day he'd get his own back on them, all of them.

Meanwhile every gleam of hope that came their way seemed to be quickly extinguished.

At the beginning of Novermber British and American troops landed in North Africa. In the streets of La Bastide they walked with a lighter step. As they queued for bread people smiled at each other, their backs straighter and their heads held higher.

"They'll be here soon, now!" they told each other at the café Terminus. The end of the war was in sight.

Their hopes were soon dashed.

In the early hours of Wednesday, 11th November, German troops crossed the demarcation line between the occupied zone and Vichy France. They had come, they said, to protect France from her enemies, from the troops which had landed in North Africa and might invade the south of France if the Germans were not there to protect the Vichy government.

The next day, a Thursday, when there was no ordinary school, Joseph was at catechism class, at the church. The children were restless as always. They let their prayer books fall on the bare tiles with a loud thud and scrabbled noisily to retrieve them. They pushed and shoved and flicked paper pellets at each other. Monsieur le curé despaired and wondered how Raoul Vidal coped with them all and why they seemed to behave so much better in the schoolroom.

Gradually they became aware of a distant rumbling, an endless mechanical grinding, echoing like thunder round the hills.

Once Luxat had been cut off from the world with only Tomas the shepherd to bring them news. Now the Coste

119

family had a wireless and everyone in Luxat knew what was happening: the sound they could hear was the sound of the German army invading the south of France.

So Joseph and his friends were on their bikes and away, up the cliff path which Robert had taken and along the edge of the forest to the Col de la Babourade and out onto the main road, the D117, which crossed France from Perpignan and Quillan in the East, to St Girons and Bayonne in the West. They emerged from the grey shadows of the forest and stood by the roadside to watch as the Germans went by: lorries, vans, motorcycles, troop carriers, guns, provisions and equipment rolled past in an endless display of overwhelming power.

Joseph had seen La Bastide on market day, crowded with carts and buses and bicycles. "But you've never seen anything like this," he told Maman. "You looked one way and the lorries were disappearing over the hill and you looked the other way and there were new ones just coming. On and on. We started counting but we counted more than thirty and they were still coming."

"More lorries?" asked Maman.

"Yes. And tanks. Tanks with the roof open and a German soldier inside, standing up, his head poking out above the roof. And they were armed, with rifles. Like they were ready to shoot!"

Maman sighed. "I hope we don't see any of them here in Luxat."

"And motorcycles. Making an absolute racket. Some of them had side cars. They had two soldiers on the bike and another sitting in the side car."

They were impressed but horrified.

On Sunday in La Bastide the Nazi flag hung from the balcony of the Town Hall and a military band played stirring tunes. The German army was on parade.

A sleek black car glided quietly to a halt in front of the Town Hall. An aide leapt to open the door for his commanding officer, who stepped out with slow dignity and glanced round the little town, drab in the bleak November cold.

"They're going to see some changes here. They'll find out now what smartness and efficiency mean," the great man declared with contempt. His aide smiled and nodded as he ran to usher his master into the Town Hall. The band struck up. With exquisite horsemanship the cavalry led the parade through the town, their horses well-fed and beautifully groomed. Then came the armoured cars, tanks and motor cycles. These were not dented gazogenes but petrol fuelled vehicles, smooth running and gleaming with polish.

The people of La Bastide, their faces thin with cold and hunger, watched the parade. Dazzled by the display, stirred by the music, impressed by this power and organisation which totally eclipsed the Valmy demonstration, they waved and clapped and smiled.

"I told you they had a lot of cars and tanks and things, didn't I?" Joseph reminded Marcel.

"I don't care. I don't like the Germans." Marcel was determined not to be seduced by this glamorous display.

"I hate them," said Joseph, hurt by the implication that he might not share his brother's patriotism.

However much he might once have been prepared to admire Marshal Pétain Joseph's sympathies now were firmly with the British, with Robert and Monsieur Vidal and their friends. But it was difficult not to be impressed by this demonstration. The German army was powerful. Joseph had dreamed of defeating the Germans. Robert had told him how they had kept the enemy at bay by blowing up bridges. It had sounded like good fun and they had played at securing the perimeter down by the old bridge in Luxat. Winning the war now seemed altogether more difficult. It would not be easy to defeat this force.

Raoul Vidal was watching the parade in grim silence. Beside him, Jean-Paul Ramel was angry. "Why do people have to welcome them? Why can't they turn their backs? It makes me ashamed to be French."

"Well, they aren't putting on this parade just for fun, are they? They're showing us how strong they are, how rich and powerful. They want us to believe we can't possibly defeat them. But we're not all cheering, mon ami. Look round. A lot of us are just watching and waiting."

After the armoured vehicles came the soldiers, impressive in their warm green overcoats. Their polished leather boots rang confidently on the cobbled street. One or two small children giggled at their goose-stepping march but they were quickly hushed.

From the top of the bakery steps, Alice Chauvet gazed with awe. They were so fit these young men, tall and muscular, so much smarter than the young men of La Bastide. She was full of admiration and tossed her dark curls and hoped that they would not all march away, that some of them might come back to La Bastide.

Marcel, unwillingly, was impressed. He had never seen such thick, smooth cloth, such shining, sturdy boots, such tall men, glowing with health and vitality. He felt humiliated. He and his friends wore scruffy boots, with old rubber tyres for soles. They were short and skinny, not tall like these arrogant invaders. Well, German soldiers needn't think they could just march through his town. He'd show them how much he cared. He squared his shoulders, stuffed his hands into his pockets and sauntered into the road, swaggering through the marching ranks with just a hint of a goosestep. Laughter flickered through the crowd.

Monsieur le Commissaire Delpech, who had been admiring this orderly display of force and was only too well aware of the German officer watching from the balcony of the Town Hall saw Marcel and turned imperiously to a subordinate.

"Stop that idiot! Bring him here!"

Laurent Barde, the young policeman, had been smiling. At Monsieur Delpech's command he wiped the smile from his face and did as he was told. He grabbed Marcel and led him back to Monsieur Delpech. The incipient laughter died.

"What the hell do you think you're doing?" Monsieur Delpech growled.

Marcel was not going to give way now. "Just crossing the road. Like the chicken. You know: Why did the chicken cross the road? Just trying to get to the other side."

Laurent Barde stood beside him, carefully impassive. Monsieur Delpech spluttered.

"Oh, you are funny, aren't you! Well, you may change your mind. This young man here is going to take you down to the police station and he is going to explain to you what respect for the law means and I personally am going to see that you get plenty of time to think about how sensible it is to show off in public. You may be sorry you crossed this road at this particular moment." He paused. "Take him back to the Police Station. I'll see him later."

Joseph watched them go and wondered what on earth he could do. Wondering what to do, frowning, trying to work out whether Marcel would be able to cope if he were running away from the police, Joseph edged his way through the crowd. The German parade was still streaming past. It was impossible to reach Marcel.

Monsieur Vidal had seen what happened and caught up with Joseph. "We'll go to the Police Station and see if we can do anything," he said. "Though I'm not hopeful. There seems to be a law now against doing anything anti-German. Defeatism they call it," he muttered bitterly.

Laurent Barde was at the Police Station. They could see no sign of Marcel.

"He's in a room at the back," the policeman told them. "You'll have to wait for Monsieur Delpech. I don't know what's going to happen to him."

They sat on a bench covered with greasy oilcloth. The room was cold and dusty, painted in a grubby institutional grey. They stamped their feet to keep the circulation going and got up and read the notices on the wall. They were depressing. Notices forbidding the population to express their opinions, ordering them to collect ration cards, warning them of the dire punishments meted out to offenders. It seemed a long time before Monsieur Delpech appeared.

When he did, Monsieur Vidal was very polite, very correct. "I would like to see the boy, if I may," he said. Monsieur Delpech shook his head. Monsieur Vidal pleaded the boy's youth. He was a bit silly, impatient perhaps, but an agitator? "No. He's not an agitator," Monsieur Vidal declared. Then there was his widowed mother. "She needs his help at home, to keep the farm going."

Monsieur Delpech was adamant. "We'll be taking him to court in Carcassonne tomorrow. Then we'll see what happens."

So Joseph had to go back home on his own, to tell Maman. "What do you mean? They arrested the boy for crossing the road? They took him to the Police Station just for that?" Maman could hardly believe it. "Are you sure that's all he did? He didn't try to kick one of the soldiers? Or throw a stone?"

"No. He just walked across the road in the middle of the parade."

"Mon Dieu! What are we coming to!" Maman was horrified and fearful for the future. "If he's in trouble for that now, what will happen when he really starts getting up to mischief? And he will. He'll do a lot worse than that."

They could think of nothing else all evening.

"You two are my sons," she told Joseph, not for the first time. "Since I lost my little Claude, you two have been my boys and I worry about you."

"He will be all right, won't he?" asked Joseph, anxious for reassurance.

"Yes. He'll be all right this time, I expect. But he does things without thinking. And I just hope that this time he may learn his lesson. Before he does something really silly."

Marcel, at the Police Station, was confident that all would be well. At court in Carcassonne next day he was the picture of innocence.

"So why did you interrupt the parade?" asked the judge.

Marcel did not try to give a silly answer this time. "I saw a girl I know, monsieur. She's been a bit unfriendly recently and I thought if I could catch her in a good mood, while she was enjoying the procession ... "

The judge was not convinced. "So what did you say to Monsieur le Commissaire Delpech?"

Marcel hung his head and tried to look contrite and mumbled an apology.

His case did not take long. The judge was convinced of the need to collaborate with the Germans and to punish any hooligans who broke the law.

"It is an offence to show any disrespect to the Germans or the symbols of their authority," he declared. "One month's hard labour."

Marcel waited in a small cell behind the court until other cases had been heard. Then, as night was falling, he was handcuffed and pushed into a van with other prisoners and driven off. It was dark and they could not see where they were taken.

A prison officer wrote their names in his register. Marcel was marched off to a big dormitory where he was shown a rough wooden bunk, with a thin matress and a worn blanket which smelt of sweat and urine. The room was cold, the stench appalling. He lay down and thought of Monsieur Bouladou who was in prison somewhere near Montpellier. He turned and twisted, scratching with increasing irritation, at the bugs and fleas and lice which gave him no peace.

In the morning they lined up for roll call. There were a lot of Spanish men there and some Italians.

After roll call they marched to the kitchens. In silence. Marcel collected his breakfast: a bowl of warm water, an unappetising brown in colour. Coffee? Whatever it was, there were no coffee beans in it and it tasted foul.

He spent the day sawing logs. It was hard work but at least the effort helped to keep him warm. The men with him coughed and wheezed. Two of them were terribly thin. Marcel wondered how they managed to cope with this strenuous work.

Somehow his family found out that he was in prison in Carcassonne. Monsieur Cambon's brother came in with some food for him: a length of sausage and a loaf of bread. Marcel shared it with a Spanish boy who had no family to bring him extra rations.

He grew used to the routine: roll call, breakfast, work, supper, bed. But it was hard. He was hungry all the time, really hungry, not just ready for his next meal. And brought up in the freedom and fresh air of Luxat the confinement and the endless regulations were torture.

"Just keep your mouth shut and count the days to your release," the others told him.

And he did. And the month passed and he came out.

Never had a town seemed so beautiful as Carcassonne that day. At the railway station he loitered, watching the barges on the canal and he thought how wonderful it was to be free and to be able to travel up and down on the water. Even the train packed to bursting, seemed luxury compared with his prison cell and when an old woman opened up her basket and handed her children bread and ham and crisp green apples, Marcel savoured with delight the good rich smell of wheat and flour and mustard and the crunch of teeth biting into the white flesh of the apples.

From Quillan he got a lift on a lorry going to Lavelanet and got off at the Col de la Babourade and walked down to Luxat, where Maman and Joseph and the Coste family and everyone was waiting for him and greeted him with hugs and kisses and they laughed and cried and wiped the tears from their eyes and were delighted to be together again.

Achille Cambon rummaged in his shirt pocket and, his rough red face beaming with generosity, brought out a battered packet of Gauloises. "The real thing. None of those dried leaves for a man who's just come from hell." He held one out for Marcel, another for Joseph, and they lit up and sucked in the tarry fumes. Monsieur Cambon wheezed, his lungs destroyed by years of Gauloises and Gitanes, Joseph coughed and spluttered, trying to cope with this assault on his throat and lungs, and Marcel with masterly control, proudly puffed like a man who knew how to cope with the good things of life.

"What was it like?" Joseph asked when they went to bed that night. "Was it awful?"

Marcel shrugged. Of course it had been awful but what could he say about it? How could he tell Joseph how bloody, fucking angry he was? He tried. "That prison was full of people like me," he said. "Those bloody men in Vichy, what are they trying to do? Ruin the bloody country! Sell out to the fucking Boche! The whole bloody country is in the hands of a senile dodderer and a traitor! "

The prisons were indeed full of men like Marcel and outside the prisons, too, the government was increasingly unpopular. The Prime Minister decided that he should broadcast to the nation, to explain why they needed to work so closely with the Germans.

Raoul Vidal was at his parents' home in Quillan. His grandmother had died and the whole family had gathered for the funeral. His parents, his grandmother's three brothers from Strasbourg, uncles and aunts, cousins, brothers and sisters, Vidals and in-laws, they were all there. The table was extended to its limit and they had emptied their larders and scoured the local markets and provided a meal which, though it might not match pre-war standards, was a feast in their present circumstances. The best linen was on the table, the best china. They had opened bottles of Blanquette de Limoux. There was a mellow feeling of family solidarity.

"We are going to hear Laval's broadcast, aren't we?" one of the uncles asked. They switched on the set and tuned in. Shushing the children, leaving the empty dishes uncleared, they prepared to listen to the Prime Minister.

Laval told them that there would be a new Europe when the war was over and round the table the family murmured their agreement.

In this new Europe Laval looked forward to seeing France working in harmony with Germany and Italy.

The Prime Minister continued. "Germany is fighting to build a new Europe. Germany is sacrificing the blood of her young people."

"And ours," complained Uncle Albert. "Did you know that they're taking young men from Alsace and forcing them into their wretched German army?"

Laval went on. "I hope that Germany will win this war ..."

There was pandemonium. Uncle Albert, a gentle academic, frail and far from young, banged his fist on the table with such force that the crockery trembled and clattered and Simone, Raoul's wife, heavily pregnant, was convinced that the baby jumped.

"How dare he!" roared Uncle Albert.

His brothers were as angry as he was. Raoul's father was still trying to hear what the Prime Minister was saying but it was useless. He had to turn off the set.

Deep into the night the argument continued. Did Pétain, the hero of the Great War, know where Laval was leading them? Was he too old to understand? Senile even? Surely he was not totally under the thumb of the Germans? That was the only argument, though. None of them could find a word in favour of Pierre Laval and his support for Germany.

In Luxat Joseph had gone round to the Coste's to hear the speech. He told Marcel what Laval had said.

"He wants the fucking Germans to win the war?" Marcel was incredulous. "I'm not going to help the bloody Boche. I'll fight the Boche and fight Laval and bloody Auguste's bloody Legionnaires and anyone else who tries to make me. If it bloody kills me," he declared.

CHAPTER 10
December 1942 - March 1943 The end of the beginning

Marie Monnier was delighted when four German soldiers were billeted on them at the Hotel du Commerce. It meant that they had four rooms permanently occupied, with the bills settled promptly. They were easy guests too, clerks who spent their days dealing with identity cards and travel documents, careful, tidy men who caused no trouble in the hotel.

Three of them were middle aged, thankful not to be fighting in Russia. The officer in charge was a younger man. He was nearly six foot tall, strong and sturdy with straight blond hair cut short at the back and sides but tending to flop into his eyes at the front. He was quite good looking and with better eyesiight would have been a formidable rugby player but he was short sighted and wore wire-rimmed glasses with thick pebble lenses which made him look timid and hesitant as he peered out at a vague, blurred world.

The Monniers made an effort to impress these German soldiers. Auguste, who had joined the Milice, paraded before them in his uniform, swaggering through the hotel in his black trousers and his khakhi shirt, with its new armband.

He saw himself as part of the military machine. "We're the local force," he would say. "We keep an eye on all the undesirables, the socialists, the trades unionists, the terrorists. We can tell you who the trouble makers are."

Marie Monnier began to put her hair in curling rags at night. She sometimes took off her overall before she came to the hotel desk and appeared wearing a dress which was suitably black but had sprigs of flowers printed on it and was padded at the shoulders and gathered across the yoke and fell in pleats from the waist. It was less seductive than she imagined and showed how skinny she was but the German soldiers were pleased to talk to her. She would lean on the counter puffing at her cigarette and was always happy to listen to their news from home. When they showed her photographs of their children she examined the pictures with interest, remembered the children's names, knew how old they were and was impressed by their progress at school.

Old Madame Monnier was scornful. "I don't know why you bother with them," she said. "They're not interested in you. They've got wives and families at home and if they want a bit of fun here they're going to find something better than you can offer them."

Louis was not bothered what his wife did. He spent his time in the bar, encouraging everyone to be happy. The Germans attracted other customers. Men like Monsieur Delpech were happy to spend their evenings drinking in the company of such important people.

There were language classes at the school in the evenings. It seemed a good idea to learn German and then go into the Hotel du Commerce afterwards and practise what you had learnt. Alice Chauvet was an enthusiastic student. She did not go into the bar after classes but when the soldiers came into the bakery she would smile and fuss over them and make a great show of speaking German, pouting and frowning and struggling to get it right.

Hans, the young officer, got a particularly warm welcome. He had lovely manners she thought. He would wait in the queue with everyone else, even though he was a German soldier and was entitled to go straight to the front of the queue. If she had baked any pastries Alice would keep one back for Hans and he began to call round after work to collect his treat.

Alice would practise her German. "Where do you live? How old are you?" she would ask, frowning and stumbling and mouthing the words with exaggerated care, forgetting what she was supposed to say and starting again a dozen times. Hans found her accent enchanting. He would reply very slowly and clearly but even if he repeated his answer again and again Alice never quite seemed to understand and they would collapse in laughter, with her complaining that the German language was simply too difficult.

Like the older men at the hotel Hans missed his family and he showed her photographs of his parents and his brother and sister. His face clouded when he talked of his brother.

"We are very anxious for my brother," Hans told her. "He is on the eastern front, at Stalingrad."

"Don't worry," Alice reassured him. "He'll be all right. It won't be long now before the Russians are defeated. And then he'll come home."

"I hope so," said Hans.

Alice thought that his parents would miss their two sons this Christmas. "What do you usually do at Christmas?" she asked him.

Hans's eyes lit up as he thought of home and remembered the idyllic holidays of his childhood. "We decorate the house," he told her. "We have a splendid meal. No rationing, of course." They laughed.

"Why don't you come here this Christmas?" Alice suggested.

Hans was delighted. On Christmas morning, he stood in front of the big old mirror in his room at the Hotel du

Commerce and carefully combed his hair with a wet comb. He was wearing a new shirt and a blue silk tie that his parents had sent him. In a jug by the washstand stood a bunch of flowers, beautiful hothouse flowers that he had bought specially in Foix the day before.

Louis Monnier smiled at him as he left the hotel, wishing him a happy Christmas. He crossed the road and climbed the steps of the bakery. As he opened the door he was greeted by a delicious smell of home cooking which drifted, tempting, from the kitchen. He went through the shop and stood at the door, shyly offering his bunch of flowers.

Alice was overwhelmed. Nobody had ever given her flowers before. It was so romantic. Like a story in a magazine. She put up her arms and drew his head down and gave him a wonderful, lingering kiss. Nobody had every kissed him like that before. As he took her in his arms all his shyness vanished and he knew that he loved her.

They had charcuterie, four or five different meats and sausages. They had rabbit in a creamy mustard sauce, roast vegetables, potatoes and parsnips and marrow. Then there was a galette, glowing with golden wheat, drenched with white sugar. They drank blanquette de Limoux from crystal glasses that had belonged to Alice's grandmother and when they had finished they sipped old Armagnac and sat by the fire, with Hans roasting chestnuts. He pulled them out and scorched his fingers as he peeled them and Alice parted her lips and he fed her pieces of roasted chestnuts. She ran the tip of her tongue round his fingers. She was so close, her perfume overwhelmed him. He crushed her to him, kissing her, and her tongue was inside his mouth, probing, and her lips were hard against his. He could hardly breathe, his whole body seemed to burn and quiver.

It was dark outside and they had eaten and drunk until they could eat and drink no more, and when they were sated, too, with kisses, Hans slowly loosened his silk tie and Alice unbuttoned his new shirt and slipped off her party dress and they lay naked on the big, soft bed and made love with a passionate tenderness that neither had known before.

They were overwhelmed by love, absorbed in each other. Hans took Alice to dinner at the Hotel du Commerce and Marie Monnier, who had been so sharp when Alice was flirting with Louis, welcomed them with a gracious smile as she showed them to a quiet table in the corner. After they had gone, though, she was less flattering.

"What's Albert Chauvet going to think about this when he gets home?" she demanded.

Louis pulled a wry face. Old Madame Monnier sniffed, pursed her lips and complained that young women to-day didn't know what duty was and they were all no better than they should be, the whole lot of them.

Alice was not worried about Albert, in prison in Germany. Their wedding photograph stood on the mantelpiece above the fire, so that when she thought of Albert now it was this photograph she saw, not a real, living man. They'd set up home together and worked together in the bakery. They'd planned to have children. When she married Albert, Alice had thought he would bake the bread and she would look after the shop and the children. It hadn't worked out like that. She was landed with the baking and the shop and no children and no fun. Now Hans had come and there was laughter and joy in her life.

Hans too was happy, irrepressibly happy. Sometimes he felt a twinge of guilt, not because of Albert, but because of his brother who was suffering on the eastern front. The news was bad. His letters home had complained about the cold.

He had no winter uniform, there was no transport because their fuel had frozen solid. Now there were no letters at all from the front and his parents were sick with worry.

They were not prepared for such a crushing defeat, though. The entire 6th Army had been lost, all the men killed or taken prisoner. In Germany, stunned by grief, the whole country observed three days of official mourning.

In France the opponents of the regime took heart. At the café Terminus more and more men huddled round the wireless in the evening, celebrating news of the German defeat.

"I told you. I said the Russian winter had defeated Napoleon. I said Hitler would be sorry he ever went into Russia!"

"Oh, those German soldiers thought they were going to plough through the country, taking over Russia like they've taken over everywhere else."

"They thought they were invincible."

"And they aren't."

"They've been defeated!"

That was the point, of course. The German army had seemed invincible. Now, at Stalingrad, they had failed to conquer. For the first time the German army had been forced to surrender.

So the men at the café Terminus were full of hope. The Italians would desert. The allies would land in France, in Provence perhaps. They would get rid of the Germans, they would be free.

In this atmosphere of hope the Spanish refugees set to work. They stole a load of gelignite and detonators from a construction site in the mountains and they blew up electricity pylons and attacked railway lines and bridges.

They destroyed a train as it waited at the station loaded with wheat ready to be transported to Germany.

The men at the bar in the hotel were enraged.

"Young hooligans!" they fumed.

Monsieur Delpech could not understand such wilful destruction. "What do they think they're doing? There's so little flour, the bread ration is right down, and these terrorists destroy a whole train load of wheat! What good will that do?"

Louis moaned about the power cuts and the shortage of candles. Auguste puffed out his chest and strutted around promising everyone that the Milice would round up all the terrorists and make them wish they'd never been born.

At Luxat Joseph and Marcel heard about Stalingrad and welcomed the news but Joseph was too young to be involved in the resistance and Marcel had other things on his ming.

"Marie-France!" he sighed. "She's gorgeous!" he told Joseph. "Golden skin! Light brown hair! Curves in all the right places!" He sighed with satisfaction. "And she likes me! Whoopee!" He flung out his arms and broke into song: bars of unmusical exuberance.

Joseph shook his head, not really interested. Maman smiled indulgently.

"Not too late, to-night, Marcel. There's work tomorrow."

Marcel had just spent a month in prison in Carcassonne. He was not going to waste time now. It was a very decorous courtship as they sat together by the fireside with her parents and her grandmother and her brothers and sisters all around them. But he could listen to the sound of her voice, smell the sweetness of her hair and he found her enchanting. It didn't matter what she said. She told him that her grandmother had made her a bonnet, out of rabbit fur. "It's so warm!" she said. "It's not just warm, though, it's really fashionable, elegant." Her lips pursed in a reflective moue and she tossed her head, her hair rippling. "Some of the boys here are very forward, you know, and one or two of them have said that a bonnet like that would not disgrace a lady in Paris. One of them says he thinks it is quite charming." Her eyebrows arched and her eyes grew wide and earnest and Marcel felt a stab of jealousy which had to be dispelled with clear assurances that she valued his opinion on this, as on other matters. "I think you have very good taste, Marcel," she confided. "I trust your opinion." He was not entirely mollified though until her voice softened and she touched his arm and told him quietly, "It really matters to me, you know, what you think." And she let him put his arm round her waist and she leant against him and he nuzzled her ear and snatched a kiss and thought that life had never been so good.

All this took a long time and it was late before Marcel left to cycle back into La Bastide and on, through the hills, to Festes and along the valley road to Luxat. The moon was shining and the silhouette of Festes Castle stood proudly above the village, dominating the landscape, though Marcel, pedalling home was not thinking of the majesty of an ancient monument. His thoughts were devoted to Marie-France.

As he climbed up towards Luxat, however, he grew aware of an unusual sound. Somewhere in the sky above was an aeroplane. He reached the village and propped his bike against the woodpile outside the Coste's house and stood, staring up into the sky, searching. The Germans had no planes in the area. Surely the British were not coming down here to drop their bombs on Luxat? Surely this was not the hoped for Allied invasion, one plane on its own, landing on Luxat?

Joseph , who had been woken by the noise, slipped out of the house to join him.

"Can you see it?" Marcel asked.

"No. What is it?"

"Yes! There!" Marcel pointed.

The plane was flying low, down the valley now towards Festes. Tousled heads appeared at the windows of the houses, doors opened and men came out to peer up, following the plane with their eyes. The engines had faded to a faint purr as it flew over the castle at Festes but it turned back towards Luxat and the noise, as it slowly circled the village, was loud and menacing. The boys ducked involuntarily as it passed overhead, a thundering iron hawk. Then, suddenly, the aeroplane had risen and sped away, over the hills to the west, and the sky was crowded, filled with parachutes which shone silver in the moonlight and floated tremulously to the ground, where they were caught in the trees above the village.

"What on earth ...?"

Something had hung, suspended from those parachutes. Without waiting to consider, they headed off, clambering up the mountainside, along paths that were scarcely more than goat tracks. The white silk of the parachutes shone starkly, clearly visible but the first one they came to was inaccessible, lodged in the branches of a beech tree growing on ground that dropped too steeply to be reached by boys on foot who had no logging gear. The second was high up in the branches of a tree. They could not reach it but they could distinguish a metal container, cigar-shaped, six feet, two metres, long.

One had slipped through the foliage and lay on the ground, the delicate silk rumpled untidily over a container which was undamaged by its fall. They stared in wonder. Joseph ran his hand along the smooth, hard metal. Something was attached to the outside: a spade. And there was a pick, too. Squatting on the ground Marcel undid the catches that held the tools and peered uncertainly at the container.

"Come on, open it!" Joseph was already scrabbling at the catches. The metal split. "It's in three parts!" he exclaimed.

The moon shed an eerie light, which filtered coldly through the forest trees. Joseph was opening one part. Whatever had been dropped, it was wrapped in a dark, protective cloth. Joseph undid the first package and stared at what he had uncovered. There before them, tightly, neatly packed, were dozens and dozens of revolvers.

"What do we do with these?" Joseph asked.

"I don't know. "We can't leave them here, though, can we?"

There was a plane tracking station at Nebias, just beyond Festes. "They'll have heard that aeroplane going over and they'll be out from Nebias as soon as it's light," Joseph said.

"I know. But where can we hide all this stuff? It's heavy."

They thought of the big cave of Mathilde's old story but that was on the other side of the river.

"It's miles away. I'm not lugging it all over there," groaned Marcel.

"Anyway, we don't want everyone to see us carting it through the village," Joseph agreed.

Then they thought of a small hollow in the rocks, not far away.

"It's not obvious from the outside. We could hide the stuff there."

So they closed the container. They discovered that it had a harness. They could each take one on their back and they picked up the third and carried it between them. Huffing and panting and stumbling across the rough ground, they reached the rocky hollow.

"There!" Marcel said with satisfaction.

Joseph was hopping around, peering at it from all angles. "You can't see a thing unless you're right on top of it."

"Right! Let's get another!"

By the time they had hauled a second container into the hollow, they wanted to sink onto the hillside, close their eyes and sleep. But they had to get on.

Raoul Vidal, in his flat above the school at Festes, had been woken like everyone else by the low flying aeroplane. Roger, who was eighteen months old, had been disturbed by the noise and started to cry. The new baby wanted to be fed. Simone saw to the baby and Raoul picked up the boy. By the time the children had settled, the plane had disappeared and, with relief, they snatched a few hours sleep before work called them in the morning.

Cycling into Luxat, Raoul could see parachutes clinging to the mountainside above the village and was not surprised when Joseph met him as he got off his bike and led him up the mountain to the containers they had hidden.

"There are still a lot in the trees, but we've hidden three of them, " Joseph explained as they went. "Do you know what they're for, monsieur?" he asked.

Monsieur Vidal was pleased to see that some of the containers had been rescued. "Whatever they were for, they're here now. You've done a grand job hiding them. I'll see what I can find out. But we'd better get back. I've got to open the school and we don't want to be found here when the Germans come. They'll have heard the plane and they won't be long now."

The climb down the steep path was no easier than the climb up. They had to watch where they put their feet and had to grasp at trees and bushes to keep themselves from falling.

When they reached the village, it was strangely quiet. The few foresters and farmers who were about seemed to disappear just before they met, or were busy working and failed to meet their eyes. Nobody greeted them, there was no word or gesture.

The boys went home while Monsieur Vidal turned into his schoolroom, to prepare for his class. Taking up his chalk he wrote on the blackboard the subject of the day's composition and distributed the books which he had corrected. The children started to arrive, nervously subdued, and took their places at their desks without the usual scuffle and chatter, arranging their pens and pencils, opening their books, waiting for the lesson to begin.

Suddenly the rustle ceased. The class was silent, totally still. Monsieur Vidal looked up and saw, standing in the doorway, a soldier wearing the fieldgrey uniform, the peaked cap and the insignia of an officer of the German army.

He wanted a word with Monsieur Vidal. There was no need to tell the children to work quietly. They may not have done much work but their heads bent diligently over their books and though they were straining to follow what was happening beyond the classroom door, they certainly did not want to draw attention to themselves.

The German officer pointed to the ribbon in Monsieur Vidal's lapel, the green and black ribbon of the 1939-40 engagement. "A soldier like me," he said, pointing to his own iron cross and shaking Raoul's hand with friendly warmth.

The interrogation was not harsh. He wanted Raoul's name and date of birth. Where did he live?

"Did you hear a plane during the night?"
Nobody could have missed the roar of those engines.

"What did you do when you heard the aeroplane? Did you contact the mayor of Festes?"

Raoul Vidal smiled. "I assume you heard what we heard. Yes, we heard the aeroplane but with two small children to pacify we had our hands full."

"Did you know that the aeroplane had flown over Luxat? Did you know that containers had been dropped?"

"I saw the parachutes in the trees as I came in."

"Was there any sign of unusual activity in the village?"

Raoul shook his head. "On the contrary. Everything was particularly quiet and subdued. The children were very quiet when they arrived at school. I think they are surprised, stunned. This is something totally unexpected and not welcome. They don't know anything about it and don't know what to do."

The questions continued. "Has there been any talk of sabotage, any hint of terrorism in the village?"

Monsieur Vidal answered as helpfully as he could. The village, as far as he knew, was solidly patriotic, anxious to support the Vichy government. He offered to show his visitor round.

"Thank you. That is most kind but not necessary."

The questions were over. The German officer was satisfied. He clicked his heels, saluted and went on his way.

Raoul Vidal took a deep breath and returned to his class. The children looked up for a moment and one long sigh was exhaled. Then their heads bent once more over their books and the lesson continued. Through the window they could see the officer and his men preparing to leave.

While their officer had been asking questions at the school the German soldiers had been busy. They went into every house and questioned the inhabitants. They searched every barn and outhouse.

Marcel had eagerly offered to help and he took the soldiers up the hillside, showing them the quick way up a vertical track which became a rushing waterfall when the snows melted. It was now muddy. It was thick with rocks. Reasonably passable for wild boar and goats and healthy teenagers, it was sorely trying for the heavily equipped German pioneer corps who slithered and slipped and stumbled up the mountainside.

The Germans withdrew. Obviously the containers had not been intended for that inaccessible slope. They reported that the village of Luxat had been startled and disturbed by the drop and they would continue their investigations elsewhere to try to discover how many containers had landed and whether any of them had been removed.

When Monsieur Vidal examined their hidden treasure they discovered that they had fifty-four well-greased revolvers, four radios, several rolls of cordite, boxes of detonators and cakes of gelignite.

Monsieur Vidal warned them sternly of the need for secrecy and the boys promised solemnly that they would say nothing.

"Not a word!"

"On my honour!"

But the villagers of Luxat knew that these treasures were hidden in the hills above the village and the boys were young and eager to boast of their adventure. Perhaps also they needed to share their secret, so that they could share the burden and the whole village could consider how to respond to this unexpected and not altogether welcome responsibility.

Joseph and Marcel were full of questions. They wondered where the containers had been meant to land and why the pilot had dropped them there, over Luxat. Who had been waiting for that precious cargo and what were they intending to do with it? Other youngsters asked them what they had found and some of the bolder ones followed them up the hillside and were honoured by a glimpse of the containers nestling in the hollow in the rocks.

The villagers of Luxat were proud of their treasure. They felt singled out by fate and believed they had no choice but to protect what they had been sent.

"If those English planes can get right down here and send us guns and ammunition and radios and all this stuff for blowing up bridges and things, well, they're powerful," Achille Cambon argued. "The Germans couldn't stop them, could they?"

"Not with us here," Marcel gloated. "We fooled them properly."

Even the oldest and most law-abiding villagers smiled and felt proud of their achievement. Luxat, their little village, which could not even boast a market or a railway, which was hidden away at the end of the valley, was part of the Allied war against the Boche.

Most evenings now a small group of villagers, including Joseph and Achille Cambon, would creep round to join Monsieur Coste straining to catch the BBC news and to hear Maurice Schumann's morale boosting 'Honneur et Patrie'. They rarely had any proper tobacco but they would puff away at cigarettes made of poisonous and foul-smelling weeds and would enjoy a bottle or two of cheap wine and Joseph, though he was considered too young to smoke, would feel that he was now part of a man's world, respected because he could speak English and because it was he and his brother who had hidden the foreign parachutes. When the programmes ended Monsieur Coste would open the door and peer out.

"All clear!" he would whisper and beckon to his friends who would scamper home, one at a time.

"Nobody in Luxat would betray us," he told his wife, "but it's as well to be careful."

She did not need persuading. The last thing she wanted was for her husband to be denounced and sent to jail for listening to the BBC.

At the café Terminus they posted a guard to warn them of any strangers approaching. Marcel and his friends rarely missed a session of Frank Bauer's jazz and with the sound turned low they would huddle round the set listening to the coded messages transmitted for resistance groups. They would look earnest and nod and rub their chins and frown and hope that they looked as if they understood these messages.

"It's important to listen all the time," they declared. "You never know when your message may come through."

At the Hotel du Commerce there was no scuttling secrecy. There they were listening to Radio France, to Philippe Henriot. His voice was rich and persuasive and he warned against Jews and Masons and communist terrorists and frightened good catholics with images of Bolshevik hordes raging across Europe, contained only by the Nazis and the German army. Louis Monnier, serving his customers and chatting with them, was glad of this protection.

"We've all seen what trouble those Spanish can cause. We don't want any more of that," they agreed.

Monsieur Delpech and his men, Auguste and his friends in the Milice, were ready to maintain the authority of the government in this corner of France.

For once Louis felt proud of Auguste and even wished that Joseph was more like him. The trouble with Joseph, he thought, was that he'd got that foster brother who thought he was so clever and had ended up being sent to prison in Carcassonne. He was a bad influence. But there wasn't much Louis could do about it now. Just hope that the boy didn't get involved in any stupid terrorism.

There was, in fact, very little sign of terrorism and resistance in the villages. But Marcel was now working in the forest with Achille Cambon and as the two of them travelled round, delivering wood to isolated farms and remote hamlets, they would talk and pass on news.

"The Allies are sending arms to France you know," Achille Cambon would tell them. Marcel was happy to hint that he was personally inolved. "Those parachutes they dropped at Luxat. You know about them?" They would look at him, enquiring. "Guns. Revolvers. Rifles. Equipment. So that we can help fight the Germans."

Their neighbours were impressed. On Easter Monday a crowd of young men from the farms and villages round

Luxat gathered, to scramble up the hillside, as the schoolchildren had done, to look into Alladin's cave and gaze at the boxes of guns and ammunition and the strange instruments of sabotage.

When they returned afterwards to their farms, those who had been initiated into the secret felt less isolated. They felt that they belonged now to a community which was arraigned against the German oppressors and the Vichy government, which took their produce and sent their men to work in Germany. They were not alone in their opposition.

So, quietly, they watched the German troops. They passed on information. If they heard that inspectors were coming to check on unregistered animals, they let the farmers know. If they saw the Gestapo or the Milice going towards a village, they warned the villagers. For the moment they might not have much to do but they were developing a sense of resistance and solidarity that was to prove invaluable sooner than they might have expected.

CHAPTER 11
April 1943 - June 1943 Supplies

While the villagers of Luxat were admiring their hoard, Raoul Vidal was trying to find the group for whom it was intended. Asking discreetly among his friends and colleagues, he discovered that a group at Quérigut to the south had been waiting for a delivery of radios. He decided to get them there as soon as possible.

So he came to collect them one Thursday morning when the children were with monsieur le curé. When he arrived Joseph stood stock still at the stable gate, his brown eyes round with wonder. Monsieur Vidal had come in a car. Not just a battered old black Citroen either: a beautiful white car, a cabriolet, with the hood down.

There was a lad not much older than Joseph who clambered out of the narrow space at the back and helped them load the radio sets, squeezing them in, so that when they had finished he had almost no room at all and had to perch in the back with his feet on one set and another clutched awkwardly in his lap.

Joseph was not interested in the passenger. He had eyes only for the car and he ran his hand lovingly along the paintwork and fingered the leather seats. The owner was flattered by his admiration.

"With petrol in the tank it can do a hundred kilometers an hour," he boasted.

Joseph whistled his appreciation.

With petrol in its tank no doubt the car could spin through the countryside at formidable speed but with a gas cylinder providing the fuel it was more difficult. This morning the gas was simply not getting through. Joseph pushed as hard as he could, heaved with his shoulder, strained every muscle to get the car moving and encourage the motor to turn. The young man in the back clambered out once more and joined him and they took one side each and pushed the car a few meters along the road. The engine coughed weakly and died. The car would not start.

Monsieur Vidal was tapping impatiently on the dashboard. "We're never going to get this car up the lane, you know. It's far too steep. We'll have to take the valley road back to Festes and come down from the Col de la Babourade. And that will take a lot longer."

Still the car would not budge. Monsieur Vidal looked at his watch. "I'm sorry," he said. "I've got to get back. I've got to see someone else and I really must see him." He looked doubtfully at Joseph. "Do you know the way to Quérigut?"

His eyes shining with excitement, Joseph nodded. It was the route Tomas the shepherd took, when he went south with the sheep, up into the mountains.

But Monsieur Vidal shook his head. "No. I can't ask you to go. It's too dangerous. You might get stopped and questioned."

"Please monsieur! Please! I'll be ever so careful."

Monsieur Vidal relented. "If you do get caught, play dumb. You're just a boy who loves cars and you don't know these people, don't know what they're carrying. They were driving through Luxat and they were lost and they asked you for directions. All right?" He looked anxiously at the driver and his passenger. Everyone nodded impatiently.

So Monsieur Vidal borrowed Joseph's bicycle and rode back to Festes. He was hardly out of sight, of course, when the engine belched and hiccupped and coughed into life. The two youngsters leapt in and Joseph sank back, wriggling happily. They sped along the valley road, waving wildly to Monsieur Vidal as they passed him on his bicycle, and turned left, back through the forest, across the open plateau of the Pays de Sault and through the hills to Quérigut. Joseph, sunk in his seat, peering out through the windscreen, pointing out the way, was bursting with pride and pleasure, exhilarated by the speed and luxury of the car.

At Quérigut they stopped at the doctor's house and took the car down the drive to unload in the shadow of the trees.

"Do you live here?" Joseph asked the young passenger.

He shook his head. "No."

It seemed a very short answer. Joseph waited, expecting him to say something more, to explain where he did live or what he was doing in Quérigut but he didn't say anything else. Silly of me to ask, Joseph thought. If he's travelling in a car with radio sets being delivered to a group of resistance he's hardly likely to start telling me all about it and if he's just an ordinary man, going to see his uncle or ask about some sheep, he wouldn't be loading up radio sets, would he? But Joseph looked at him with more interest. It was the first time he'd met one of the resistance, he thought. Unless you counted Monsieur Vidal and he'd never really thought of him as one of the resistance.

They got back into the car but now there were only the two of them, Joseph and the driver. "Is he not coming back with us?" Joseph asked, nodding towards the back of the car, where the young man had been.

"No. I was asked to bring him with the radio sets. I don't know any more than you do."

The journey back went only too quickly. The driver, now that he had delivered his cargo, was more relaxed. With the noise of the engine and the wind snatching at their words, they did not talk and Joseph simply relaxed and enjoyed the journey.. He had only been in a car once or twice before and never in an open car. He was almost disappointed when they reached the forest and passed through the narrow cliff tunnel above the village before plummeting down the twisting lane. When he reached home he flew into the house, eager to tell Maman all about it. For weeks afterwards he would find himself thinking about that wonderful car ride and sometimes he would remember the young man who had gone to Quérigut with them. Of course, he did not expect to see him again.

Most of the time, though, Joseph was too busy to think about anything but school and homework, the garden and the livestock.

There seemed to be rules and rations for everything. Even pigs had to be registered and only if you had filled out the right forms could you buy feed for them. Then, when you came to the pig killing, the authorities took their share for the army. The German army.

So, like anyone else with any sense, Maman kept another pig, out of sight of the authorities. It all added to the work and the worry, because it was difficult to find extra pig food and because it would certainly be confiscated and they would be in trouble if it was discovered.

Everyone suffered from the shortages. There were days when you could not get meat, even in a restaurant, and days when you could not be served alcohol. And far too many days when even if the shop was allowed to sell you something and you had all the right papers and ration cards, you could still not buy it because it was simply not available.

Maman and the boys were fairly self-sufficient but Madame Vidal's colleague at the school at Festes was distraught sometimes. Her husband was a prisoner of war in Germany and she tried to send him parcels to make his life easier. But he had no idea how difficult it was now in France.

"He's written again, asking for tobacco and chocolate and soap," Fernande wailed one morning. "Soap! When did you last see soap, Simone? I'd send him some if I could find some but there isn't any. As for chocolate, I can barely remember what it looks like." She shrugged her shoulders and shook her head and went off again to scour the countryside, hoping that she might be able to find something for him.

In the bakery Alice Chauvet's customers got angry and shouted at her when she ran out of bread. It did not help that they knew Hans could get things for her. One morning the smell of coffee, real coffee, wafted through the shop from the kitchen behind. She had perfume, too, that Hans had brought back after a trip to Toulouse. They had no perfume or coffee. Only German soldiers could get luxuries like that or rich people paying black market prices.

Alice loved these treats. She loved Hans, of course.

"When the war's over," he told her, "We shall get married."

It was like a fairy tale. Alice believed him and knew that they would always be happy together but there was a problem, of course.

"When the war's over…"

Hans smiled at her, doting, and put his arms round her and smothered her in kisses and told her that he loved her more than anything in the world.

"I know," she protested. "And I love you, Hans. But …" She had to say it. "When the war's over, the prisoners will come home."

Hans understood but it was not a problem. "And your husband will come home, of course. He will come back to the bakery. And you and I will go to Germany." It seemed an unimportant detail. "And I will buy you silk stockings and beautiful dresses and a fur coat." He covered her in kisses, as if to seal his promises.

And, as she drank the coffee Hans had brought her and ate the cake his mother had baked for them, Alice forgot her worries and was persuaded that everything would be all right and they would live happily ever after.

If life was hard in Luxat and La Bastide it was far worse in Paris even for rich people like Monsieur and Madame Fournier who could afford to buy on the black market. In her elegant apartment, Gabrielle Fournier grew tomatoes in her window boxes and kept rabbits on the balcony. Jacqueline, remembering her days in the country, happily watered the tomatoes and on her city walks snatched up morsels of greenery to give to the rabbits. They could not grow much, though.

Whenever she could, Gabrielle would take the train into the country and come back with butter and eggs and fruit but these trips were wearisome and the reward was meagre. When she suggested another visit to the mountains, her husband did not refuse her. He had his work in Paris. As long as she did not expect him to go with her and as long as she made proper arrangements for his well-being in Paris, she was welcome to go and visit her family. In fact, he thought it was a good idea, for they badly needed something to fill their empty larder and provisions would be much easier to find in the Pyrenees.

This time the journey was easier. They went overnight, by train to Toulouse and this time the family was prepared and was expecting them. Marius, her nephew, was ten now, and met them with the cart at the station at La Bastide. Jacqueline and Philippe were enchanted. A great plough horse, with shaggy fetlocks, leather harness and a warm, country smell! Philippe gazed, enraptured.

"He can sit up on her back if he wants," Marius said.

They lifted the little boy heavenwards and he sat, enthroned, viewing the world from a mighty height.

Jacqueline was allowed to sit at the front of the cart, watching the great, rolling haunches, sharing the bench with her beloved cousin, who let her, once, put her hand on the worn leather reins. As for Marius, he basked in the admiration of his two little cousins, savoured the perfume of his elegant aunt and drove out of the station and up the road to the hotel, where they took the turning to Festes. His heart was bursting with pride.

Louis Monnier was out on the steps of the hotel and caught sight of them and recognised them before he turned and went back to his work in the bar. Joseph was in town that day, hovering by the cycle stall in front of the bakery, and looked up and recognised the lady and guessed that the little boy on the horse was her son and the little girl at the front of the cart must be her daughter. He did not think of them as his brother and sister though he knew the lady was his mother because Maman had told him so. He watched with a twinge of sadness as they turned off for Festes. He wondered if she would come to Luxat to see him. He knew that she would not bring the children with her and, somehow, he felt that she had seen him once and would not come again.

155

A middle-aged woman, coming out of the baker's, paused to watch the proud equipage. "Wonder what Louis Monnier makes of that then," she quipped to her friend.

"I see he's gone indoors fast enough. Must have recognised her!"

"Recognised her! I should think he would! Saw enough of her once upon a time, didn't he!"

They laughed, enjoying a good joke.

"Mind you, he may have taken advantage of her when she worked at the hotel and she may have left with Marie Monnier calling her every name under the sun, but Gabrielle Peyrou has done well for herself since she left La Bastide."

"She has indeed. Chased out of the hotel, an unmarried mother with a bastard child, more or less disowned by her family who never helped her much - not that they've ever had two pennies to rub together the Peyrous - and now look at her!"

"She's a fine lady now, isn't she? Two children tarted up like dolls and a rich husband in Paris!"

"She's got a lot to thank Louis Monnier for! If he hadn't done what he did, she might not be a fine lady in Paris now. She'd still be here in La Bastide, struggling to make ends meet."

"Like us!"

The two women cackled again and went cheerfully on their way, still laughing, quite unaware of the boy at the bicycle stall, whose face was turned from them.

Joseph stood stock still, his body rigid, his face expressionless, frozen. It was as if his heart stopped beating and the blood turned to ice in his veins. He knew now. He did not need to ask Maman. He knew. It made sense.

That was why Madame Monnier was always so nasty to him. That was why Auguste had bullied him and called him a bastard. That was why Monsieur Monnier had liked him to help in the bar.

That fine lady, his mother, who came from the farm at Laurac, near Festes, she had come to La Bastide to work at the Hotel du Commerce. She had waited at table in the restaurant, served in the bar, helped Monsieur Monnier. Helped, as Joseph had helped. And Monsieur Monnier had been nice to her. But he had betrayed her. He gave her a baby. And then Madame Monnier shouted and threw her out and Monsieur Monnier had watched her go, just as he'd watched when Madame Monnier had thrown Joseph out of the hotel. She had no money. Then the baby was born. That was how he, Joseph, had come into the world. And Monsieur Monnier had not helped. So she had gone to Paris, to find work, to make some money, like Maman had said. Leaving Joseph behind. And Monsieur Monnier had not helped.

He had pretended. He had seemed to welcome Joseph to the hotel. But he had betrayed him. He had sent the police out to Luxat to find Robert. How could he? Joseph was angry and hurt and, though he did not put it into words, he was ashamed. He was ashamed of himself, that he mattered so little that he could be ignored like that. He was ashamed of his father that he could be so weak and uncaring.

A sob rose in Joseph's chest, a hard, choking sob, that did not dissipate in tears. To think that once he had thought this man was his friend. Once he had wanted to know who his father was. He had dreamed of meeting him. And now he knew. This was his father. Louis Monnier.

CHAPTER 12
June 1943 - February 1944   Preparing the maquis

It was Joseph's last week at school. He would be fourteen at the beginning of September and would not go back when the new term started Maman certainly needed more help but he was hoping to do work for other people in the village too.

"I shan't have any trouble finding something," he told Maman. "Everyone says they need extra hands."

His last few days at school were relaxed. Monsieur Vidal gave him the run of the book cupboard and he spent his time tidying the shelves and reading whatever took his fancy. He found an old book about the Cathars and the siege of Montségur in the 13th century.

"They were very brave, weren't they?" he said to Monsieur Vidal.

"They were."

"But I think they were stupid."

"Do you. Why?"

"Well, they thought everything was so wicked! It's alright going off to be a saint and help other people. And I reckon it's alright to say that priests should live simple lives and not dress up in fine clothes. And I agree that the rich shouldn't oppress the poor. But to say you're a sinner because you eat and drink, that's just stupid."

"Well, they did think that everything physical belongs to the devil and is evil and I'm inclined to agree with you about that. But they were called 'the pure' because they tried to live good, simple lives and were not greedy and self-centred. And, as you say Joseph, they were brave. When their fortress at Montségur finally fell, they were promised that they would be free to go if they did as the church told them, you know. They could have come down from the top of their hill, renounced their faith and walked away. But they didn't, did they. They kept their faith and did what they thought was right. They came down the hillside and climbed onto the funeral pyre and were burnt to death. All of them. Two hundred and seven of them."

Raoul Vidal had spoken seriously, with obvious respect.

"So do you think they were right, monsieur?" asked Joseph.

"I think they were prepared to live by their beliefs, and die for them, Joseph. That's their legacy to us. We must stand by what we believe is right, whatever anyone else says. Even though we know that we may be attacked for it. We may have to suffer and even die for what we believe. We must still do what we think is right."

Joseph nodded. He understood perfectly well what Monsieur Vidal meant. Just as the Cathars at Montségur had resisted the catholic church, so Monsieur Vidal would resist the Germans and the Vichy government. He knew that it was dangerous and that he might suffer and even die in the resistance but that was what he felt was right and so that was what he would do.

"I think, after all, I'm quite proud to be from the Cathar country," he said shyly.

"So you should be, Joseph."

It was true, as Monsieur Vidal had said, that there was a sturdy independence in this part of France. People mistrusted authority. They could make their laws but people would do what they thought was right, whatever the government said.

The hardships and injustices of the German occupation were affecting everyone and the Vichy government had much less support now than when Marshal Pétain first offered to serve his country. People put up with all the problems for a long time but when young Frenchmen were called up to go and work in Germany there was serious opposition. They did not want to leave home. They did not like the Germans. They were afraid that they would be killed in the bombing raids on Germany. They would not go.

Hans, overseeing the arrangements, was very critical of the French authorities. "It's a shambles," he told Alice. "They've sent out 200 letters telling young men to report for their medical and nearly half of them have been returned 'Not known at this address'. Most of the small villages haven't even managed to send out any papers at all."

By October, as fewer young men reported for their medical and fewer still actually left for Germany, Hans began to realise that he had met deliberate sabotaging of the scheme, not inefficiency. "Our quota for last month was 200. And do you know how many actually went?"

Alice could tell that there weren't many.

"Five!" he wailed.

The French were impossible, frustrating his efforts at every turn. His commanding officer was demanding action, men to go and work in Germany, but Hans was happily absorbed in his love for Alice and his plans for the future. Alice was pregnant and he was happy.

They lay in bed one morning, snuggled up togther, thinking about getting up but well aware of the ice covering the inside of the window panes and reluctant to leave their warm bed for the freezing chill of the unheated room.

"We'll go and get dressed by the kitchen stove," said Hans.

"Mmm." Alice was still sleepy. "Not yet."

Hans lay his hand on her swollen belly, proud and loving. "What are we going to call him? We could call him Frantz, after my brother. And it sounds French and you're French."

Alice pouted. "No. Not Frantz." She did not want to name her baby after a young man who had died a horrible death at Stalingrad.

"Or Jean. That's the French version of Hans."

"No. It doesn't sound in the least like Hans."

He took her fingers and kissed them, one by one, and felt an overwhelming love and marvelled that he should have found such happiness.

"It might be a girl anyway," Alice reminded him.

"It could be twins!"

"No!" That was altogether too much for Alice. "Not twins. How would I ever find clothes and food for twins? It'll be bad enough to get what we need for one baby."

"Don't worry," Hans told her. "I'll look after you. Both of you. You and the baby."

He felt so proud and confident.

He did not realise that all over the country young Frenchmen were refusing to go and work in Germany and there were thousands of them. They could not stay at home. The police and the men of the Milice would hunt them down. So they headed south. Some of them risked the arduous crossing over the mountains into Spain and went on to Algeria, to join the Free French Forces there. Others 'took to the maquis' as they called it and camped out in the hills, working as woodsmen or helping on farms where they found work easily because so many men were still prisoners of war in Germany.

Some of them were eager to join the resistance and fight the Germans but even the least belligerent knew that they were outlaws now and might be forced to take up arms simply to save their own lives.

When a couple of young men in Luxat got their papers to go to Germany they asked Monsieur Vidal for help.

"I know an old farm at Aunat, near Festes," he told them. "It's miles from anywhere. There's a track up to Laurac and that's a god-forsaken, isolated place, run by a couple of women and a boy and Aunat is even further into the forest. Very isolated. Nobody would find it if they didn't know the way, so you should be safe there."

"How would we live, though?" they asked. "What about food? Money?"

"Well, you could chop wood and sell that. You could help a bit, around the farm at Laurac. I dare say they'd be glad to give you an odd chicken or two, for a couple of days' work."

So, early in October, the two young men from Luxat and half a dozen other defaulters moved into the abandoned farm. It was not ideal, however, for the place was so isolated it was difficult to get food up there and the young men could not risk coming down into the villages very often. Even more important, there was no water on the site.

By December Monsieur Vidal was worried. "They look terrible. They're all skin and bone. And what are we going to do if the weather's bad this winter? Food may keep once it gets there, but if the weather's really bad we won't be able to get to the place."

Mathilde Barthez helped. Her pigs were ready for slaughter. Pig killings were not the happy communal parties that they used to be and there were no celebrations now, since nobody was going to let people see exactly how many animals they had fattened. But the four of them, Mathilde and the two boys and Achille Cambon, with no jokes, no theatrical knife sharpening, heaved the pig into the trough and Achille cut its throat. They hauled it out and sliced it up as quickly as they could and even after she had given a few bits to neighbours, Mathilde and the boys still had plenty of meat left, so she was happy to send some sausage out to Aunat.

"Can I take it?" Joseph asked. Maman looked at him. "I'd like to see Laurac," he explained. "It's where the lady from Paris came from, isn't it?"

So Maman agreed and Joseph, curious to see his mother's home, cycled back on the route she had taken when she went out to Luxat to see him. He bumped along up the uneven track and arrived, as Gabrielle had done, amidst a cacophony of barking and clucking and bleating, while Marius shouted at the dogs which danced around the bike.

"Thanks," said Joseph. He had not expected to meet another boy and, just for a moment, he wondered if this was another child left behind by the lady from Paris. He smiled doubtfully. "I've brought some food for the men in the forest," he said.

"Right. I'll show you the way if you like."

Joseph nodded.

"There are two tracks up to the old farm," Marius told him. "This one's quicker."

Joseph followed Marius up the narrow track. "Do you live here?" he asked.

"Yes. With my mother and my grandmother. My father's a prisoner in Germany. I don't really remember him very well." He sounded proud of his father, wistful that he was away from home.

Joseph was relieved that this boy was not an unknown brother but he felt he had to match his confession.

"My father was killed in the war," he declared and drawing boldly on his memory of Robert's stories, he added: "He died at Dunkirk, blowing up bridges to secure the perimeter. He was decorated for bravery."

Marius was suitably impressed.

"Do you have any brothers or sisters?" asked Joseph.

"No." Then Marius remembered the one impressive part of his family. "I have an aunt in Paris and two cousins. They've been here to stay because Paris is a terrible place to live in, though it's very smart. My aunt's here, staying with us, now."

So that was it. This boy was his cousin. Joseph appreciated that Paris was indeed very smart but he didn't tell him they were cousins.

"Where do you live?" Marius asked.

"Luxat. Did you hear about the parachute drop a few months ago?"

Marius shook his head, then remembered the night when a plane had flown low over the castle at Festes. Was that the one he meant?

Joseph nodded, tight-lipped. "Can't really say anything about it. Security. We have to be careful."

Marius could understand that. Obviously this boy who was not much older than him played a major role in the resistance. "Do you know many maquisards?" Marius asked.

Joseph nodded. "Some," he said, modestly.

"Are there any other boys your age in your group?" asked Marius, wondering whether there might, perhaps, be a place for him. "Nothing ever happens here," he complained. "I wish I lived somewhere like Luxat, where things happen."

In Luxat, it seemed, even boys were involved in the war and could take part in heroic deeds.

"Well," said Joseph, rather grandly, in words which would haunt him for the rest of his life, "You never know. There's the maquis here. They may want you to help them."

Marius considered this, wondering how he might possibly help the maquis. It seemed unlikely.

"What's your name?" he asked, changing the subject.

"Joseph. But you musn't tell anyone I've been here."

"Joseph what?"

For a moment Joseph hesitated. "Joseph Peyrou," he said.

Marius stopped in his tracks. "That's my name. I'm Marius Peyrou."

"Well, there's lots of them around." Joseph tried to dismiss the coincidence.

"What about your mother?" Marius asked.

Joseph was saved from answering as the narrow path turned and they found themselves suddenly in the courtyard of the old farm, where half a dozen men were chopping wood. Pleased to see their visitors, they stopped work and turned to the boys, stretching tired muscles.

Joseph showed them what he had brought and they exclaimed happily when they saw the sausage.

"That'll give us something to chew on!"

"And bread!"

There was even a rabbit.

"You're a saviour, Joseph. Come again! Any time!"

"And be sure to thank Madame Barthez."

They took the longer way back, a wider, more open track, waving to the men as they finally disappeared from sight. Their delivery completed they returned more slowly.

"Here!" Joseph was conspiratorial. "There were some fags in those sacks." Like a magician with his white rabbit, Joseph drew out a packet of cigarettes. "I'm dying for a fag now," he said grandly.

They made themselves comfortable, propped against a tree beside the pathway and lit up, taking shallow, inexperienced puffs.

"This is the first time I've smoked a whole cigarette," Marius confessed.

Joseph nodded, understanding. A younger brother, always following after Marcel, he was enjoying this chance to show how grown up he was, basking in his cousin's admiration.

Their cigarettes finished, they went on their way, dawdling. When they reached the farm, Marius's mother and his aunt were there. Monique went on with her work but for a moment Gabrielle stared at them, transfixed.

"Bonjour, madame," said Joseph, nodding politely.

"Bonjour." Gabrielle was impressed. The boy was bright, he was not going to blurt out that they had already met. She smiled. He was charming, at that delightful age, just before manhood, just before the awkward surliness of adolescence. Handsome. Fresh faced. With a mop of thick dark hair, big, brown eyes and wonderful long, thick lashes, that blinked shyly as he looked at her. A boy any mother could be proud of, she thought, and felt a twinge of regret, remorse even.

"My aunt comes from Paris," Marius explained proudly.

"Perhaps I may see you there one day, madame," Joseph responded, surprising himself with the words. He had no plans to go to Paris. Gabrielle's eyes widened in surprise, her lips parted. What would she do if this bold boy turned up at her flat in Paris?

There was plenty for Joseph to think about on the way home. He was glad he had met Marius, but why had he exaggerated the importance of his role in the resistance? That was silly. But he was glad he'd seen his mother. She was beautiful. And he knew he'd made a good impression. Perhaps he would see her again. Perhaps he would go to Paris. He'd see Marius again, anyway. He was sure of that.

Joseph said very little about the visit when he got home and Maman, understanding that it might have been more difficult than he expected, did not press for details.

As it happened there was no reason for Joseph to return to Aunat because just before Christmas Laurent Barde, the young policeman at La Bastide, warned Jean-Paul Ramel that the men at the derelict farm had been denounced.

"There's been a letter from Festes, saying that there's a group of defaulters hiding in the forest, who come into the village sometimes selling wood. We don't know exactly where but we'll be sending out patrols and it won't take us long to find them."

Jean-Paul passed on the warning to the men who left immediately and went their separate ways, joining other groups elsewhere.

"I thought it was such a good place," Raoul Vidal explained , "because it was isolated. But it wasn't really very good, was it?"

The war was turning in favour of the allies and resistance was growing, adding to the numbers escaping from the German draft. They needed to provide for these volunteers. With constant rumours of allied landings in Provence Jean-Paul and Raoul were determined that in their corner of the country they would be ready to fight when the battle began. So, with greater understanding than previously, the two men began to look for a good site for a maquis camp.

"We musn't make the same mistakes again as we made at Aunat," said Jean-Paul.

"So what do we need?"

"Well." Jean-Paul thought. "There must be water. That's essential. And they must be able to work, to earn money and buy food."

"Which means they must be able to trust the people around them, be sure that they won't be betrayed. As sure as they can be, anyway," Raoul added. "And it's not enough for them to be safe and secure. They've got to be able to do the work of the maquis. You thought Aunat was good because it was isolated but it was too isolated you know, when you think about it. If the Germans do come after them they've got to be able to escape. They've got to have plenty of different paths, in and out and plenty of roads round the site, so that if they find themselves under attack they can get away."

They thought about all the places they knew.

"There's one thing more, too," Raoul added. "It's no good if the Germans can surround the place. It's got to be big enough."

They thought about the countryside round Festes, round the castle, but the approach from the north was far too easy for an attack. They thought about the area round Ste Agathe, where there was plenty of water, but there were not many pathways in and out.

"The best place is the forest above Luxat," Raoul decided. "There are plenty of streams, so there's water. "

Jean-Paul agreed. "The men can work in the forest and there are tracks and footpaths all over the place."

"And it won't be difficult to defend. You can get along the valley to the village but the cliff then is almost vertical. There are just a few goat tracks, no vehicles can reach them that way. And coming in from the forest road, there's just that narrow tunnel in the cliff. That wouldn't be hard to defend."

"And you said it had to be big enough so that the Germans can't encircle us. Well the forest there is vast."

Raoul had just one slight reservation. "The Pays de Sault, to the south. It's a bleak, barren plateau and you could see any enemy approaching but it would be more difficult to defend."

"Perhaps so. But there's several roads there, there'd be a choice of two or three roads if you had to escape that way."

The deciding point was the local population.

"The people of Luxat can be trusted," Jean-Paul said. "More than that. They'll help. Achille Cambon and Marcel have already sounded out supporters."

So it was decided and Achille Cambon and Marcel now set about getting firm promises of supplies of meat, bread, eggs. The man who ran the garage at La Bastide promised to help with the maintenance of any vehicles.

They were not simply going to camp out in the forest though. They intended to fight. For that they needed weapons and ammunition and readio sets. They had to get in touch with someone who could supply these.

Raoul Vidal had a friend, a teacher in Quillan, who was in touch with a wider group of resistance and promised to help them. Then Raoul heard that the Gestapo had called at his friend's school one morning, walked into his classroom and arrested him. He was devastated. He waited anxiously for news, praying for his friend, afraid that other men might be arrested, that the Gestapo might come for him one day. It was weeks before he heard that his friend had been executed and only much later did news reach them that on his last day in prison he had managed to pass on a message to say that he had not talked.

This man's courage and the tight security with which he worked had saved Raoul Vidal but that tight security made it difficult for him to re-establish contact. Eventually someone who claimed to have been working with his friend got in touch and arranged to meet Raoul and Jean-Paul at a café opposite the railway station at Quillan.

"I'm using the name 'Jules'. What do I call you?" he asked, a pencil ready in his hand, his notebook on the table in front of him.

"I don't think we want a record," said Raoul.

"Don't worry, I'm not stupid. I don't write minutes. I use code names and symbols and abbreviations. Nobody but me could make sense of what I write."

Reluctantly Raoul suggested that he might be called 'Serge'. Jean-Paul took the name 'Etienne'. They discussed what Luxat might be able to offer and what they would need to establish a useful fighting unit. They told him that the butcher in La Bastide had storage space and would be willing to keep things for them.

'Jules' left them and took the train back to Montpellier. As he stepped down from the train he saw the Milice and SS checking papers. He hurried, hoping to join the crowd while it was still busy and they might be checking papers less carefully but this was no random check. They were watching for him. They caught sight of him as he approached and moved to close in. Dropping his suitcase he made a dash for freedom.

"Halt!"

The other passengers looked round, alarmed by that abrupt command.

"Halt!"

'Jules' dodged behind a loaded trolley, put his hand in his pocket and drew his gun. He fired but missed and a German bullet caught him in the shoulder. As he peered out from behind his shelter, hoping for a second shot, he was caught in a hail of bullets. He was dead before the soldiers reached him.

When Raoul and Jean-Paul heard the news they grieved for their comrade but they were anxious for themselves, too. 'Jules' could not have said anything, he had died too quickly for that but what of his notes? Had they fallen into the hands of the Gestapo? And how easily would they be deciphered? They went about their work as usual but with a nagging fear and uncertainty and the resistance leaders in Montpellier ordered that there should be no further activity and no more parachute drops until they had sorted out how far their security had held.

So when there was a short holiday in February they were pleased to be getting away for a break. The Vidal family was going to stay with Simone's mother in Limoux. Simone who had been dreading that terrible knock on the door, the Gestapo calling for her husband, was thankful to be getting away. Some of her anxiety may have shown as she said good-bye to her colleague, Fernande, who like them had a flat above the classrooms.

"Take care," Fernande said.

Simone smiled. "And you, take care." Then she added. "If anyone comes ..." She was not sure what she wanted to say. "Well, let me know," she ended, lamely.

Fernande seemed to understand.

It was Monday, 21st February. The first day of the holiday. They came at dawn. Not, at first, to the school at Festes, but to Jean-Paul's lodgings in La Bastide. They asked for Etienne Butcher. They obviously had the notes 'Jules' had made but they had been confused by his symbols and abbreviations.

Jean-Paul, like the Vidals, had gone home for the holiday. When they asked his landlady about Etienne Butcher, she shook her head. No Etienne Butcher here. The Gestapo searched the house. There was a young man lodging there, a young bachelor, though his name was not Etienne Butcher but Jean-Paul Ramel and he was away at that moment, staying with his parents in Festes. They went in search of him.

As soon as they left, the landlady phoned a friend in Festes. "Please, take a message to Madame Ramel. Urgently. Tell her they're looking for Jean-Paul."

It is not far from La Bastide to Festes. The friend who warned Madame Ramel had scarcely left the house when the Gestapo turned into the village. Jean-Paul was still in bed, in that deep, lazy sleep of the young who had fun last night and have no responsibilities to get up for this morning. His mother, used to rousing him, shook him firmly.

"Jean-Paul! They're here! The Gestapo!"

He was awake in a flash, pulling on his clothes.

"Out here!" his mother urged, opening the window and letting in the freezing February air. The hillside rose abruptly behind the house. Jean-Paul jumped and ran with all the speed a rugger wing could muster. His mother shut the window, shoved out of sight anything belonging to her son and was hoping to regain her breath when they knocked at the door.

"Where's your son?" they asked. Her grey hair uncombed, her teeth mislaid, her face unwashed, dressed in a shapeless black cotton garment, Madame Ramel was ready to play the scene of her life. She cupped her hand behind her ear and shouted at them in impenetrable patois.

"What? Who are you?"

They struggled to explain that they were looking for her son. Lighting with joy on a photograph of Jean-Paul they finally seemed to make her understand who they were looking for.

In what was clearly the young man's room, they found the bed still warm. The French interpreter told her the game was up.

"He's just left. This bed's still warm!"

Madame Ramel was indignant. This was her bed. She had only just got up. At her age she had the right to lie in bed for a few hours, surely. She had been up early enough for years, getting everyone off to school and to work, doing the household chores, managing everything. Now she was old, she could surely stay in bed for an hour or two in the morning.

The police interpreter pointed to the splendid matrimonial bed in the other room. Madame Ramel gave him a withering look. What was he thinking of? At her age! When she was young, no doubt, it had all been good fun, and left energy enough to spare. Now? She needed a bit of peace. Her husband coughed all night long and was up and down with the trouble with his bladder. She needed a good night's sleep.

The policeman who was wilting under the difficulties of shouting to be heard and straining to understand the thick patois, gave up. The Gestapo accepted that if this was the home of the man they were looking for, they had obviously missed him.

The Ramel family treasured the tale for years, laughing till their sides ached and tears streamed down their cheeks.

The Gestapo left, to continue their search elsewhere. This time they had no name but they were looking for the husband of the schoolteacher at Festes.

Fernande opened the door. She was cool, elegant, charming, a generation younger than Madame Ramel and well-educated.

"Where is your husband, madame?" they asked.

Fernande looked at them in amazement. "He's in Germany. A prisoner of war," she told them.

They demanded proof.

"A photograph. Here!" She plucked from the table a photograph of her husband in his infantry officer's uniform.

"If this is your husband, yes, he is an army officer but how do we know he's your husband?"

More photographs. A wedding picture showing the same young man, with Fernande, his bride, at his side. The Gestapo were beginning to have doubts. The young woman seemed supremely confident.

"This does not prove that your husband is in Germany now."

Carefully, Fernande went to the walnut dresser, opened it wide and from one of the drawers took out a bundle of letters. The translator, glancing through them, could see that they were from an officers' camp in Germany and the correspondent was clearly the lady's husband.

They shook their heads, suspecting that their information had been faulty and they left, their boots clattering down the wide stone stairs, wondering whether the note book had been deliberately misleading or whether it had been wrongly deciphered. It did not occur to them that there might be another teacher at the school, another married woman teacher, and one whose husband was not a prisoner in Germany.

Fernande hurried to the post office, to telephone Simone's mother in Limoux. She spoke to her friend. "You've had visitors," she said.

Simone heaved a sigh. "Thank you."

Like Jean-Paul, Raoul wasted no time. He went into hiding. Simone was on her own, with a full time job and two small children to care for. Fernande helped when she could but much of her spare time was spent scouring the countryside in search of food, to send parcels to her husband in prison in Germany. Supplies were increasingly erratic and Simone, like Fernande, spent hours queueing for food or trying to find someone to supply milk for the children or a little extra bread.

Ration cards were changed yet again. Simone and Fernande went together to the Town Hall to collect their new cards, Simone wearily carrying the baby, while Fernande tried to cope with the fractious toddler. Roger decided to sit down on the dusty stone floor and, drumming his heels on the ground, declared that he would not, absolutely not, move. His mother was too tired to bother. The queue wound up the stairs and out of sight. She could not lose her place. She could not take him home.

"Just stay there, then, my little cabbage. We'll collect you on the way down." Roger fell asleep and they did indeed collect him on the way down, fortunately relaxed and in a better temper.

Simone, by then, was seething with anger. She had waited three hours in that cold queue, stamping her feet and rubbing her hands to keep the circulation moving. Fernande had taken the baby from time to time but the child seemed increasingly heavy.

At last they reached the head of the queue and handed in their ration cards for renewal. Simone had four: one for herself, another for her husband and one each for the children. Brusquely, with a tight sneer, the mayor's secretary handed back Raoul's ration card.

"He's not here, is he? Tell his friends they can feed him."

Tears stung her eyes. Simone struggled not to cry in front of this bitter, hateful woman.

At that moment, though, when this little group of resistance seemed on the verge of collapse, they were, on the contrary, about to struggle into life. Raoul Vidal and Jean-Paul Ramel had gone to Luxat. They were living in a cave up above the village, that secret cave of Mathilde's story, where the young wood-cutter had hidden his little girl to protect her from the wolves. The real Luxat maquis, so yearningly desired by those who brought it into life, had suffered a long, slow gestation. It was now about to face the world.

CHAPTER 13
February - March 1944 Help arrives

Raoul Vidal had been everywhere trying to get the materials they needed to fight the Germans. Without weapons and ammunition and radio sets there was not much they could do. His contact in Quillan had been arrested, 'Jules' had been shot and now the organisers in Montpellier had stopped all further activity until they found out what had gone wrong with their security.

But six months ago he had arranged for a young man to go to Quérigut and now he was back. He had crossed into Spain and travelled on to Algeria. There he had been summoned immediately to meet General Giraud, the commander of the Free French Forces. They were going to land in France and Geeneral Giraud needed to know what support they might find in Provence and Languedoc. Were there already groups of men who might join the army in fighting the Germans?

So, for four days the young man was given instructions. He learnt how to work a radio transmitter, how to use codes. Then he was sent off to Barcelona and crossed the mountains once more, back into France this time, returning to Quérigut, to the village which had always been a centre for smugglers and was now a centre for refugees crossing the Pyrenees.

That night, at the doctor's house, they sat round the fire, the blazing logs constantly replenished, as the snow fell outside and the wind moaned in the chimney. The doctor and his wife were joined by the schoolteacher with whom the newcomer was to lodge. They drank their toasts in

Blanquette de Limoux. The wine sparkling in their glasses lifted their spirits and their hopes. The young man from Algeria had seen the world outside, a world already free and they were thirsty for his news. Even his name, 'Victor', brought hope.

"So, over there in Algeria, what are they doing?"

"Are they going to come?"

"Will there be landings in France?"

"Are they going to land here, in the South, on the coast of Languedoc?"

He told them what little he could. "Yes. They'll come. That's what I'm here for, to get information in preparation for the landings. I can't give you any details. But they'll come."

For security reasons an operator never travelled with his radio, his 'piano' as he called it, but the next day Tomas, the old shepherd, shuffled past, leaving a parcel at the schoolhouse. Trembling with excitement, Victor unwrapped his precious 'piano', set up the aerial and started testing the radio. It worked like a dream. The needle jerked impatiently and inside his headphones the world throbbed out its messages. Then it was time for him to contact Algeria. He prepared to receive.

Titi-ti-ta! Titi-ti ta! BJK from TUR! BJK from TUR!. QRK, QRK, ta-tita. He had made contact! Excitedly he replied. TUR from BJK! TUR from BJK! QSA4. I am receiving you.

As he settled down to transmit, there was a flash, a bang, a terrible smell of burnt bakelite and Victor stared, aghast. Angry and impotent, he reeled in the aerial. He could have wept with rage and disappointment. He had come all this way, only to have the mission abort before it had even started. He had filled his head with codes and procedures.

He had struggled over the mountains. He had come back to France, where he was wanted by the French police and the Gestapo. All for nothing!

"Everything all right?" the schoolteacher asked when he came back from his classes.

"No. All wrong," Victor told him. "The thing blew up."

The teacher refused to despair. "I've got a colleague at a school near here, who's a radio ham. Mad about the things. We'll see if he can help."

The friend came over and looked at the wrecked machine. "You've got one valve and a circuit burnt out. Someone's sabotaged this, so that it would work for a few minutes and then break down. You want to warn them back in Algeria."

"Can you mend it?" Victor asked anxiously.

"Mais oui! Of course I can mend it. We can't get new parts but we can rummage around and find something. No problem."

So the wizard went to work and Victor was back in business.

"This isn't the best place to broadcast from, though," he told the teacher. "It's right in the middle of the village. Too many people around who may hear what I'm doing, too easy to miss a stranger coming to investigate."

So he moved to a house on the outskirts of the village, where an old soldier of the '14-18 war was living in retirement and was delighted to help. "I did my bit in the last war and I'd like to do something useful now," he said. "Anyway I get lonely sometimes, out here on my own."

"It could be dangerous," Victor warned him.

"Of course it's dangerous. But there's only me, so there's nobody else to bother about. And it'll give me a bit of excitement. There's no danger growing vegetables but it gets a bit dull sometimes."

So they went round the garden, setting out the aerial, hiding it among the plants and shrubs. At the appointed time Victor prepared once more to send his message. The old man, who was frail and bent, stiffened with amazement, his eyes sparkled and his cheeks creased with joy as he heard the response from Algiers.

They had to be careful. The Germans had vans equiped to intercept broadcasts and three vans worked together to pinpoint the location of the set. So they kept messages short and posted a look out.

Victor had just started his transmission one morning when the old man came in. "They're here!" he warned. Someone had spotted a lorry parked on the hill above the village, with two men standing beside it, scanning the landscape with binoculars. Victor was prepared, they had already rehearsed their response. In a flash the equipment was dismantled and the aerial hung out in the open, an innocent line for washing.

They had acted before they could get an exact siting but the Germans knew they were in the village and it would not take long to find them if they broadcast again from Quérigut. So Victor moved to Ste Agathe and broadcast from there until another suspicious vehicle was spotted and he had to move once more.

For Victor it was a life of unceasing vigilance and constant moves. Meanwhile he was doing what he had been sent to do, collecting information about the area and the strength of local resistance.

He went north to Luxat, met Joseph and discovered that Raoul Vidal was in hiding but when they knew what he wanted Joseph took him to meet Raoul Vidal.

It was bitterly cold. Thick snow covered the ground and the snow drifts were dangerously deep. The frozen surface cracked under their boots and their feet sank into the soft snow beneath. The wind whipped against their faces which were blotched red and blue.

Joseph enjoyed his trips up to the cave and with a sympathetic listener he happily repeated the latest joke. "Have you heard about the Jew who was supposed to have killed a German soldier in Quillan last week?" he asked. "They took him to court but he got off."

He paused, giving Victor time to absorb this impossible scenario. "You see, the chap was killed at nine o'clock at night and whoever killed him chopped him up and ate his heart. So they knew it was all a load of lies. Because Jews don't eat pigs. Anyway a German soldier doesn't have a heart. And nine o'clock at night? They'd be listening to the BBC!"

Joseph chortled with glee. Victor had heard the joke before, more than once, but he pursed his lips and shook his head and laughed.

Raoul and Jean-Paul were delighted to meet him. They gave him details of safe hiding places and of groups of men ready to fight.

"But what we need are weapons and ammunition," Raoul Vidal urged. "And gelignite and fuses and sabotage material. We've got men round here raring to go but we can't fight tanks with our fists and we can't cut down electricity pylons with nail scissors. You give us the materials and we can provide effective opposition to the Germans."

Victor said he would pass on the message. "Don't worry, I'll tell them," he promised. "They've got the material you need. And men to show you how to use it."

Joseph had a more personal message for Victor to pass on. "A message for Robert Maclachan, of Alan Brooke's 240 corps. Please, please find out if he got home safely. And let me know," he pleaded.

Victor promised to do his best.

"I'll need some details from you if you're going to get your supplies," he told Raoul. "We need a Michelin map number and a landmark which the pilot will be able to see in moonlight."

That was easy. "Map number 86 and the landmark will be the ruins of the castle at Festes."

"And how far is that from the Landing Zone?"

That was more difficult. The Landing Zone had to be on flat ground. And not too close to the tracking station at Nebias.

"The valley below the village, where the lane turns off towards Luxat, the end of the valley there, that's the best place isn't it?"

They agreed.

"That's three kilometers from the castle."

"In which direction? North? South?

"South."

"Then there's the message for the BBC to broadcast," Victor said.

They thought about that for a few minutes. It had to be simple but memorable and not too short or they might miss it. They finally decided on : 'The sun rises in the east on Friday.'

"If you hear that, it means the landing is on for that night," Victor said. "So you will have to listen every time there's a full moon."

"Are you going to tell them about this in Montpellier?" asked Jean-Paul. Raoul said nothing. "I know we need the stuff but the Gestapo are looking for us and the people in Montpellier have told us to lie low for the moment."

"Oh do shut up!" said Raoul Vidal. "If we're being offered help, I'm not going to refuse it. The committe men in Montpellier have shown little enough interest in us and I'm not going to suffer now just because they've lost their nerve."

At Luxat they were ready. They saw themselves as the chosen people singled out to receive that earlier flurry of parachutes and to protect its precious treasure. They had enjoyed outwitting the Germans. They knew that what they did was dangerous but they accepted the task willingly.

Achille Cambon prepared his cart and oxen so that they could transport the material. Marcel would help drive the animals.

"They need me there, anyway," he boasted, "because of my experience with parachutes and things."

Marie-France thought she had never met anyone so brave, so clever and so handsome.

Joseph, provoked by Marcel's assumption of glory, went to see Monsieur Vidal to remind him that he too had experience with parachutes. Maman, accepting that she could not stop them going out with the reception party, warned them to be careful and told Joseph to make sure that Marcel did nothing foolish. She hoped that Monsieur Vidal and Monsieur Cambon and the men with them would see that good sense prevailed.

For it was dangerous, this planned parachute drop. They could be betrayed. Too many people knew what they were doing. The Germans, watching from their aerial surveillance post little more than a mile down the road from Festes, would certainly hear the plane and come in search of its cargo. If they were caught there would be no mercy. They would be shot.

The drop was expected on a night of full moon. It was Wednesday, 15th March. "The Ides of March!" Monsieur Vidal noted wryly. They listened to the BBC. 'The sun rises in the east on Friday.' It was their message. The plane was coming!

Rumour of the drop had escaped, of course. They had been too proud and too excited to keep the matter entirely secret. They had boasted to wives and sweethearts. Children had overheard whispered conversations. It was not only the maquis who heard the broadcast message, someone else heard and understood its importance and told Monsieur Delpech at the police station at La Bastide. He sent out patrols, looking for suspicious activity. Laurent Barde warned Monsieur Vidal.

"There'll be patrols out tonight. I'll be on duty. We've got people all round Festes, along the valley to the south and east. I'll be above the castle, to the north, on the way to La Bastide."

"We're expecting the drop at the end of the valley, just below Festes, by the turning to Luxat." Raoul Vidal looked at the policeman, questioning.

"That's no good. They'd soon pick you up there."

"What about the other side of the castle, where you are?"

Laurent Barde thought about it.

Raoul persisted. "If we went high up, well above the castle? To the east? There are no houses, are there, no farms, only one small track. It's not quite as flat as the valley and it's a bit further for the men from Luxat but it could be a better place."

"It might work. There's only two of us, me and my partner, on patrol between Festes and La Bastide and we would swear we saw nothing."

So they decided to move to the other side of the castle and hope that the pilot would see their signals and make the drop to the north.

In the last broadcast that night the BBC repeated the message: 'The sun rises in the east on Friday.' It was cold. That morning a flurry of snow had carpeted the ground. If they went ahead, the tracks of their cart would be clearly visible. They could still stand down and avoid the danger.

"So, we've been told not to have a parachute drop. We've got patrols out everywhere looking for us and there's snow on the ground to help them find our tracks," said Jean-Paul.

"I thought you agreed to go ahead," said Raoul sharply.

"Just try and stop me! I've waited four years for this and I'm not pulling out now."

Achille Cambon was equally determined. "Bugger the police, bugger the snow and bugger the blighters in Montpellier. The plane's coming and I'm going to be there to meet it."

So Joseph and Marcel, Monsieur Cambon and a dozen men from Luxat were out that night, waiting for the plane. They moved quietly and spoke in whispers. Monsieur Vidal had warned them that the police were there, hidden, watching. Smoking was forbidden. They waited anxiously. Joseph looked up and saw the silhouette of an old chapel darkly outlined against the brightness of the moon. He could see clearly, it was so bright, it looked light enough to read. Marcel was with the oxen which stood waiting patiently, their grey hide gleaming silver in the moonlight. They were standing so still they looked like a pair of silver charms modelled for a bracelet.

Then from the north the faint thrum of engines came through the silence and grew louder as the plane approached. It found its landmark, flew over the castle at Festes and on, to the south towards the Landing Zone.

Desperately they switched on their torches and turned them up towards the sky. Joseph wanted to call out to them, to warn them of the policemen hidden in the valley, of the villagers of Festes who might betray them, above all of the German look out post just down the road. He wanted to remind them of the danger and beg them to hurry.

The torches flickered round the field and the plane turned. Like a sudden black cloud, it cut out their view of the sky and the stars and its engines were thunderously loud. Then, while they still held their breath, the parachutes were released. Containers were drifting down, nuzzling into the earth.

Like children romping in the first snow of winter, they caught the silk of the parachutes, buried their faces in the soft texture and ran, exploding in delight, to take their presents to the waiting cart. They heaved and pushed and pulled and struggled, encouraging the oxen which had to be harnessed to help extract the containers which were half buried in mushy snow, mud and undergrowth.

Achille Cambon, with Marcel beside him, drove his cart to the caves where they hid this treasure, while Joseph, with branches from nearby trees and bushes, swept away the traces of the night's activity. Before dawn came they were back in Luxat, weary but proud and excited. As Joseph fell asleep he thought happily that perhaps, after all, he was at the centre of resistance, as Marius had believed.

The station at Nebias had tracked the plane of course but the police patrols had reported no sighting of the parachutes and enquiries in Festes and La Bastide brought no results. Everyone had heard the plane but nobody could tell them who might be involved and the snow was melting, leaving no trace of the landings.

The café Terminus was crowded that evening. Regular clients were being careful, aware that there might be informers among them but the wine flowed freely and there was a hum of excitement.

The mood at the Hotel du Commerce was quite different. Monsieur Delpech, angry that they had found no sign of the parachutes, was grumbling about terrorists and godless left-wing teachers who corrupted the youth of the country.

"You want to take a look at Luxat," Auguste suggested.

His father was uneasy but Monsieur Delpech was interested.

"Don't forget that British soldier they were sheltering out there."

"You don't know that. They never found him," Louis objected.

Auguste ignored him. "Remember the boy who walked through the procession in November?"

Monsieur Delpech remembered that cocky idiot and his silly joke about the chicken.

"Marcel. And I wouldn't trust that little bastard Joseph Peyrou either. You try out at Luxat," Auguste advised him.

"We will," said Monsieur Delpech, setting down his glass.

Louis was not happy. He no longer felt proud that his son was in the Milice. They were getting a nasty reputation for violence and he'd even heard of revenge attacks on the families of Miliciens. The parachute drop the previous night had worried him, too. "Do you really think those peasants in Luxat can bring the RAF down here to help them?" he asked his wife.

Marie Monnier disliked Joseph as much as Auguste did and was not happy to think that he and his neighbours might have powerful friends. Somebody, though, had been able to command the RAF and it might be them.

"And I'll tell you another thing that worries me," said Louis. "The Germans couldn't stop it could they? Where was the Luftwaffe? What about anti-aircraft guns? Delpech had his men out last night, so how did they not find anything?"

Louis did not want any harm to come to Joseph but it troubled him to think that possibly Joseph was on the right side now and no longer in danger. He could hardly bring himself to express his doubts but was it possible that Germany might not win the war? Was it possible that he had boldly shown himself as a supporter of the losing side and Joseph would be on the winning side?

At 5 o'clock next morning Madame Barthez was startled from her sleep to answer a knock at the door. It was the Gestapo. "You. Dress. Come."

Marcel and Joseph were bundled out, handcuffed and marched off to a barn at the end of the village, while a couple of soldiers searched the house. Maman knew there was nothing hidden there, no weapons, no leaflets, no hidden messages. She was still afraid, though, afraid simply to have the Germans in the house and afraid what might happen to the boys.

Every house in the village was surrounded and searched. All the men were lined up, facing the church wall, with armed guards standing watch behind them.

Monsieur le Commissaire Delpech had lost no time. He had called in the Gestapo. The Milice often passed on false information to settle old scores with people they disliked but the Gestapo had still taken the information seriously and were searching the village and questioning all the men.

The policeman from La Bastide had told them about Marcel, so they started with him. Joseph, facing the wall of the church, could just see the corner of the war memorial, where the list of Luxat heroes who died in the last war began with the name of Jean Barthez. He recalled how he had enjoyed playing the hero in front of Marius and how proud he had been when he got back, only yesterday morning, after collecting the parachutes. Now he no longer wanted to be a hero. He was simply frightened. Terrified. He could hear sounds from the barn where Marcel was being questioned, voices sometimes rough and loud. He could hear thumps. He could hear Marcel screaming.

Joseph screwed up his eyes and clenched his teeth and prayed. And it was silly but he was so nervous he was afraid he was going to piss in his pants. And then everyone would know how scared he was and think he was just a baby.

There was the sound of the barn door opening. One of the guards grabbed Joseph's collar and kicked his shin, pushing him inside the barn. He caught sight of Marcel, crumpled on the ground outside, his face swollen, his eyes closed with bruises, a cut on his temple pouring blood. His hands were still tied, handcuffed behind his back and every muscle of his bent body proclaimed the agony of the beating. A guard stood over him, pointing a rifle at his head, as if they feared he might try to escape.

Joseph tried to stand up straight in front of the Gestapo.

"Name?" they asked.

"How old are you?"

"So you have just left school. Monsieur Vidal was your teacher?"

Joseph had not been expecting that question.

"Yes," he replied.

"And you knew he was a terrorist?"

"Well, yes, but not until he disappeared."

The questions went on. It was easier to answer them after the first few minutes. Joseph almost convinced himself that he knew nothing about the activities of Monsieur Vidal and that Wednesday night had been as innocent as any other night and though they slapped him with the butt of a rifle if his answers were slow in coming, they treated him less roughly than they treated Marcel. He was younger and had no record of being a trouble maker. They had no evidence against him.

There was no evidence against anyone and despite the beatings and threats nobody gave anything away. Eventually the Germans lowered their guns, removed the handcuffs and released their victims.

Marcel was the only one who had been really hurt and his friends helped him home and set him down by the fire and neighbours called to wish him well. They brought small gifts to comfort him, candied fruit and cake and their best wine and finest liqueur. Marie-France came and fussed over him and they played cards and laughed and when he began to recover Monsieur Coste brought his gramaphone and some records. Marie-France felt that this was real sophistication.

"I expect it's like this in a night club in Paris," she said, giggling as she sipped a glass of armagnac.

CHAPTER 14
March - May 1944   Action at last

It could have been their radical tradition, their history of opposition to authority: it could have been the arrival of Robert or the accidental parachute drop: it could have been the influence of Monsieur Vidal at the school: whatever the reason, Luxat was firmly united as a centre of resisitance.

La Bastide was bigger and there were certainly collaborators there. Joseph knew this perfectly well but he was still shocked when he saw a Frenchman chatting happily with German soldiers, smiling, offering to buy them a drink.

On the Saturday after the Gestapo affair he had gone in to market as usual and had wandered over towards the bakery. He was hungry. There was no bread, he knew, and he had no ration tickets anyway. He was simply roaming around, thinking about food.

The door of the bakery opened and Alice Chauvet came down the steps, followed by Hans in his uniform. Alice paused and Hans took her arm and Joseph watched as they crossed the road. He could hear their voices though he was not near enough to catch what they were saying. Alice laughed and flicked back a stray curl. It was a cold day. Her cheeks were rosy and she clung to Hans, perhaps to share the warmth of his heavy overcoat, perhaps to keep herself steady, for her gait was awkward. She was heavily pregnant.

Joseph had heard that she was having an affair with one of the soldiers at the hotel and there she was, brazenly walking through the town on the arm of a German officer whose child she was bearing. A woman whose husband was a prisoner of war in a German camp.

The Germans had been out at Luxat that very week, had lined them up and threatened them with guns. They were bullies. They took their wheat and their livestock. They sent their men to work in Germany. How could anybody French even speak to them if they didn't have to? How could any French woman sleep with a German soldier? Joseph was outraged. He kicked away some cabbage stalks and broken boxes that littered the path, thrust his hands deep in his pockets and went on his way, scowling.

Joseph was not the only one that morning aware of Alice Chauvet and her lover. Louis Monnier was on his way back to the hotel and he saw them too. He'd always had a soft spot for Alice and he wondered how she and Hans would cope if the war turned out badly for the Germans.

That parachute drop near Festes had worried Louis. When the armistice had been signed there had been no choice. They'd had to support Pétain and collaborate with the Germans. He hadn't asked to have German soldiers billeted in the hotel, they'd just been sent there and he couldn't be rude to them and pick a quarrel with hotel guests, especially important guests like that. But he knew the hotel was seen as a centre for Germans and collaborators and he was beginning to wonder if he'd picked the wrong side. If the Germans now lost the war he might have problems. And if he might have problems it would be a lot worse for Alice Chauvet.

It was because they were both preoccupied with Alice and not watching where they were going that Louis and Joseph ran slap into each other. Joseph tripped and fell awkwardly among the rubbish by one of the market stalls and Louis bent down to offer his apologies before he recognised the boy.

"I'm sorry," he began and then beamed. "Joseph! Are you all right?"

Louis Monnier was the last person Joseph wanted fussing over him at that moment. Still angry and contemptuous about Alice Chauvet, he wanted nothing to do with any collaborator. They didn't just betray their country these collaborators. Alice Chauvet had betrayed her husband. Louis Monnier had betrayed Joseph himself, his own son. So when Louis held out his hand to help Joseph get up, the boy shrugged him away.

Bewildered, Louis looked down and saw the big brown eyes glaring at him with implacable hostility. He was fond of the boy. He'd enjoyed having him there at the hotel, helping in the bar. He hadn't wanted to turn him out but his wife didn't like Joseph, he could understand she didn't want his bastard boy around, usurping the place of her son, Auguste. He couldn't do anything about that. He was sorry his wife had told the police about the British soldier. He hadn't been happy when Auguste had sent Monsieur Delpech out to Luxat to look for the parachute party. But whatever his wife and Auguste had done, he hadn't done anything to hurt the boy. When Joseph turned from him with such bitter fury, Louis was dismayed.

"Joseph," he pleaded, "I've never meant to hurt you."

"Oh no, I'm sure you didn't," Joseph spat at him. "No. You never meant my mother to get pregnant. You never meant Madame Monnier to shove me down the steps of the hotel. You never meant to tell the police we had a British soldier staying with us. When the Gestapo line us up against a wall and shoot us, you won't mean to hurt us. But you won't move a finger to help us, will you?"

"That soldier, you know..." Louis began.

"Yes, that soldier, you call him. Well, his name's Robert. And when the war's over, he's going to come here and take me back home with him, to join his family. And you can go and rot in hell. I hate you."

Joseph struggled to his feet and flounced away. "And you just wait until Robert hears who betrayed him and see what happens then!" he flung over his shoulder as he left.

Louis shook his head, stunned at the depth of Joseph's passion. What could I have done, though, he wondered. Nothing! But Joseph's accusations echoed in his ears. Nothing! That was what Joseph couldn't forgive.

Unhappily, Louis crossed the road and went up the steps of the hotel and along the dismal corridor.

Joseph had boasted to Marius, exaggerating the importance of the resistance at Luxat, but things were beginning to happen now. Within a month of the first parachute drop they were expecting another.

"Let's make it a bit easier, though," Achille Cambon declared. "Let's change the Drop Zone. Somewhere further from the eyes of the police and the tracking station at Nebias."

So they cut down the trees in front of his cabin up in the forest and cleared the land and waited for the BBC to announce: 'The rabbit will fly at midnight.'

That afternoon, far away in Algeria, four radio operators gathered on the edge of an airfield. They turned out their pockets, to check that they were carrying nothing to betray them. They were going back to France and they each took a flask of cognac, so that they could celebrate when they arrived, but saying farewell to the Englishmen who had trained them, they toasted their departure in a more English fashion, with tea and biscuits.

Up in the forest above Luxat the reception committee was waiting. The plane passed overhead. The pilot checked the site, wheeled round and then returned. The Halifax engines filled the sky with thunder and then the plane roared away leaving four parachutes drifting down, with four men swinging helplessly on their fragile ropes.

The men below saw one of them land in the Drop Zone and begin to reel in his parachute.

"Come on!" Marcel and Joseph headed into the forest where another parachute had landed and another airman was skidding down the branches of a pine tree.

"Salut!" he greeted them, overwhelmed with excitement.

"Welcome!"

It was incredible. A French airman, a radio operator, had flown here to Luxat, brought by the RAF to fight the Germans.

"Can one of you go up that tree and get my parachute?"

Marcel hitched Joseph into the lowest branches and he scrambled up and reached out to pull in that soft white silk.

"Here!" The airman pulled out his flask and Joseph gulped and felt the fire surge through his veins. "To the resistance!"

They gathered on the edge of the Drop Zone, the four airmen and the men from Luxat who had come to meet them and they slithered back down the hillside, down the almost vertical path to the village below and to the beds prepared for them.

One of them, Emile, was staying with Mathilde Barthez and the boys. "Is it safe here?" he asked.

"For tonight," she said. "They'll come tomorrow, though, to look for you."

When he went to bed that night Emile slipped his pistol under his pillow. As he fell asleep he wondered what he would do if the Germans came and caught him there. Would he fight or try to escape? Whatever happened, he was excited, delighted to be back in France and back in action.

The two boys were excited, too. When Robert came to the house, they had simply given a home to Monsieur Vidal's friend, without thinking about it. Now they were part of the resistance and they knew they were going to be fighting the Germans.

Maman lay awake for a long time. She was frightened. The Germans had been to the village before and they would come again now. If they caught this young man in the house, they would all be shot. She slept fitfully and woke early, to see Emile on his way before the Germans arrived.

They were still doubtful about Luxat. The tracking station had followed the plane and in the morning the Gestapo were out once more, questioning people in Festes and La Bastide and Luxat. This time they took Marcel to the police station and questioned him there, while Maman and Joseph waited nervously at home. There was still no evidence though and he was back before nightfall.

Since Raoul and Jean-Paul had gone up to the cave, volunteers had been flocking to the maquis. There were now forty or fifty men living and working in the camp above Luxat and the cave could hold six at the most.

"We'll clear out the cabin and you can use that," Achille Cambon offered. So they harnessed the oxen and loaded the cart with axes and scythes and sickles and a shepherd's crook and a couple of ploughs and squeezed it all into the stable at his house in the village.

The floor of the cabin was only bare earth but they had hay to sleep on and well-wishers bustled round and found some blankets and plates and spoons and forks for those who needed them. They took wood from the trees they had felled to clear the landing field and made tables and chairs and benches, so that they could sit and eat properly and Monsieur Vidal used a corner of the hut as his head quarters.

It was quite snug inside the cabin. It had thick, stone walls and though the roof leaked at first there were plenty of men to repair it and they mended the door and put new shutters on the windows.

They were altogether better organised now. Raoul Vidal went to Toulouse and came back in high spirits.

"At last! We're free of that pathetic lot in Montpellier. We've linked up with de Gaulle's Armée Secrète, in Toulouse."

"What difference is that going to make?" asked Achille Cambon.

"We're no longer relying on Victor and his friends to see we get supplies. This lot will liaise with the RAF for us."

"What about La Bastide?" asked Jean-Paul.

"They've joined the Francs Tireurs et Partisans. The RAF won't supply them. They say the FTP are communists."

"Shame!" said Achille Cambon.

"Why? It doesn't matter, does it?" asked Raoul.

Achille Cambon looked doubtful. "Not really. But one of our radio sets disappeared yesterday. And we think it was the men from La Bastide who took it."

"Who cares?" asked Jean Paul. "Good luck to them. We're all fighting the same enemy."

The BBC, at least, seemed to recognise this in its news bulletins. They no longer talked of the 'maquis and the 'resistance'. They were now the FFI, the French Forces of the Interior, the army inside France, waiting to join up with the rest of the troops when the Liberation came.

Longer and longer lists of coded messages were broadcast, announcing the arrival of more and more parachute drops and even round La Bastide hardly a day passed without reports of another attack on a railway or an electricity supply. It was the Spanish refugees, though, who were the real saboteurs here. With their experience of guerrilla warfare at home, they had organised themselves into batallions of Guerilleros and they travelled by bus round Quillan, Limoux and Carcassonne, carrying suit cases full of explosives with which they blew up railway bridges and electricity pylons.

At the Hotel du Commerce they knew what was happening.

"It's all these foreigners – Spanish, Italian. Rubbish they are. And communists. If they had their way there'd be anarchy here."

"You can't live without law and order."

They took heart from the defeat of the maquis at Glières, in the Alps, where armed with supplies from the RAF the resistance fought off the local police and Milice but were wiped out by the German army..

"Over four hundred of them killed, there were," Monsieur Delpech noted, with relish. "The German army knows what its doing. They don't stand a chance, those gangs of terrorists, when they're faced with a proper army."

"String 'em all up, that's what they deserve."

"Shooting's too good for them."

"Someone needs to teach them a lesson."

"Come on!" they called to Hans who came in at that moment. "Let's drink a toast to the defeat of all terrorists."

"With pleasure!" he said, a wide grin on his face. "But there's something even more important to celebrate. Let's drink to the health of my son. Baby Henri!"

Louis uncorked a bottle of Pasti and poured out the glasses.

Monsieur Delpech took his and held it up. "To Henri!" he called.

The others drank, but without enthusiasm. They were all good Vichy men and they knew that they were depending on the Germans to protect them from the terrorists but they were not eager to celebrate the birth of this child. After all Albert Chauvet was their neighbour. They'd known him since they were children together. It didn't seem right to be celebrating his wife's affair with a German soldier while he was locked up in a German prison.

Others made their feelings clearer. That night someone threw a stone through the bakery door. The noise of shattering glass woke Alice and she went to see what had happened. She picked up the stone and unfolded the paper wrapped round it. 'Welcome Home Albert!" she read, scrawled in red crayon on a grubby piece of paper from a child's exercise book. She was trembling as she went back to the bedroom and showed the paper to Hans.

"What's going to happen?" she cried. "What'll happen to us if the allies invade France? What'll happen if …" she clung to Hans and sobbed. "What'll happen to Henri and me if the allies invade and the maquisards take over?"

Hans kissed her and stroked her hair and told her everything would be all right. "The maquisards at Glières didn't take over did they? The German army is unbeatable. We didn't lose the war in 1918. We were betrayed. And you saw what happened in 1939, 1940. None of them could stand up to us."

"I know," Alice said. And added anxiously, "But look what happened at Stalingrad."

"Yes. But that was just one battle. Hitler has a secret weapon. He's told us so. When the time comes, he'll use it. We'll win the war, you'll see."

Henri began to whimper. Hans looked at his little son. With a shock of dark hair and skin so pale, almost transparent, he was such a tiny, fragile creature. Slipping his hand under the baby's head, he picked him up and handed him to Alice. Henri opened his eyes for a moment, then with a purr of contentment took his mother's breast and began to feed.

CHAPTER 15
May 1944   With the maquisards

Men were flooding into the forest. By the end of May there were more than two hundred of them and just finding enough food was becoming a problem. Even if it was available in the shops they had no ration cards and they could not wander round the markets. Supplies were short anyway, because so much was taken by the Germans to feed their soldiers in France or to send back to the people in Germany.

But the maquisards did have friends. The mayor worked closely with Hans and his men. He knew when troops would be going out to a farm to collect cattle and he had details of where they would be held and how they were to be transported. And Madame Roux, his secretary, was sympathetic to the resistance.

Achille Cambon was in charge of provisions and she would let him know when the Germans were going to collect their supplies. He would warn the farmer and they would slip down during the night and snatch a few animals. Not enough to alert the enemy that Madame Roux had passed on information but enough to feed their men for a few days.

"What about paying me?" the farmer would ask.

"No money now but an IOU. I give you a receipt and you get paid after the liberation."

If the farmer still had doubts there was always one fruther argument, particularly telling if he had been a friend of the Germans.

"And we won't forget your help. If there's any problem after the liberation, we'll remember you let us have these cattle. You'll have the receipt anyway, to prove it."

There were arguments sometimes, of course. A family in La Bastide lost their pig and swore the maquisards had taken it, though there was no evidence. One day they bought a couple of sheep and were making arrangements with the butcher at La Bastide when the young shepherd erupted into the store room, blazing with anger.

"What the bloody hell are you playing at?" he yelled, thumping his crook on the tiled floor. "I sold you two bloody sheep, good and honest, and you sneak round and take another bloody lamb, without a bloody by your leave."

His eyes were bazing and his face was as red as the old cotton scarf knotted round his neck. "I'll denounce the lot of you. I'll tell them who's up there with you. And where they can bloody well find you. I'll take them there myself!"

"Bloody idiots!" growled Achille Cambon, clapping the young shepherd on the shoulder and chewing on his cigarette to move it to the other side of his mouth. "You did well to come here, mon vieux. I'll find out who it was and they won't get a bite of meat for a week, I can promise you."

He paid the shepherd for the stolen lamb, shared his packet of cigarettes with him and went back to the camp to knock a bit of sense into the thick heads of those young fools who didn't understand that they couldn't afford to quarrel with the local people. They relied on them.

They provided corn and meat and poultry and vegetables and they supplied services, too. The butcher at La Bastide cut up the carcasses and prepared their meat for them. The miller at Festes ground their corn and the baker there baked their bread. The garage at La Bastide serviced their vehicles for them and the owner of the garage at Espezel had a brand new tanker and let them use it for collecting water, now that there were too many of them for the well up in the forest. They couldn't have survived without all this help.

It was a hard life for the men in the camp, though, and those like Joseph and Marcel, who could get away to the comforts of home, would savour every spoonful of proper cassoulet and lentil soup, whenever they could.

"Look," said Marcel, at dinner time one Sunday, spearing a carrot on the end of his knife. "This is a carrot. A real, genuine, earth-grown carrot."

"And this," said Joseph, "is meat. What sort of meat? Mouse? Rat? Hedgehog? No, my friends, this comes from that old-fashioned pre-war delicacy, a rabbit!"

Maman laughed. "You do talk rubbish."

Marie-France was there. "You haven't really eaten rats and hedgehogs, have you?" she protested.

"We haven't eaten rats but some of the maquisards have and we've had hedgehogs."

Marie-France shuddered.

"We have. And the other day we caught a fox and it made quite a good stew."

Joseph was telling the truth and it sounded convincing.

Marie-France decided to admit to some of the horrors she had enjoyed. "We had a grass snake a few weeks ago. It wasn't bad. My brother caught it in the wood pile. And we've eaten mangel-wurzels that were meant for the horses."

"I'm hoping we'll catch a deer. I love venison." Marcel licked his lips, hopefully. They spent a lot of time dreaming about food.

They spent some time growing food too and looking after livestock. There were far too many of them now for Achille Cambon's cabin. Other Luxat families who had land above the village had cleared out their forest cabins and let the maquisards use them and those who did not want to spend their time practising with the new weapons or tearing through the villages in their cranky old vehicles, were happy to help the farmers who had given them lodging.

Once a sleepy little cluster of houses that never saw a stranger, Luxat was now host to an international community. There were Spanish and Italian refugees, there were British and American airmen, there were even some North Africans who had been recruited into the French army at the beginning of the war and had been stranded in France since 1940.

Joseph was in his element. Few of the allied airmen spoke any French and Joseph, armed with a thick dictionary, became their translator, their navigator on trips beyond the camp, their guide and authority on all things French. He was busy and happy with his new friends and even more delighted when Emile called him one day to say there was a radio message for him from Colonel Robert Maclachlan.

Joseph jumped up and bombarded Emile with questions. "Where is he? What does he say? Is he here in France? Is he coming to see us?"

"Hang on," said Emile, "military messages are very short, you know.

"Please! What does he say?"

"He just says to tell you he's safe and well and will see you when the war's over."

Joseph did two somersaults, he was so excited.

Marcel too found life with the resistance more exciting than anything he had ever done before the war. He was helping Achille Cambon with supplies but where the older man was talking to farmers and negotiating deals, Marcel was out in the lorries, armed with a rifle, impressing the girls and frightening peaceful villagers for miles around.

His latest project was typical of the boy.

"We need some tobacco, you know," Marcel declared.

"Perhaps we do but I'm thinking more about bread and meat. Essentials," Monsieur Cambon told him dryly.

"Yes, but one quick excursion could give us a real haul. And if we had some tobacco for our friends it would encourage a bit more generosity with bread and meat, wouldn't it?"

Monsieur Cambon considered. "So where would we get this tobacco?"

"From the depot at Limoux."

Monsieur Cambon had his hands full but they agreed that Marcel and his friends should take a couple of lorries and stock up on tobacco.

"You'll need an armed guard, though," Jean-Paul warned.

Half a dozen young men had leapt into the lorries almost before he had finished speaking and they set off happily, waved on by the men at the camp who were looking forward to smoking to their hearts content.

They set up their machine gun at the crossroads, broke into the depot and started loading the bales onto the lorries. They had nearly finished when a German convoy appeared.

It was bedlam. The maquis blazed away with their machine gun, the Germans returned the fire, the young men leapt onto the lorries and they raced away, guns rattling.

Within a few minutes there were shrieks of alarm.

"The tobacco's on fire!"

Smoke was pouring from one of the bales. Little flames were already flickering across the surface of the bale.

"We've got to get rid of this!"

They swarmed towards the dangerous bale and shoved and pushed and heaved it over the side of the lorry just as they went round the corner. The burning bale toppled into the road and rolled into a culvert.

"Hey!" Marcel yelled.

One of the young men had been clutching the cargo with too much enthusiasm and he hadn't let go. As the lorry swerved round the corner the young man had been carried away with the burning bale. They couldn't stop. He had to crawl into an old shed and hide until nightfall and then make his way back on foot.

He trudged into the camp next morning with blistered feet and a foul temper which was not helped by the laughter and mockery that greeted him. "Where's the tobacco then? I thought you'd got off to save it."

"You haven't smoked all that on your own, have you?"

"Get lost!" he muttered and stomped off to try and get some sleep.

He was tired and disgruntled but Marcel and his friends were elated. Resistance work was important and patriotic, no doubt, but it was good fun. Even that shoot out with the Germans had been a laugh. Nobody'd been hurt and they puffed away happily through a haze of tobacco smoke, with that cheerful confidence in their own immortality which young men have.

The Spanish men of the 5th batallion of the Guerilleros were older and more experienced than the group at Luxat and there were fewer of them. They had moved into the old camp at Aunat, above the Peyrou farm..

This was not like the small group of woodcutters who had stayed there previously. This group was armed and organised. They had transport, bicycles and motor cycles. They roared down the track with rifles slung over their shoulders and Marius was delighted to see them come and go, waving as they passed. He no longer felt isolated from what was happening in the world, he was at the centre of things now.

These men had fought in the Spanish Civil War and they knew about explosives and about sabotaging electricity pylons and railways lines. But they were prepared to attack German soldiers when they got the chance.

One day, returning to their camp across the empty hills above the ruined castle at Festes, they spotted a German car coming down from La Bastide.

"No escort?"

The car was on its own.

They fired a volley of shots as it came out onto the last stretch of road before the village. The vehicle overturned. All four passengers were killed.

They wasted no sympathy on their victims. "Next time, we'll get more of them," they declared.

They considered where they might find a good target. "There's no point in attacking a convoy but when they come off duty they often send a lorry to take them into town."

Within a week they had found a lorry bringing troops down from the mountains and they attacked, killing fourteen soldiers.

This was too much for the Germans who scoured the countryside, asking questions and listening to rumours, determined to find those responsible for these deaths.

A few days after the attack on the lorry a young Spanish refugee went into the café Terminus and was soon talking to Juan Almagro and his friends.

"Where are you from?" they asked.

"From the coast, near Perpignan."

"What are you doing here?"

"We got caught by the Gestapo. I managed to escape but a lot of my friends were taken."

Most of the Spaniards in the south of France were Republicans, anti-fascists who had fought in the Civil War. Juan accepted him as a comrade and was sympathetic. "I heard there'd been trouble."

"How did you get away?"

"I wasn't there are the time. I'd gone into town for supplies. I was lucky."

They nodded, they all knew about running from the Gestapo.

"Anything going on here?" he asked.

"We always need help," they said and Juan introduced him to a young man who took him out to Laurac, where they waved to Marius as they passed and went on, down the little hidden pathway, to Aunat. The new recruit who said his name was Pablo was shown a place where he could sleep.

"What were you doing with your group?" they asked.

"Explosives, mostly," he replied. "I've got some stuff that I managed to salvage when we were attacked. It's in Limoux. I'll go and get it tomorrow."

The next day Pablo left the old farm. He went to Limoux. But not to collect sabotage material. He reported to the Gestapo, giving them details of the camp at Aunat.

Early in the morning, a few days after this, just as he had woken up, Marius heard the dogs barking and looked out to see one of the men riding back towards the camp. Barely two minutes later the dogs went wild, barking and racing round in circles. The chickens and geese joined in. It was bedlam. His mother came out of the house to see what was happening.

A troop of German soldiers in marching order was waiting on the track leading up from the main road. At their head were six French men in the dark uniform of the Milice. One of the Frenchmen called angrily to Marius. "Here! You! Stop those dogs!"

Marius reassured the animals. The Frenchman continued. "There's a terrorist camp up in the forest here. You can take us to it."

"But monsieur ..." Marius was trying to think of an excuse. " Monsieur, I have to feed the animals." And he had to go to school. Could he say he did not know where the camp was?

The man from the Milice walked over, with long, deliberate strides. And hit him. Hard. Across the face. His lip was cut. His mother moved to protest.

"And you!" The militia man pointed his gun at Marius's mother. "Get back inside. He's coming with us."

Monique Peyrou knew the man, had known him since he was a baby. A nasty little boy whose father could not keep his hands to himself and who had fathered Gabrielle's child as well as this young thug. "Auguste ..." she began.

He turned on her, and casually slammed the butt of his pistol across her head. Blood poured from her nose. Auguste smirked. No Peyrou woman was going to tell him what to do. "Get inside," he commanded. Hurt, fearful, bewildered, Monique allowed her mother to pull her inside the house.

"Now," said Auguste Monnier. "Don't bother with any more excuses. Just take us to the camp."

Marius could have taken the narrow path but if they went that way they would come out suddenly into the courtyard at the old farm and catch the men unprepared whereas if they took the wider track, they would come out into a clearing where the men might see them and have the chance to escape.

For Marius the men at the camp were his heroes and his friends. They waved to him when they went by. One of them had given him a ride up to the camp in the motorcycle side car. Joseph, the boy from Luxat, was not much older than him and he was part of a maquis like this and had even told him that one day he might be able to help the maquis here. Marius was not going to let anyone take his friends unawares. Still frowning as he worked it out, he led the Germans and the Milice across the muddy courtyard and on to the wider track.

With Marius at the head of the column they marched towards the camp. The boy knew what would happen if the men there were caught. They beat them up to get information and then they hung them and left their bodies dangling. Or they shot them. There were a lot of German soldiers marching behind him. He'd not had time to count them but he knew that it was a big group, too many for the men at the camp to fight off.

Perhaps they would take prisoners and the maquis would be interrogated at La Bastide or Limoux. Everyone knew what happened there. Marius stumbled as he remembered what he had heard. They tortured people. They held them in baths of cold water, their heads submerged until they nearly drowned, then they pulled them out and started all over again. They hosed them down with freezing water and then gave them electric shocks. They pulled out their nails. They broke their fingers.

Marius choked as he thought of the terrible things these men could do. Oh God, please save my friends, he prayed. Please let them see us coming. Please let them be safe.

At Aunat the men were getting up. Still half asleep they were pulling on their boots, shaving, preparing coffee for breakfast.

They slept upstairs, on the first floor of the old farmhouse, in what had been a huge, undivided storage space. At the end of the building, overlooking the farm yard, there was a big, unglazed opening. One of the men was standing there, shaving, taking advantage of the light from the window. It was he who saw the approaching column: a young boy followed by those terrible dark blue uniforms of the Milice and then the 'feldgrau' of the German army.

"The Boche!" he yelled, dropping his razor and running. Every man in the building snapped into action as if fired with electric current. In a few seconds they were downstairs, out of the farmhouse, cowering in the forest.

The soldiers covered the building from all sides and advanced, going from room to room, blasting their way through with grenades, then rushing in, firing wildly. The building echoed with the putter of gunfire, the thudding of grenades, with cracking wood and falling plaster and the barked shouts of troops high on danger, recording their progress through the buildings. The men hiding in the forest could hear the commotion. Marius, terrified by the noise and violence, was knocked to the ground by the militia men, who laughed angrily and warned him that he would suffer if his friends had escaped.

All day the guerilleros hid in the forest. At the farm, at Laurac, Monique and her mother fidgeted, trying to get on with the day's work, unable to settle, waiting for news of Marius, pacing backwards and forwards, going out into the farmyard and immediately returning indoors.

Towards five in the afternoon they heard the soldiers returning. They were singing German marching songs and the music, inexpressibly haunting, drifted down to the farm. The two women came out into the courtyard. The chorus grew louder as the men approached and hearing such singing they were encouraged, for men who could sing so sweetly must surely have kind hearts, must surely be incapable of brutality. The music rose to a climax and the men surged into the yard, crowding together, elated.

"Right! Food and drink for the troops!" they commanded.

Auguste Monnier and the other Frenchmen translated when necessary but the soldiers made their demands with rough gestures and threats rather than with words. The two women warily served them, bringing up wine from the cellar, cutting ham from the joints which hung from the beams, hunting for eggs to make more omelettes. The soldiers ate well and drank copiously, not caring about the effect on the family's meagre provisions. As night fell they roistered off down to the main road, singing lustily.

There was no sign of Marius.

Monique had visions of the boy lying wounded, alone at the old farm, waiting for help. Why did she not ask the men where the boy was? More than once she was on the verge of framing her question, but she caught a cruel, mocking glint in the eyes of Auguste Monnier. She feared what he might tell her and shied away from asking. She would go herself and look for the boy.

When the last soldier had left, she took a lantern and stumbled up the path towards the camp. Juan Almagro and one of his men were emerging from the forest, returning to see what had happened and whether there was anything to salvage from the wreckage of the farm.

The building had been destroyed, blasted by grenades and gutted by a fire which was still not quite extinguished.

There was a continuous crackling. Embers were still stirring into life. Blackened timbers were still falling and settling. There was nothing here to salvage.

Monique, going through the charred remains, was whispering the name of her son. "Marius! Marius!"

They found him on the ground floor, in a room next to the entrance. His small, thin body was half hidden by charred beams which had collapsed, still burning, and fallen across his legs. They kicked and tugged and shifted the blackened wood. The fire had caught the boy's clothes, had scorched his body which lay burnt and twisted.

His mother stared, aghast, her left hand fluttering at her lips, her right hand wavering in the sign of the cross. She repeated a prayer: Ave Maria gratia plena: Dominus tecum: benedicta tu in mulieribus et benedictus fructus ventris tui.

The men turned over the body of Marius Peyrou. He had been terribly beaten and tortured. His fingers had been broken. His eyes had been gouged out. He had been shot in the back of the head.

Monique, her eyes wild with grief, her lips stretched in a rictus of despair, collapsed beside the body of her son. "Oh, my poor child!" she cried. "My poor Marius! Oh, my son, my son!"

The two men made the sign of the cross and joined Monique in the Lord's Prayer: Pater noster qui es in caelis...

Juan was beside himself, overwhelmed with grief and anger. How could they do this to a child? A boy of twelve! This was the boy who waved to them so happily when they passed the farm. A boy with his whole life before him. He had saved their lives. He had taken the open path and given them the chance to escape and while they escaped the boy had been tortured, on his own in the deserted farm with a horde of German soldiers and French Milice. Grief for the boy and his mother mingled with a sense of humiliation and guilt because Juan Almagro had not been there to help the boy who had saved his life.

In the courtyard they found a plank of wood. Gently they picked up Marius's body and laid it on this makeshift stretcher. Juan took off his shirt and covered him. Once more he made the sign of the cross. Monique touched her son's wounded face, tears pouring silently down her cheeks. The three of them stood, head bowed, then the men picked up the stretcher. They carried him back home, faltering, stumbling in the uncertain light of the lantern.

They laid him on the table in the kitchen. That night the two women watched beside the body. Monique held a photograph of Marius as a baby, six months old. She gently stroked the picture. She prayed, trying to escape thoughts which jumped from images of the past to images of her son now, tortured, in front of her, and to images of a future without her child, growing old unsupported and alone. There was no comfort in these thoughts.

Her mother dozed at her side. The men could not stay. "It won't help any of us if they come round and find us here," Juan told her. "But this boy saved our lives. We can't undo what has been done but we shan't forget your son, madame."

Monique looked at him, bleakly.

"We shan't forget what they did to him either. When this war is over, we'll hunt them down and make them suffer, like they made this child suffer. That's a promise. I swear." He made the sign of the cross. "We'll get them!"

Monique and her mother heard what they said. It did nothing to ease their present grief.

CHAPTER 16
June 1944 The Battle of France begins

Next day the men from Aunat came to the camp at Luxat. One of the sentries brought Juan Almagro to the cabin where Raoul and Jean-Paul were working. They could see that something was wrong. Juan was a small, wiry man, full of bounce and vivacity, a man who would burst through a door with such energy that everyone would look up and smile. To-day he just stood in the doorway, his shoulders drooping, his expression grim.

Jean-Paul was on his feet. "What's the matter?" he asked. "What's happened?"

"They came to Aunat," Juan told them. He spoke slowly, as if it was hard to articulate words.

"The Gestapo?"

Juan nodded. "And the Milice."

It was the worst combination, the one they all dreaded. Thugs and bigots both, the Germans had power and the Milice had local knowledge.

"How many did they get?" asked Raoul, fearing that the guerilleros battalion must have been wiped out.

"Oh, none of us." Juan's voice was dry. "Young Marius from the farm was guiding them. He brought them up by the wider road, so we saw them coming." Juan stopped.

The two Frenchmen felt a chill of fear. "So what happened?"

"They killed Marius." The words flowed now. "Those filthy Boche and those Milice swine, they took a little boy and they killed him." He gulped, a sob rising in his throat. "And they didn't just kill him. They tortured him first. They'd broken his fingers. And ..." Even the words were brutal. "Do you know what they did? To a little boy? They poked out his eyes! Just a young lad he was and his mother went up there afterwards and found him. And the building had been burning, so his little body was burnt and charred and broken and there was blood all over him and his eyes ..."

Juan covered his face with his hands and sobbed, his whole body shaking.

Raoul Vidal found a drop of armagnac and poured it into a glass. "Here," he said. "You need this."

"What sort of men could do a thing like that!" Jean-Paul asked in disgust.

"Auguste Monnier! You know him? He was there, leading the Milice."

Raoul and Jean-Paul stared at Juan in horror. They'd never liked Auguste, they'd always known he was a bully, but it was still hard to accept that someone they knew, a young man from La Bastide, could do this. It was Raoul who found his voice first.

"When this war's over, men like Auguste are going to have to account for what they've done," he said quietly.

He was thinking. "Marius Peyrou was the boy's name, wasn't it?"

Juan nodded.

"I don't suppose Joseph knew him. It's the same name though. "

Jean-Paul, who came from Festes, was trying to dredge up anything he might have heard about the Peyrou family. The two boys were probably not close, but they might have met. Joseph had taken supplies out to Aunat he remembered.

"I'll go and see if I can find him," Monsieur Vidal said.

Joseph was with the English airmen, playing cards, some silly game. They were slapping their cards down on the table and roaring with laughter. Monsieur Vidal stood watching them for a moment and Joseph looked up and caught his eye.

"Were you looking for me, monsieur?"

Monsieur Vidal nodded. Joseph shoved his cards into his neighbour's hand and got up, with a quip to his friends that made them all laugh. He came towards Monsieur Vidal, still grinning.

Should he have left him alone, Monsieur Vidal wondered, let him find out accidentally what had happened? But he was here now and it might be easier for Joseph to be told directly.

"Bad news, I'm afraid," he said. "From the farm at Aunat." And he told Joseph what had happened. How Marius had led the men to the Spanish camp and had given his friends the chance to escape and how the Germans had killed the boy.

"You met him, didn't you, when you went to Aunat?" Monsieur Vidal asked.

Joseph nodded. He remembered how he'd boasted about his work with the maquis and how impressed the younger boy had been. And how grandly he'd suggested that Marius might be able to work with the maquis at Aunat.

"It's all my fault," he muttered.

Monsieur Vidal's voice was sharp. "No Joseph. It's not your fault. Marius did what he thought was right. He saved a lot of men. It's the Gestapo, the Milice, who are to blame for what happened."

News of Marius's death spread quickly. He'd been in Madame Vidal's class at the school in Festes, where she and Fernande struggled to find words of comfort for his friends whose parents wondered what consolation there could ever be for his mother.

At the Hotel du Commerce even Monsieur Delpech was shaken by what had happened and found it hard to justify the death of a child, though he was convinced the attack on the camp was justified.

"Those terrorists were killing German soldiers," he reminded everyone.

It was Hans, the German soldier, speaking awkwardly in French, who voiced what they all felt in the Hotel du Commerce. "Yes. And if they had killed the terrorists that would be right. But they killed a boy. A boy even who may have seen the terrorists but who was not a terrorist." The men in the bar murmured their agreement. "Besides they killed like an animal. That is wrong."

They all knew that Auguste had been there with the Milice. Monsieur Delpech looked down at the floor. Louis polished a glass, twisting the cloth with ferocious energy. They were ashamed of what Auguste had done, felt contaminated by their connection with him.

They had no respect now for the Milice. They were brutal. They betrayed their countrymen. There was no enthusiasm for the Vicy government either and as for the German soldiers, nobody wanted anything to do with them.

So it was Alice Chauvet who bore the brunt of their guilt and hostility. She had never hidden her love for Hans and now there was the baby, Henri, evidence of their affair for all to see.

Marie-France for one condemned her. "She should have more pride," she declared to Marcel, tossing her head.

"She should think of her reputation. How can a man respect you when you let him take advantage of you like that?"

They were sitting close together on one of the stone seats by the bridge at La Bastide and to show what she meant Marie-France removed Marcel's hand which was on her knee, dangerously near the hem of her skirt. Marcel protested that he would never fail to show respect for Marie-France.

"What's going to happen to her now?" she asked, fully aware of the practical difficulties facing Alice. "How's she going to explain that baby to her husband when he comes back after the Liberation? And where will her handsome German soldier be then?"

Marcel moved even closer and put his arm round her waist. "I'll never leave you," he swore.

With this promise firmly declared, Marie-France rested her head on his shoulder and allowed him to kiss her.

Unlike Marie-France and the men at the Hotel du Commerce, Joseph did not turn against Alice Chauvet. When Monsieur Vidal told him about Marius he had not mentioned that Auguste had been leading the Milice but it was not long before Joseph like everyone else knew that he had been there and had hit Marius and his mother before setting off for the old farm.

Joseph knew who to blame and his anger was implacable. Auguste was an old enemy. It was Auguste who had hit him and punched him when he was a child, Auguste, the favoured son, who had strutted through the hotel when Joseph was thrown out, Auguste who had found out about Robert and betrayed him. And now he had tortured and killed a boy who was helping the maquis.

The Liberation was coming, though. Men like Auguste would be held to account and Joseph would have his revenge. He was often busy, helping the allied airmen or practising with the new weapons, but when he was free, Joseph could be seen with a knife in his hand, whittling at a piece of wood.

"What's that?" one of the airmen asked.

"Beech." Joseph was not the cheerful, talkative boy he had been. He was altogether sharper since the death of Marius.

"Beech. Quite. But what's it for? What are you making?"

With slivers of wood dusting his lap, Joseph held out his open palm, the wood resting on his hand. A lovely warm russet colour, a narrow box, tapering slightly at the end.

"What is it?"

Joseph looked up, his eyes hard and cold.

"A coffin."

He went back to work, chipping away with his knife.

"I'm going to put his name on it: Auguste Monnier. And the date: 1944." There was grim satisfaction in his voice. "Then he'll know what to expect after the Liberation. And I'm going to sign it: JP. So that he knows it's me and I'm going to get him."

Joseph finished the little coffin. He sanded the wood so that it was smooth beneath his fingers. He polished it carefully, enhancing the grain of the wood, its rich colour. Neatly, he carved the date and the names. He wrapped it in brown paper and wrote on the outside: Monnier. A young man from the camp slipped into the hotel one morning when the coast was clear and left it on the desk outside the bar.

Janine found it when she went to sweep the floor and she took the parcel to her mother. As the paper fell away from the beautiful polished wood, Marie Monnier's hand dropped to her side.

"What's that you've got there?" her mother in law asked, putting down the peas she was shelling and pulling the paper towards her. She read the inscription and sniffed. "So they're threatening Auguste."

She was a tough woman, Louis's mother. She was fond of her grandson but she was not going to weep and wail. "Well, if other folks have been able to go into hiding for the past few years, that's what he'll have to do now, isn't it?"

She glared round at the family about her.

As if she was touching something filthy and smelly, Marie Monnier picked up the miniature coffin and turned it over. She peered at the initials on the back.

"So who sent it then?"

"JP. That little bastard, Joseph."

"Or someone else in the Peyrou family," the old woman countered. "They've got precious little reason to love Auguste, have they, any of them, not after what he did to that lad of theirs."

"I wish it was the little bastard himself they'd caught, that's all I can say." Marie Monnier was bitter but some of the fire had gone. She was worried. "They mean it. Auguste won't be safe here after the Liberation. I just hope they don't take it out on the rest of us."

There had been rumours that the maquisards were attacking the families of men in the Milice. As she said to Louis afterwards, they could all be in danger.

"It may not be easy," he agreed. "What with Hans and the soldiers living here, they may well make life difficult for us." He was beginning to wonder if this might be the moment to renew a few old friendships. After all some of the maquisards were his neighbours, he'd known them for years. The trouble was they weren't around any more, they'd gone into hiding.

And perhaps there wasn't much time left.

They all knew that the Liberation would not be long now. They were waiting for news of the Allied invasion. For days the BBC had been repeating Verlaine's haunting lines:

Les sanglots longs
des violons
de l'automne ...

The long sobbing of the violins of autumn ...

Even the Germans were tense, waiting for the closing of the phrase, the lines which would complete the verse and announce the allied landings.

It came on the nine o'clock news, on Monday, 5th June.

Les sanglots longs
des violons
de l'automne
bercent mon coeur
d'une longueur
monotone.

The same questions were on everyone's lips. Where would they land? In the north, in the Pas de Calais? In the south on the mediterranean coast? And would the invasion succeed or would the Germans hold them back?

It was the following day, the 6th June, that the Allied troops landed, on the beaches of Normandy, and that evening Charles de Gaulle broadcast once more. "Battle is joined ... the battle of France."

Raoul and Jean-Paul remembered discussing the speeches of 1940, when de Gaulle had foretold the defeat of Germany and insisted that France must be there on the day of victory, Frenchmen must play their part and must join the fight to crush the German army.

"Well, we're ready, aren't we?" said Raoul with satisfaction, looking at the men gathered round the radio.

"Been ready for weeks!" one of them declared stoutly.

"Weeks? More like months!"

They were not just ready, they were impatient for action. They had been training with the new weapons. They had kitted themselves out. Some of them had unearthed old army uniforms from the days before the occupation, others had raided a factory at La Bastide and taken uniforms intended for a Vichy youth camp. Some of them, like Marcel and Joseph, hadn't got uniforms but they wore patriotic armbands decorated with the cross of Lorraine and round their necks they tied lanyards of white silk parachute cord.

The older men warned them that they were daft to wear their uniforms and insignia outside the forest. "You meet a German patrol and you're just asking for trouble if you advertise that you're in the maquis," they told them. "They won't hesitate to shoot you, will they?"

The real hot heads simply didn't care. They were looking for a fight.

Now that the Allies had landed the maquis, the French Forces of the Interior, had a recognised role. It was their job to harrass the German troops and keep them occupied in the south, so that they could not link up with those trying to stop the Allied armies coming down from Normandy.

So they sabotaged the railways and the electricity supplies. They attacked German soldiers, too. There were casualties. Some of the maquisards were killed in these battles. Others were caught by the Germans and executed. But they were causing havoc. The Germans no longer felt safe on minor roads and on the D117, the main road that crossed France from Perpignan to Bayonne, they could travel only in daylight and even then only in convoy.

For the Germans this was intolerable. They could not let the despised terrorists dictate their movements. They decided to make an example of La Bastide.

They arrived early in the morning and set up road blocks. Most of the young men fled into the surrounding hills and woods but one, a boy of sixteen, got over the stream behind his house and was spotted in the middle of a meadow on the other side. His mother saw a German soldier shoot him and watched all day as he lay there in the open field, with the sun burning down, pleading for help, begging for water while the soldiers would not let her go to him. In the evening when the Germans left she was preparing water and bandages to take to him, when a soldier went out into the meadow and shot him through the head.

The Germans had gone through the town, house by house. At one of the first houses they searched they found a motor cycle with the engine still warm.

"Who does this belong to?" they asked.

"To my nephew," said the old man who lived there.

"And where is he?"

"I've no idea. He comes and goes. I don't see much of him."

They shouted at the old man and shoved him around but he had nothing to tell them. They marched him up the hill to the Town Hall and left him standing there all day, with a dozen or more other men, mostly elderly.

At midday the officers went to the hotel for lunch and the soldiers took out their sandwiches and sat on the stone seats by the bridge and on the steps of the bakery and of the other buildings that lined the street up to the Town Hall.

An elderly woman in black leaned out of an upstairs window and shouted at them. "Go and have your lunch somewhere else. This is my house and I don't want you here." She waved her hands, shooing them away, and they stood up, looked at her in surprise, and moved on to another doorway.

One of her neighbours was a veteran of the first world war and spoke to the intruders in fluent German. "What are you doing here, wasting your time bothering us? You should go and join your friends in Normandy. God knows they need some help up there."

They had ignored the old woman but this was too much and the man was taken, complaining loudly, to join the line outside the Town Hall.

The people of La Bastide were lucky that no evidence of resistance was discovered. The men lined up against the wall of the Town Hall were not shot but were led away in handcuffs, loaded into an army lorry and taken to the prison at Foix. The Germans had proved their point. Whatever was happening in the north, they believed they had demonstrated that here, in La Bastide, the German army was still in control.

Rumour of what was happening at La Bastide had soon reached the camp at Luxat but with road blocks on all the roads into the town they could get no firm information and spent the day hoping that no harm would come to their families and friends and dreading that they might hear of some fresh atrocity.

In the late afternoon two of the men who lived there crept over the hills into the town just as the Germans troops were leaving. They found people shaken but, as Joseph said later to Maman, "There are such terrible things happening all the time, you've no tears left."

It broke her heart to see him so quiet, without any of his old chirpy enthusiasm. He had taken the death of Marius very hard and now, every day there seemed to be news of someone else caught in an ambush or shot by the Boche. "I just want it to end," Joseph said. "It can't be long now, can it?"

CHAPTER 17
July – August 1944   Luxat joins the battle

It was midsummer. Scattered through the forest were clearings, small meadows where families from the village grazed their cattle, little fields where they grew a few crops. Not all the maquisards were military men. Some were simply hiding to escape being sent to work in Germany and they were happy to help the farmers. They cut the hay and heaved the bales onto the sledges. They watched the cows and the sheep. One or two of them even helped with the milking or learnt to make cheese.

Other men were more interested in the vehicles. They had half a dozen cars now, two lorries, the water tanker and a fleet of bicycles, all of which had to be kept in working order, at a time when no spare parts were available.

The radio batteries had to be recharged, too. They spent hours pedalling away on a bicycle fitted up to supply electricity. It took hours of muscle power to keep the batteries charged.

The RAF kept them busy too. Soon after the Normandy landings fifty containers were dropped. They all had to be cleared away and then the men had to learn to use the new weapons.

Accidents were inevitable. They was an explosion one afternoon in one of the guns. Five wounded men were rushed down to Quillan hospital where a sympathetic surgeon operated on them while their friends kept watch in the corridors and waited anxiously to take them to the doctor at Quérigut when the operation was completed.

For Marcel and Joseph the pace of life had changed completely. Marcel, still helping Achille Cambon with supplies, learnt to drive. Since the British airmen were helping to show the men how to use the new weapons, Joseph joined them and was becoming a surprisingly good shot.

Monsieur Vidal was in charge of the training. "We can tell you've been shooting rabbits all your life, can't we?" he said as he watched Joseph.

"He's got a good eye. I reckon he'll be one of our best snipers," Jean-Paul agreed.

Joseph accepted their praise happily and crawled once more through the old leaves and twigs that carpeted the forest floor, concentrating on hitting a moving target.

When Laurent Barde sent a message that the Milice had been called out to escort a petrol tanker from Quillan to Carcassonne, the men at the camp forgot their practice at once. This was the real thing. This was what they were practising for.

Juan Almagro was going to be in charge of the attack. Marcel came up with a car and they grabbed a machine gun, a couple of automatic rifles and half a dozen Gamon grenades and were on their way.

Joseph dived into the back of the car and squeezed between two Spanish guerilleros before Juan had a chance to realise what he was doing.

"Hé! I don't think this is a job for you!" Juan said when he saw him.

"Why not?" glared Joseph, daring Juan to say that he was too young. After all, if Marius could fight, so could he.

Marcel was impatient to be off. They didn't want to miss their quarry. "Oh, he's all right," he siad. "He's a good shot."

And he pressed his foot firmly on the accelerator and rattled off down through the tunnel and out of the forest, with two motorcyclists following behind.

Marcel drove as fast as he could along the D117, twisting down the mountain into Quillan, impatient that the steep bends forced him to go cautiously. Then they were off again, hoping to make good time to the gorge where they planned to catch the tanker but they met an outsized generator which was inching its way along the narrow road and a crowd of skipping children came to watch the fun. A van towing a generator then a car and a motorcycle, they rarely saw so much traffic in one morning.

"Any minute now those children will be peering into the car and will see the rifles," muttered Juan.

"And one of them will rush home to tell its mother."

The tension was unbearable.

"We've only got fifteen minutes," moaned Juan.

The motorcyclists decided to do something about it. Overtaking the car they squeezed up beside the van. "Can you move over, mon ami? We're in a hurry." The driver took one look at the two anxious men, guessed what they were doing and nodded. As soon as there was space at the roadside, he paused and the car raced past.

"Fifteen minutes," Juan said, looking at his watch. "Five minutes to get there, five minutes to prepare the ambush and with luck five minutes to spare."

Sweat was pouring down his face.

Joseph too was sticky with sweat. He lent forward and twitched at the damp cotton of his shirt, nervously trying to create some ventilation. Inside the car it was stifling. The windows were open but it was hot air that was siphoned in as they sped along the road and it hit with a fierce blast that brought no relief.

"We're coming to Couiza," said Marcel. "Hold on because if there are any signs of German soldiers at the depot there, we don't want to go through a check point and I'll make a quick turn."

Joseph sat tense and still but there was no check point at the depot at Couiza and none at the bridge either. "Are we coming back this way?" someone asked.

"No, we'll turn off left just before Limoux and come back that way. It's a quiet road, through the vineyards."

They reached a little gorge and Marcel braked and reversed the car up a path where it would be hidden from the road. Grabbing the guns and grenades they charged up a stony track to the edge of the cliff overlooking the road.

To their right was the entrance to another gorge, the Gorge d'Alet, to the left the road led back to Couiza. There was a ditch running along the road at the foot of the cliff.

"Damn!" said Juan. "If they get into that ditch they can fire straight up at us. Or worse, crawl along it and come up the track and attack us from behind." He wished they'd had more time to prepare the ambush. "Joseph," he barked. "Come here, on the right. Keep your eyes open and let us know at once if anyone starts crawling along the ditch."

They had been told that the lorry with the Milice was leading the convoy. Then there was the tanker and a motorcycle was bringing up the rear. Juan pointed to the two Spaniards. "Wait here, next to Joseph. The lorry with the Milice will come first. Wait until it's level with you, then throw your grenades. Try to get a direct hit."

Marcel was next in line. "Just shoot at the Milice. Get anyone who moves." Then there were the two men with the machine gun. "Try to get the tanker. But if you can't get that or if the others haven't stopped the Milice, then go for them. I'll take the motorcyclist bringing up the rear, if I can.

We don't want him rushing back off to Couiza to raise the alarm."

High up, on the open plateau, they were exposed to the sun. It beat down mercilessly and seemed to be reflected from every surface, from the cliffs opposite, from the road, from the stones and rocks around them. The heat was burning, the light painfully brilliant. Joseph brushed his arm across his eyes and a lizard, startled by the movement, stopped in its tracks and looked round, its flanks heaving.

Down below, on the other side of the road, he could see the river, an earthy green, reflecting the vegetation of the bank above, gently flowing, its surface scarcely rippled.

They had their instructions. They were ready, waiting, breathlessly still and silent, each second slowly passing. Joseph had his finger on his gun and waited, tense and alert, prepared to catch the slightest sound or movement. Nothing. Only the thudding of his own heart.

Then he heard the faint throb of an engine and from the left, from Quillan and Couiza, came the convoy they were waiting for. The lorry first, with the Milice. Then the tanker and finally, bringing up the rear, the motorcyclist. The lorry disappeared into the deep curve of the road below them and Joseph felt a sick emptiness in his stomach.

Then the man beside him was on his feet, the heavy grenade ready in his outstretched hand. He paused, weighing his weapon, adjusting his balance. Marcel was peering over the parapet. With a thunderous clamour the grenades exploded. In front of the lorry. Too soon! The bonnet was flung open and the lorry reared up, like a startled horse, and crashed back onto the road, in a cloud of dust.

Men in blue uniforms leapt out and, crouching low, ran for shelter. From up above, they fired. "The machine gun!" yelled Juan. It had jammed. Carefully, the men unloaded, checked, reloaded, aimed, fired again. Nothing.

Juan fired at his target but missed and the motorcyclist blazed off, back to Couiza, to warn the guards. Beside the lorry, two miliciens were trying to set up their gun and, with Marcel and Joseph firing away, the two Spaniards crept to the edge of the cliff, spat the pins from their grenades and hurled them down into the road. The grenades burst and the two men disappeared in a storm of dust.

Behind the lorry someone moved. Marcel aimed, fired. So did Joseph. A man, in a white shirt, flung up his arms and seemed to call to them. Shots rang out. From Marcel? Joseph? One of the Spaniards? The man fell back behind the lorry. A civilian driver, caught in a bloody battle.

Two or three militia men had dropped down into the ditch and were creeping along, to cut off their retreat, not to the right where their car was, where Joseph was watching, but to their left. Someone shouted a warning.

"Clear out! As fast as you can!" yelled Juan. A few more rounds and then there was no more firing from below. They should go down and destroy the petrol tank, but there was no time. They raced back to the car, the Spaniards protecting their rear.

Joseph tumbled in, panting. Juan and Marcel slammed the doors. They were all grimy, sweating and panting. Without a word, they raced off towards Limoux: through Alet, across the old bridge over the River Aude and on, through the bends of the gorge, tyres squealing and burning. They had to reach their turning before the German troops arrived, alerted by the motorcyclist. If they were caught here, on this narrow, twisting road, they wouldn't stand a chance. Did they even have any ammunition left?

Despite the heat, Joseph felt ice cold. He closed his eyes and prayed that they would make it. He could feel the men tense beside him. Finally the road straightened out. They were through the gorge and they began to relax, though Marcel's foot was still hard down on the accelerator. They could see the turning, five hundred yards ahead.

Then, bang! With a sudden explosion, the car swerved. Marcel's hands danced on the wheel and the car returned to the road, but limping, clattering and creaking like rusty iron. And stopped. They fell out of the car, guns ready. A burst tyre! The rubber had split, the tyre was in shreds, the car was useless, a couple of hundred yards from their turning.

Blindly they stumbled into the vineyards. The low growing vines, planted in neat, straight lines, offered no shelter. They had to get over the brow of the hill. Racing up the steep slope, Joseph could feel his boots clogging in the thick, clay earth, dragging his pace. He reached the top at last and threw himself, exhausted, on the ground, his legs trembling, his heart pounding, his throat parched.

Looking down he could see the car, on the road below, a tin toy, shining in the late afternoon sun. As he looked, the Germans arrived, the reinforcements called up by the motorcyclist. They stopped, got out to inspect the car and looked up, searching the countryside for signs of the escaping maquisards. Joseph turned away. They had made it, but only just.

As he lay, still panting with exhaustion, Juan was already urging them forwards. They had to find better cover. They had to move.

Marcel leading, they walked until it was too dark to see their feet and until they were too tired to take another step. Then they shuffled into a barn and collapsed on the hay, while Marcel went out again and called on a farmer who gave them bread, fruit and water. They were up early next day and trudged through rain all morning, doggedly following Marcel, carrying their precious weapons. By midday, as they arrived in sight of Festes, they were soaked. They were plagued with blisters and the sole of Joseph's right boot was flapping dangerously loose.

"No good going into the village," Juan declared. "The Germans could be waiting for us." They carried on, following the stream, keeping away from the road until, towards the end of the afternoon, they reached Luxat. Joseph stopped to reassure Maman, who clasped him wordlessly in her arms, tears streaming down her cheeks.

Trudging across the hills, hungry and exhausted, drenched by the rain, Joseph had kept his mind free of thought. Images of the ambush came to his mind but he brushed them away, like the raindrops that ran into his eyes and threatened to obscure his sight.

Now he was back home, seated safely at the familiar kitchen table, a bowl of soup in front of him, Maman hovering, her anxious questions unspoken, the anaesthetic of physical exertion was wearing off.

Joseph had been so angry. Auguste Monnier and his friends in the Milice had killed Marius, the cousin whom he had barely met but might have hoped to know one day, a boy like him. As he got into the car he had been so determined to avenge Marius. They must ambush the Milice. They must kill them all. They were traitors, murderers, they deserved to die.

But the voice of his schoolmaster echoed now in his mind: Monsieur Vidal rebuking the children, telling them that a soldier might have to kill other soldiers but it was not something to boast about. And there was the man in the white shirt. He was no milicien, he had been calling to them.

It was all too much for Joseph. He put his head on the table and longed to sleep, longed for an end to all this drama and suffering. Maman put her arm round him, offering whatever comfort her love might give. Joseph finished his soup and set off back up to the camp. He couldn't stay in the village. The Gestapo might come looking for him.

Next day the local paper carried the story of how a hundred armed terrorists had attacked the forces of law and order on the road below Alet. After a spirited response, the report declared, the terrorists had been forced to withdraw, taking with them their dead and wounded. The report was illustrated with a picture of their abandoned car, which had been put on display in the Place Carnot in Carcassone, as a warning to anyone else who might be tempted to tangle with the authorities.

They all knew that the Germans would not ignore the attack on the tanker. When the guerilleros at Aunat had killed German soldiers, the Germans had gone out to Aunat, burt down the old farm and killed Marius. When the allied landings had been followed by sabotage of railways and electricity supplies, the Germans had moved into La Bastide. Now they would come to Luxat.

Meanwhile life continued.

Saturday, 5th August was market day. The week end was, perhaps, slightly special, because the next day, Sunday, was the day of the Luxat Fête. As Mathilde Barthez prepared for market she wondered if the boys would come down to join in the festivities. She wondered if there would be any festivities. She was worried but they had lived with anxiety for so long now. Anxiety which would deepen into fear and recede and then return, like rain which could at any time dissolve into clear blue skies or break into thunder and storm.

The market that day was subdued. Business continued. Farmers needed to sell their produce, housewives needed to buy food for their families but there was not the usual relaxed chatter and gossip, the friendly exchange of news, which was normal on market day.

Mathilde caught sight of Marie Monnier, looking drawn and anxious as she skuttled between the stalls. She seemed to have grown old suddenly. She had lost the pride that she used to flaunt when she strolled round the town, daring anyone to gainsay her, she whose husband ran the hotel, who was the friend of important people like Monsieur le Commissaire Delpech. Mathilde remembered the coffin Joseph had sent to Auguste and knew that his mother had plenty to trouble her. The allied troops were moving down towards Paris. Liberation could not be far away and it would bring no joy to the Monnier family.

There was no joy for Alice either. Louis Monnier, with genuine kindness, had unearthed the old pram that had been used for his two children. Alice pushed her tiny son through the town in this battered perambulator, riding high on big, old-fashioned wheels. The warm maternity that would have come so easily to her was checked by fear and shame. She scarcely dared to smile at her small son. La Bastide had taken sides and Alice was an easy victim. Neighbours drew away as she passed, not stopping to peep kindly into the pram, to admire the new baby.

The market packed up early that morning. Nobody wanted to linger away from home. On the way back to Luxat the crowded bus was quiet. Farmers wives returning to their isolated homes were usually eager to enjoy this last opportunity to laugh and gossip with their friends but to-day they were withdrawn, each silently rehearsing their fears.

They knew that the Germans in the south were nervous, eager to move north, to join the forces fighting against the Allies but were kept in the south, waiting for another landing that might come, on the Mediterranean coast, and constantly harried by French resistance forces. Only a fool would expect the Germans to win this war but they were not yet defeated. The passengers on the bus knew that for the moment the Germans were still in control in the south of France and that the coming battle could be bloody.

The women returning from market that day had brothers and husbands and sons up in the forest with the maquis. There were rumours that German convoys had been seen in the area. If the German troops moved against the camp at Luxat, what would happen to the men trapped in the forest? What would happen to their families? Would the villages be safe? Nervous troops can be dangerous and brutal.

As they left the bus they exchanged the usual greetings.

"Take care! Look after yourself!" they said.

"See you next week!"

The familiar phrases seemed to have a sudden new intensity.

The maquis knew that the Germans were approaching. Troops were moving openly through the countryside and their intelligence was good, warning them that the 11th Panzers had been seen advancing towards the forest.

In his headquarters overlooking the open Drop Zone Raoul Vidal went over his plans once more.

To the north of the camp the land dropped abruptly. The steep cliff which led down to the village was almost vertical. There was a treacherous little footpath up the side of the cliff but that would be no good for armed soldiers. There was the lane which zig zagged, in a series of hairpin bends, from the village up to the forest road, but from this road the only way into the camp was through the tunnel cut in the rock and the tunnel, mined and guarded, would give no access for enemy troops. The Germans were unlikely to attack from the north.

To the east and west there was thick forest. Tanks and armoured vehicles would be useless here. Even infantry would be able to advance only slowly, constantly threatened by maquisards who knew the terrain so much better than their enemies. The danger lay to the south. Here the forest was bordered by the open plateau of the Pays de Sault. This was where they were vulnerable. Their most experienced troops, Juan and his Spanish guerilleros were posted here, armed with mines and grenades.

That Saturday night the men in the camp were uneasy. The Germans would not attack during the night but they would advance next day. All of them slept fitfully that night, waking to the sounds of the forest and in the cold hours before the sun rose, shivering, trying to foresee what might happen, to imagine how they would react if they were caught in the gunfire. If they were wounded. If ...

"I'm scared," Joseph confessed to Marcel. They were all afraid, of course.

Raoul Vidal was responsible for the men in the camp and there were now nearly four hundred of them. He knew that in March the maquis at Glières had been wiped out. Now news was coming through that a bigger group, at Vercors, had suffered devastating casualties. The lives of so many men depended on the decisions he would make. He believed that he and Jean-Paul had assessed the dangers sensibly. He knew they were short of weapons but they had

239

to do what they could with whatever resources they had. Attack. Retreat. Regroup and return to the attack. That was the plan. For the moment he must try to rest and sleep.

Sunday. The early morning air was clear and cool. Emile, the radio operator, cycling along the lane towards Festes enjoyed the solitude and the sense of freedom, the escape from the tensions of the camp. He rode up the incline towards the main road, skirted the village of Festes and then along the untidy gorse-lined lane that led to La Bastide. For good reception and for reasons of security his radio equipment was hidden in a barn beyond La Bastide. This morning his news was urgent but he was enjoying the ride.

As he approached La Bastide he dismounted. An old woman was leading a couple of cows to graze in a roadside field. She was short, slightly bent, her weathered face brown and wrinkled, puckered round her toothless mouth. She waved her stick irritably at him, shooing him away.

"You can't go any further along this road!" she cried. "The Germans have got road blocks all round La Bastide."

Emile turned his bike in a flash. "Thanks!" he called, as he cycled away, pedalling furiously. At Festes he got off his bike and climbed up the hill by the castle to see whether the main road, the D117, was still clear. With a terrible sense of foreboding he saw that in the short time since he had first passed that way the Germans had set up a road block at the junction leading to Luxat. The upper road, the road from the tunnel, joined the D117 further west at the Col de la Babourade. Emile heaved his bike across the rough terrain and sighed with relief when he saw no road block there. He was soon on his way again, to report to Raoul at the camp.

By midday they had news of another road block, on that upper road, at the Col de la Babourade which had been free when Emile passed. There were reports, too, that Belvis, to the south, was blocked and that maquisards in the village there had been taken by the Gestapo. Their leader was reported dead. Espezel, where the upper road came out to the south, was still apparently free. Juan and his patrols were watching carefully but could find no sign of enemy troops.

It was at Espezel that they were most vulnerable. Raoul Vidal was troubled. "They could be trying to fool us. Encourage us to break out to the south, then close in on us. They can't close the whole perimeter, they don't have enough troops. But we need to know where they are, where they're going to attack."

" I could go down to the village and see what's happening there," Marcel offered.

"I'll go with hiom!" clamoured Joseph.

Raoul Vidal was doubtful. Joseph, he declared, could watch with him from above. But a young man who knew the village well might be able to find out if there were German troops in the forest. Nothing had come along the valley road, they were watching that from their hideout at the top of the cliff but there might be German soldiers hidden in the forest above the road.

"I could go down with an armoured car," urged Marcel. "They could give me cover with a machine gun."

So, armed with rifles and grenades, Marcel passed through the maquis control at the tunnel and set off carefully down the lane, round the hairpin bends that led towards the village. Crouching low, taking advantage of protecting undergrowth, sometimes slithering straight down to avoid a sharp zig zag, he went down. The armed car followed. Slowly, with the engine barely turning, ready to offer him protection or a quick escape if needed. From above, Joseph and Monsieur Vidal watched through their binoculars.

The young man reached the village. The long, straggling street was quiet. The villagers were staying indoors, keeping away from trouble. Maman came out, pleased to see Marcel. She pressed him to take a couple of apples The car turned and waited at the edge of the village, ready to go back to the camp.

"Nothing here!" Marcel declared. Everything was still and quiet. Nobody in the village reported seeing any German soldiers. With a cheerful wave, Marcel jumped into the car. "No point in slogging back up on foot!"

They called good-bye. They all knew that a battle would come but there was no sign of enemy troops, no need yet to worry. The road was steep and the car moved slowly round the first sharp bend.

They were just above the village, carefully negotiating the second bend, when shots rang out. Marcel was flung from the car and rolled to the side of the road, hurling grenades up into the trees. The driver put his foot down and raced away, tyres squealing, his companion beside him shooting wildly through the open window. Wounded, bleeding badly, they tumbled out further up the hillside and fell into undergrowth that hid them from the Germans.

Marcel was not so lucky. From the top of the cliff a mile away, Joseph and Raoul Vidal watched in horror as Marcel, wounded, tried to drag himself across the road into the shelter of the wooded bank. But the enemy, hidden in the trees, was still shooting and his body soon lay lifeless in a pool of blood.

Raoul Vidal turned to Joseph who stood motionless beside him, his face a ghastly mask of terror. Of all the young maquisards, Joseph and Marcel were the two closest to Raoul Vidal. They had been with him since Robert first arrived at their house. Marcel was young and perky, full of life. He would have mourned the death of anyone in the camp but the death of Marcel hit him hard. Jean-Paul was at his side as he left the cliff top look out and strode, grim-faced, along the forest track towards his cabin. The attack had not yet started and already they had lost one man.

     Joseph stood immobile, his knuckles white, his fist clenched on the binoculars through which he had watched his brother die. One of the airmen heard the news and came to find him. He took off his jacket and wrapped it round the shivering shoulders and led Joseph back to their hut where they tried to revive him with hot soup. But his teeth were clenched. He huddled motionless in the corner of the hut, saying nothing, making no response to their gestures of sympathy.

CHAPTER 18
Agust 1944   The Germans attack

Late in the afternoon half a dozen partisans from La Bastide stumbled into the camp. They had been caught at the road block at the Col de la Babourade. It was their own fault. They should have kept to the forest and walked along the lanes but they had stolen a lorry and driven along the D117. As a result three men had been killed and four more wounded, one seriously.

Their arrival added to the tension in the camp and Jean-Paul decided they could not sit there all evening getting increasingly nervous.

"Let's go and do something. Have a look at that road bloack and let them know they can't have everything their own way."

Glad for something to do, a small group of men set out at dusk. From the camp they could hear the exchange of fire. When they came back later they were brighter, pleased with their night's work.

"We've got a few scratches but nothing serious," Jean-Paul said. "We did more damage to them than they did to us and it's done us a power of good."

They went off to eat and have their wounds bandaged.

But even before Jean-Paul and his men returned from the attack at the Col de la Babourade, Emile was clamouring for attention, warning that the nine o'clock news from the BBC had confirmed their drop for that night. Five planes. That meant 75 parachutes. The reception party had to be out and ready. Ready to pick up and unload 75 containers.

There was no rest for anyone that night. The wounded who were too ill to get to their feet might be excused duty but everyone else was needed.

Extra sentries were posted at every path into the forest. Men with torches were out round the Drop Zone, ready to signal to the approaching planes. Every available man was detailed to head off to find the parachutes and collect the containers as soon as they landed.

Joseph, acutely aware that Marcel was no longer beside him, was behind the cabin, in the trees on the edge of the open field, waiting for the parachutes to drop, waiting to run out, find the containers and bring in the precious cargo. He stood still, ready to do what had to be done but without the intense excitement with which he had greeted earlier drops.

Faintly at first, he heard the familiar sound of the approaching engines, which grew, reaching a tumultuous crescendo as the planes roared overhead. His whole being was caught up in the thunderous vibration, his heart throbbing. He trembled with fear, apprehension, desolation. He had been out before, waiting for the planes to come. But then it was two, three, four planes. This time there were five planes and they filled the forest with the sound of their power.

Raoul Vidal remembered that first drop, when they had waited in the snow above the castle. They had stolen out at night. The police had been out, watching and when they'd finished they'd brushed away all traces from the snow.

This was no secret drop. They had a proper Drop Zone now, in the middle of their own camp. The Germans were out there watching. They would see the planes and the parachutes but they would not try to come into the forest until daybreak. To-night the maquis could work freely, collecting the guns and ammunition they so badly needed.

The first plane swept round towards Festes, preparing to return for the drop. The whole line followed. Fire streaked out from German guns at Festes and one plane broke free, leaving the formation, diving to attack the German guns. Then the plane rose again. The German artillery was silent.

Raoul Vidal held his breath. Would the pilots call off the drop? Would they decide that the enemy was too close for safety? Frantically, the men round the field repeated their signals. He peered out through the trees and up into the sky above the open field. The planes were returning and his heart leapt as he saw the blossoming parachutes. Glowing in the moonlight, they filled the sky. There were so many containers so close together that they swayed into each other and he could hear the metal clanking as they touched. Then the planes had gone and they were all out on the field, prising open the containers, straining to free the weapons and ammunition.

Raoul was waiting with his gunners. Out on that moonlit field he wasted no time. Six new Hotchkiss guns had landed. By dawn, when the Germans attacked, they would need those guns. They had a few hours only for the men to practise how to load, aim, fire.

Joseph, whose work for the night was completed, lay on the ground beneath the trees and fell into a troubled sleep, punctuated by Monsieur Vidal's instructions and by the disciplined rattling and clunking and firing of weapons.

He woke to a frenzied tumult of dawn chorus as the forest birds, oblivious to the urgent fears of the men, came alive to a new day.

Joseph was to take messages between the cabin and the look out post at the top of the cliff. Before he reached the cliff top ledge he could hear the German tanks rumbling by on the upper road, from the Col de la Babourade. At the entrance to the tunnel, the maquisards blew up the road, stopping their progress towards the camp.

A stream of lorries trundled along the valley track and through the village. Armed soldiers jumped out and swept up the hairpin bends above the village, where Marcel had been caught in the German ambush. Others tried to scramble up the cliffside path and from above Joseph saw them fall back, caught by French snipers hidden in the trees.

All day long the battle raged on the edge of the forest above the village. Grenades and guns and rifles rattled and spluttered and exploded in constant uproar.

At the tunnel, the Germans made no advance but on the other side of the village they had given up trying to climb the cliff and moved back and entered the forest further up the valley. One of the new guns had jammed and before they could replace it the enemy had penetrated some way into the trees and could threaten them from above. The maquis would not be able to hold out there much longer.

As the afternoon drew to a close, they looked down into the village and saw the German troops regroup, clamber back into their lorries and return along the valley road to Festes. Up in the forest they cheered.

Raoul Vidal went round the camp, reporting the good news to those who had not yet heard. Every attack had come from the north of the camp. In the south, where they were more vulnerable, Juan and his Spaniards had heard the distant gunfire but had seen no sign of the enemy.

With the village clear of German troops, Joseph slithered down the cliff path, white-faced, his eyes wide with exhaustion, desperate to see Maman before the fight resumed. At the bottom of the cliff he broke into a run, and ran along the river bank and across the rickety old bridge.

The village was deserted. He ran through the fields and down the road from the church and burst into the house, running upstairs and calling out as he opened the door. But there was no sign of Maman.

In the empty kitchen, Marcel's body lay on the table. Joseph looked at his pale face, framed by his dark hair, his quiff carefully combed. He was glad that someone had taken the trouble to comb his hair. He was covered with a sheet. that Maman, as a girl, had embroidered with her initials. It was part of her bottom drawer, prepared for her wedding. Maman had given him her best. But Maman was not there.

The silence was unbearable. There was no fire crackling in the hearth, no water simmering on the hob. There were no pots rattling. There were no sounds of movement, no footsteps, nothing from outside even, no cries from neighbours, no distant murmur from the village at work.

Only his own breathing, his own breath coming in halting gasps. Joseph sat on the bench beside his brother's body, took Marcel's hand and was overwhelmed with grief. Grief for Marcel, whose life had been cut short. Grief for himself, bereft. Grief for Maman, who had feared that she might lose Marcel. "She knew you were a fool!" he shouted and stamped out of the house. Where was Maman?

Outisde the church he saw Picart, waiting patiently, and he knew where he would find her. She was sitting on a bench by the door, resting her back against the wall but sitting upright, her eyes dry and unblinking, staring at the altar through the dusty light. Joseph did not notice her at first and was turning to leave when he saw her. He stumbled forwards and knelt on the floor and put his head in her lap and felt the warm softness of her body. She offered the comfort she had always given him and she welcomed his love and his need.

"You're all I've got now," she murmured sadly. Then, with fear and sadness beyond tears, "You're a good boy. Take care." She brushed her eyes with the sleeve of her overall and took a long, deep breath.

As darkness fell Joseph climbed back up the cliffside path.

The evening was close and heavy. There would be a storm later, no doubt. Meanwhile it was too hot inside a cabin and he lay where he had fallen at the top of the path, cushioned by the soft moss and leafy mulch that covered the ground beneath the trees.

There was no time to sleep, though. Jean-Paul gathered them together, his troop of men, recruited from farms and villages around Luxat. "Well, lads, this is it!" He glanced at the twenty or so men round him. "We're moving out. To-night."

They were not surprised. Attack. Retreat. Regroup. That had always been the plan.

"The problem is, though, that if the Germans get any idea of where we're going, they'll move in and concentrate their forces and they'll cut us to pieces." He paused to make sure eveyone understood. "We're going to walk out of this forest, all four hundred of us. Without a cough, a sneeze, a laugh, a word. We're going to walk out of here in silence. Not a mouse will hear us move. No lights. No matches. No cigarettes. No torches. We'll move by the light of whatever moon God gives us. And we'll move in silence. In formation, but in silence."

They formed up and followed Jean-Paul to the Drop Zone in front of the headquarters. Joseph, beyond exhaustion, tramped mindlessly. On the track beside the cabin their little stock of transport, their lorries, cars and motorcycles, stood waiting, loaded with their heavy weapons and ammunition. In the last lorry were a dozen men, men who had been badly wounded and could not walk. The doctor and a pharmacist from La Bastide were looking after them.

Jean-Paul and Monsieur Vidal and the leaders of the various groups, the allied airmen, the north Africans, the Spanish, the partisans, gathered for a final consultation. The men sat on the ground, tense, disturbed by the sudden whoosh of shells exploding in the forest, the snap of broken branches. They had seen the troops leaving along the valley but there were still Germans round the forest who were keeping up the pressure.

In panic, half a dozen men clambered onto one of the lorries and refused to move.

"Nobody travels in these lorries, except the wounded," Raoul Vidal declared. "We need the lorries for our supplies and for heavy weapons."

The men glared back at him, frightened and defiant.

"We keep together and we walk together out of the forest. Not one man separates from his group. If the Germans catch one man, just one, they could discover where we are, in which direction we're leaving. And if they know that, they can direct their forces and destroy us." It was the message Jean-Paul had given them. "We leave here together. On foot."

The men on the ground watched and waited. The men in the lorry, their faces set, did not move.

"Get off that lorry." The command was quiet but clear. Raoul Vidal fingered his pistol. "Our lives depend upon our discipline. My orders will be obeyed. I shall not hesitate to shoot anyone who disobeys."

Slowly, calmly, he withdrew his pistol from its holster. The silence deepened. He released the safety catch.

Joseph watched, mesmerised. Would Monsieur Vidal use his pistol? Would he shoot one of his own men? His hand on the gun was barely visible, a pale blur, ghostly in the moonlight. Staring at the still figure, watching the slightest movement of his hand, Joseph was convinced. Monsieur Vidal would shoot. He would raise his gun and fire. And the men would fall. Their arms would fly up. They would stagger and drop. Dead. They would die like Marcel and Marius. Monsieur Vidal was going to shoot them.

One of the men on the lorry shifted. Joseph watched, barely breathing. Slowly the man climbed down. Raoul Vidal waited. Another followed, strained and anxious. Joseph watched. The tension in his shoulder eased. As if punctuating the commander's orders, a clap of thunder rolled above them. The other men left the lorry. Raoul Vidal put away his pistol.

The line of vehicles set off, slowly, showing no lights. The men followed, along the forest tracks leading south towards Espezel. As they left the forest of Luxat, Juan and his Spaniards, who had been patrolling the southern border of the forest, fell in behind them, ready to protect the rear.

The storm had broken. Heavy rain was falling now and they were soon soaked to the skin. Around midnight they heard the roar of engines, of planes circling overhead. A drop. Intended for them but they would not be there to receive it. The planes would have to turn back to-night.

The forest track joined the road just before Espezel and they approached cautiously, fearing a road block. But the road was still open as they marched on silently for a few hundred yards before turning off onto a lane that led down towards the river Rebentry, off across the meadows, into the woods and on beyond Rodome.

It was dawn before they stopped in the woods south of Rodome. They were exhausted. It was their second night without sleep and they had marched through the night with nothing to eat or drink. Still soaking wet, they burrowed into the ground and fell asleep.

The next morning, as the weary maquisards succumbed to sleep, the doctor at Belvis was operating on two of their wounded colleagues, while German tanks thundered past on the road outside.

The German army was moving in to attack. Their main thrust was from the south, from Espezel, as Raoul Vidal had predicted. Tanks manoeuvred down the forest track, negotiating the narrow twists and turns. The forest hut where Juan and his guerilleros had been based was pounded by artillery, was assailed by the supporting infantry and was soon ablaze. From Luxat, in the north, soldiers on foot advanced cautiously through the forest. From the west, German artillery kept their fire trained on the tunnel. From the east, from Belvis, more tanks moved up to the edge of the forest.

Every road was blocked. Confident that they had trapped the terrorists inside the forest the German troops advanced. Shots echoed through the hills. Though they did not see the maquisards, the Germans were encouraged: they were making good progress.

It was late in the afternoon when the units made contact, meeting at the centre of the camp, by the clearing in front of the headquarters. They had swept through the forest from all sides and now as the net closed they realised it was empty. The French had escaped! They had left nothing behind. There was no food, no equipment, no ammunition. All their vehicles had gone. There was no sign of any Frenchman remaining, no sign of the route they had taken.

Angrily the Germans destroyed the maquis headquarters and set fire to dry undergrowth, hoping in vain to start one of those dangerous forest fires that can take hold of acres of precious woodland. They set out to search through the villages and woods nearby.

The maquisards were already further south, higher up in the mountains than the Germans thought of searching. That night the maquis of Quérigut brought in their lorries and they moved higher still and settled into new quarters close to the Spanish border. Not one man had been lost. The Luxat maquis had escaped unscathed. They had regrouped and were ready to attack again.

On Wednesday morning the Germans returned to Luxat. They called at every house in the village.

"Fifteen minutes! Out!"

"Fifteen minutes! We set fire to all the houses. We burn everything!"

"Out! Out!"

"Fifteen minutes!"

What do you take? Children and grandparents were gathered together and hustled away up the hillside. Animals were released. Any small store of money was snatched from its hiding place. But photographs? Mementoes of family history? Linen, carefully prepared for the bottom drawer? A child's chair, generations old? The pots and pans and ordinary necessities of daily life? These were all left behind as the villagers scrambled helplessly to escape.

The Germans went from house to house. The villagers watched as petrol was poured into their homes, as each house burst into flames. From the shelter of the woods, they stood, staring helplessly at the destruction. Wood and plaster and brick and stone crackled and burnt and split asunder. Sparks flew. Heavy black smoke rose into the summer sky and hung over the houses. Poultry and cattle scattered, cackling and moaning, scurrying to escape the infernal flames. The villagers wept as the fire devoured their houses.

In those flames they lost their homes and the tangible history of their families.

The villagers of Luxat, simple peasants and foresters, had looked after the maquisards, providing them with food and shelter, protecting them. The maquisards were safe. Three hundred and ninety six men had escaped. But they had lost their village.

CHAPTER 18
August 1944: Liberation

Though Juan and Jean-Paul and Raoul no longer spent their evenings in the café Terminus those who still gathered there followed the news avidly and were impatient for Liberation.

"Where have they got to now? It's a month since the allies landed and they're still in Normandy."

"Haven't even got to Paris yet."

Not that Paris meant much to them. They'd never seen the place. But St Tropez now, that was more like it.

In the middle of August they were jubilant.

"They've landed on the Mediterranean. Round St Tropez."

"The French army!"

"With General de Lattre de Tassigny!"

This was more like it.

"They've brought the Americans too. Half a million of them."

"Well, they'll find a good welcome here."

They did indeed. The French Forces of the Interior, Fifi, as they were affectionately called, led the army swiftly north, up into the Alps, and all through the south of France the maquis surged forth, sabotaging the railways, blowing up lines and engines, destroying bridges, cutting telephone wires, attacking German soldiers.

Raoul Vidal and his men came down from the Spanish border to patrol the D117 and clear the road to Carcassonne.

The forest cabins where they had sheltered were now only piles of rubble with low uneven walls and charred beams pointing starkly skywards. Joseph dug his toe into black ash and burnt undergrowth.

"What's this?" he asked.

"They lit fires. They wanted to destroy the forest," said Raoul.

Joseph was shocked. "That's wicked. A forest fire's a terrible thing. It can burn for days and destroy everything."

The people of Luxat depended on the forest for their livelihood.

"But there was a storm the night we left. Remember? The fires never took hold."

They walked over to the little graveyard beside the old headquarters. Marcel was not here. He had been buried in the churchyard in the village. But the men killed when the gun had exploded and others who had died while working with the maquis were buried here. There were mounds of freshly dug earth, in two rough ranks, each marked with a simple wooden cross. It was as if the men were sleeping there, lying stiffly wrapped in a blanket of forest earth. Raoul Vidal made the sign of the cross and Joseph did the same.

" 'There is no happiness without freedom and no freedom without courage'," quoted Raoul. "Do you know who said that?"

Joseph shook his head.

"Pericles. A Greek. More important, do you know what he meant?"

Joseph nodded. "Same as the Cathars. You may have to die for what you believe is right."

Monsieur Vidal liked his answer. "Yes. And we must never forget what they fought for. Freedom."

He crossed himself once more and quietly repeated the prayer for the dead: "Lord grant them eternal rest and let perpetual light shine upon them. Amen."

"Amen," said Joseph.

The camp in the forest had been destroyed and the men had moved around so much that they had lost touch with those who had been supplying them with food and water.

"It was bad enough when we were in the camp at Luxat," Achille Cambon complained. "And there we had all our friends round us to supply us with meat and bread. The more we move the harder it is. And all these new recruits are fine, I'm sure and they're doing a good job. But they have to be fed." He looked sternly at Raoul and Jean-Paul. "Of course there is food to be had." They waited. "At Couiza."

So that was what the old rogue wanted.

"A month's rations for 100,000 men, the Germans have, stored at that depot there. Good French food that belongs to us by rights."

"So how do we get hold of it?" asked Jean-Paul.

"That's your job," Achille told him.

So they sent out a raiding party. Juan and his guerilleros who were to attack the guards defending the depot. They took any men they could spare to load the stores and all the vehicles they could muster to transport them back to their new camp.

They approached the depot cautiously. The lorries and the men with them waited down the road and Juan and his guerilleros spread out, with machine guns and snipers covering each entrance.

"You looking for the German soldiers then?"

They turned, startled. A skinny boy, about eight years old, slid down from the cart where he was perched and addressed Achille Cambon.

"You won't find them here. They've all gone along to the school."

The French forces relaxed. It was the boy's great moment. Skinny, rather grubby and dressed in worn old clothes, he took them proudly down to the village and pointed to the school. A heap of German weaponry was propped untidily against the wall by the door.

Achille Cambon went in, with Juan. Achille's rifle was slung casually over his shoulder but Juan was still on guard, his rifle ready, a pistol in his holster, cartridges at his waist and a couple of grenades hanging from his belt.

The boy called the teacher who came down from his flat above the schoolroom and unlocked the door. The elderly conscripts who had been guarding the depot were perched uncomfortably on the worn wooden desks and rose to their feet, hands up, anxious to be accepted as prisoners.

"So how come they're here?" asked Achille.

"They just walked in this morning. They'd left their weapons outside and they asked for protection." The teacher looked doubtfully at Juan. "I said they'd be safe here."

One of them spoke some French. "We surrender," he said. "The war is finish."

Achille took the keys to the depot and they left a couple of youngsters to guard the Germans. "I think he's right," he said. "When men like that are so desperate to surrender that they go to a village schoolmaster, the war is finish." He spoke with satisfaction.

They unlocked the depot. They knew that it was full of food but they had not expected the treasure that was stored there. "Butter! Chocolate! Pâté!" Their eyes grew wide and their voices rose in amazement as they registered each new delicacy. "It's disgusting. We've been scraping together just enough to live on and look at all this!"

They did not waste time though and the men filled up the lorries with as much as they could take. "We'd better leave a guard here, I think," Achille decided. "We don't want looters taking what's left and selling it on the black market. We'll have a word with the mayor as we leave and he can arrange what happens to it now."

The band of elderly guards at Couiza had surrendered independently but the German occupation was coming to an end throughout the region. The German army was leaving Toulouse, Montpellier, Foix.

It was not an orderly departure. The railway was in chaos, it was hard to get petrol, there were no spare parts for vehicles that broke down and local enthusiasm which had sent the allied army so swiftly north from St Tropez was working eagerly to hamper the Germans. The maquisards heard the stories and passed them on gleefully. "They're leaving Toulouse and they're having to use carts and bicycles!"

Joseph remembered the proud parade which they had watched from the edge of the forest when the Germans arrived with an endless stream of vehicles. Jean-Paul wanted to savour the moment. "Come on! Let's go and see them leave!"

This time it was very different. There were a few tanks and lorries crammed with men but the vehicles were dusty and dented, the soldiers' uniforms looked old and worn and many of the men were trudging past on foot.

"It's worse on the road from Toulouse," an old woman told them happily. "Someone put sulphuric acid in their petrol and everything's broken down. The road's choked. They can't move!"

Not all the news was good, though. Raoul Vidal warned his men not to provoke the Germans to retaliate.

"The maquis near St Girons attacked a German column and they've destroyed houses and killed civilians. We don't want that to happen here."

In the café Terminus they knew what the Germans could do.

"Bastards to the end"

"They've killed prisoners at Carcassonne. They took them to the ammunition depot and blew them to bits!"

They were anxious for their own friends and neighbours.

"What's going to happen to our men in the prison at Foix?"

As the Germans left there were Frenchmen anxious not to be left behind. Auguste called in quietly to see his family.

"It's no use hanging around here," he told them. "Joseph sent me that coffin, they mean to kill me. I'm lucky to have escaped so far."

There was no point in arguing. They all knew that Auguste would not be safe at home.

"Where will you go?"

"They've laid on transport for us from Carcassonne."

"The roads are bad. What if you can't get there?"

Auguste shrugged. "I can always go and join a maquis. Somewhere in the north, where they don't know me."

They gave him some money and some food and sent him on his way.

"He joined the wrong side, didn't he," Louis said to his wife when Auguste had left. "There was a moment when I was quite proud of him, you know. Thought he was on the side of law and order."

"You don't think they'll come here do you?" his wife asked.

"Looking for Auguste?" Louis was surprised by the question. "Of course they will."

"No. For us."

"For us? What've we done?" For the life of him Louis couldn't imagine why they would be a maquis target. "No. We've nothing to worry about. But Auguste always was a bully and he turned into a real thug once he joined the Milice."

Marie Monnier had been going to suggest that perhaps Louis should lie low for a few weeks. She remembered the British soldier who had been betrayed and recognised that they had, after all, been at the forefront of the Vichy supporters, the collaborators, in La Bastide. She'd felt the hostility of her neighbours in the market and was not at all sure that they were safe. But she was angry that Louis could only criticise Auguste.

"You've never had any time for him. You've always prefered that little bastard Joseph."

Louis had heard the accusation before. He didn't bother to reply.

For Auguste the decision to leave was not difficult because he knew what to expect if he stayed. Hans was much more troubled. He had orders to go to Carcassonne to join his unit but there was no transport to take him there. It would not be safe for him to try to make his way across the country on his own and the other soldiers billeted at the hotel had already found reasons to go to Limoux and like the guards at Couiza had not waited for orders.

Perhaps Hans did mean to leave and join his unit in Carcassonne. He saw Auguste at the hotel and knew that he'd come to say good bye to his family   That night Hans told Alice that he must leave.

She gazed at him in misery. "I know," she said, clinging tightly to him.

"Will you be all right?"

What could she say? The neighbours wouldn't speak to her. There had been the message scribbled on the wall of the bakery, 'Welcome home Albert'. And Albert would come home and what would he say when he saw Henri? Would he turn her out of the bakery? How would she live then?

She buried her head in Hans's shoulder and wept. And the baby was distressed and began to cry. He was hungry and Alice didn't have enough milk for him. Poor mite. Hans picked up his little son and held him close and patted his back and rocked him in his arms and whispered soothing nonsense but the baby still cried.

"I won't leave you," he declared.

"You must."

"No. I can't get to Carcassonne anyway. It's far too dangerous. I'll stay here. You can hide me for a while and then I'll surrender. I'll be a prisoner of war. And one day, perhaps, we can be together. Really together. A proper family."

Liberation came. In the north of France allied troops arrived in tanks and lorries to liberate the towns and villages. Here it was the French Forces of the Interior, the maquis, who announced their liberation.

Shaved, bathed, his hair trimmed, his uniform starched and pressed, his puttees neatly tied and his boots polished to perfection, Raoul Vidal marched into Festes at the head of his men. They carried the French flag and the Marseillaise blared triumphantly from loud speakers outside the Town Hall where the Tricolor had joyfully replaced the Swastika.

They stood at the war memorial, in a moment of silent tribute and Joseph, looking round the square, could see only happiness. Even through his mourning for Marcel and Luxat, he could feel the joy and excitement of victory. They had torn down the German flags and smashed the signposts with their menacing Germanic script. The Germans had gone.

Adjusting his tie and brushing down his best suit, Monsieur le Maire stepped forward to express his satisfaction that the German occupation was ended. He paid tribute to all the men of Festes and of the neighbouring communes, who had fought so bravely to bring them to victory. Raoul Vidal made a speech. The French was faultless, the phrases well-turned, the sentiments impeccable. There were stern warnings, though, that anyone found to have acted against the interests of their country would come before a military court and receive just punishment.

The sun was hot, the speeches long and predictable. Joseph was not listening. He was trying to come to terms with the horrors that had shattered his life. Marius. Marcel. His home and his village destroyed. As the words of the speeches echoed round the square, he heard the promise of punishment for traitors and he remembered the coffin he'd sent Auguste.

When the speeches were over Festes celebrated. Jean-Paul looked at the boy who had done so much and suffered so much. "Right lad," he declared. "It's time for you to grow up. There are girls out there just waiting to get their hands on Fifi." He looked at him, appraising. "Washed. Clean, you know, they might take to you."

Joseph sniffed and wiped his nose on the back of his hand.

Jean-Paul was shocked. "Oh dear! Not the manners of a gentleman. The youth of to-day! I despair. What do they teach them in their schools?"

Joseph almost smiled.

Jean-Paul was right. Girls were dancing in the square, walking round the village arm in arm, singing the Marseillaise and robust, lilting love songs. They flung flowers at the men from the maquis and kisses, to which Jean-Paul responded with enthusiasm. Old men were offering wine, grand bottles of blanquette de Limoux.

"Here, try this!" he said, holding out a glass sparkling with blanquette.

Joseph tried it. And tried again. And again. He stopped counting and put his arm round a young woman with beautiful, painted lips and curves in all the right places..

He was too tired that night to go home. He collapsed onto the floor of the schoolroom, below the Vidals' flat and fell, snoring, into sleep.

Next morning he went back home. Older men, who could be spared by their families, went on to continue the fight. Raoul Vidal went. And Jean-Paul Ramel. And Achille Cambon. They joined the French army and crossed the Rhine and fought in Germany and they were there, as de Gaulle had wished, when Germany was defeated.

Joseph was too young to join the army and he returned to Luxat.

"Mon Dieu! You look terrible," Maman cried when she saw him, still bleary eyed. "What have you been doing?"

"Celebrating," growled Joseph, his tongue thick and the uncertain voice of adolescence betraying him.

Maman shook her head and pretended that she might be cross and was glad that he had been able to enjoy himself.

She even found an egg that a hen had left in the debris that had once been their home.

There was no celebrating in Luxat. They were glad enough that their war was over but their village had been destroyed. They were living in charred ruins, sheltered by tarpaulin. They had no beds. They prepared their meals, crouching beside a fire made of a few sticks laid on the ground. Their cooking pots were black and dented. They had very little food.

All day long they worked to clear away the debris, to restore their gardens and to hunt for their livestock. Maman and Joseph were grieving too, for Marcel, who could never be restored to them. The devastation of war was all around them in Luxat.

Maman would not have been able to cope without Joseph who cleared away charred beams and stones that were too heavy for her. But it was not just the physical labour that meant so much to her.

"If you weren't here , you know, I'd have no reason to sort out this mess and no reason to get on with things and get the dinner every day and try to prepare for winter."

Joseph was surprised to hear this confession and perhaps faintly embarrassed but he knew that they needed each other. They both presented a cheerful face to the world but sometimes as he was doing work he usually shared with Marcel, or if he came downstairs expecting to see his brother, Joseph would find himself overwhelmed with grief and Maman would put her arm round him. And one day when she was serving soup Maman found that she had put out three spoons and she stopped, with the ladle poised, remembering that there were only two of them now. This time it was Joseph who put his arm round her.

CHAPTER 20
August 1944   Settling accounts

The following Saturday Maman was not going in to the market.

"We've got nothing to sell. I'll be better off clearing up here, but you go," she told Joseph.

He offered to stay and help.

"No. You need to get away from Luxat," she said.

La Bastide, when he got there, was in an ugly mood. As in Luxat, the reminders of war were all around them.

At the liberation of Foix the old men who had been taken prisoner in July had been released. They came back to La Bastide, the embodiment of all that Frenchmen had suffered at the hands of the enemy.

The ironmonger's father sat on the pavement outside his son's shop, his head nodding with weariness. He was thin and unshaven, his lips swollen, his face cut and bruised. He moved cautiously, suffering agony from cracked ribs.

Others also were reported to be distressed and news soon spread that one of the prisoners, an elderly factory worker, apparently fit and vigorous when he left La Bastide, had not survived the barbarities of prison in Foix.

The prisoners had spent weeks crammed together in small cells. Released now they sought each other out, gathering at the café Terminus and in the bar at the hotel, where they provoked pity and anger.

"At least the prison guards didn't get off scot free," said Laurent Barde, the young policeman who no longer needed to hide his support for the maquis. "One of them was strung up on the gates of the prison."

"Best thing to do with buggers like that."
"What about Delpech?"
"Raoul Vidal told me to lock him up. He's in a cell at the police station."
"Good man!" His friends congratulated him.
"Give the bugger hell!"
"There are others here who need to be taught a lesson. Alice Chauvet for one," someone said. Alice was an easy target.

The morning distribution of bread was coming to an end and the women still queueing knew that they had little chance of collecting their ration. They were hungry and disgruntled, angry with Alice, with the Germans, with everything that was making their lives difficult.

The men in the bar had been liberated. They had celebrated with a few glasses of Pernod. A friend of theirs, Albert Chauvet was still languishing in a German prison and it was not right that his wife had been playing around with an enemy soldier. In St Girons and Foix they'd made a public spectacle of such women. They'd do the same in La Bastide.

The queue at the door gave way when they approached and the men charged in, shouting for Alice. She might have stayed in the shop and let them take her but she ran instinctively to the room behind the shop. She had to protect her baby. She needed Hans to protect her.

The crowd followed. They stopped in their tracks when they saw Hans standing there.
"You swine!"
"You rat!"
"Filthy Boche!"

They screamed at him, their faces twisted with hate. They grabbed him by the collar, they clouted him round the head, they punched and kicked him down the steps in front of the shop.

Hans was on his knees, his eyes wide with terror, his hands shaking, trying to protect himself from the savage blows. One of the men put a pistol to his head and shot him. He keeled over in a pool of blood and the crowd sighed with satisfaction.

It was not enough, though. The crowd had scented blood. They surged through the bakery, taking whatever was to hand. They took the flour. They took the tins and trays in which the bread was baked. They helped themselves to linen and to crockery. They staggered out with tables, chairs, beds. What they could not carry, they smashed, wrecking and destroying.

But they still wanted their scapegoat. Alice was to be put on trial. A table was set up on the pavement outside the Town Hall. Three men, good honest citizens, sat at the table and questioned the young woman who stood, bedraggled, before them.

"You were a collaborator. You sold secrets to the German troops."

Terrified and confused, Alice denied treachery. "We loved each other," she claimed, simply. "We loved each other."

How was she to know that the jeering, baying crowd could not forgive this love. That enemy whose body lay on the pavement beside them, had deserved to die. They were in no mood for touching tales of young love. They wanted punishment, suffering.

"Shave her head!" they yelled.

"Let everyone see what a slut she is!"

They brought out a cut throat razor and sharpened it on a leather strop, as Alice watched, mesmerised. They took her hair, the curls that had charmed so many men in La Bastide, and they tugged and sliced. They shaved her scalp, closely and roughly, so that her head was cut and bruised. When they'd finished a young boy, laughing, tossed the shorn locks in the air for everyone to see. They put the baby in her arms and hung a placard round her neck and paraded her through the streets and the crowd pelted her with tomatoes.

    Joseph was reminded of the dreadful day when war was declared, when Marie Monnier flung him out of the hotel. He remembered the hurt and the anger, the humiliation, and felt sorry for Alice. It was not Alice he wanted to see there, it was Auguste, who was guilty of far worse crimes than hers.

    The crowd was already looking for him.

    "Auguste!" they cried. "Auguste Monnier!"

    "Auguste Monnier!" Joseph roared with the crowd.

    Laurent Barde went with them, though he knew that Auguste had already left the town. Raoul Vidal and Juan Almagro had charged him, when they left, to arrest Monsieur le Commissaire Delpech and Auguste Monnier. By the time he reached the hotel Auguste had already fled.

    "You won't find him there. He's gone," he told them.

    But they paid no attention. The crowd swarmed into the hotel. They went into every room, opening cupboards, flinging aside anything which might be hiding him. Auguste was not there.

    Joseph went into the kitchen where Madame Monnier was sitting at the kitchen table, with Janine beside her. She stared at him, impassively. He wanted to smash her face in. He picked up a plate and flung it at her.

    "You bloody bitch!" he yelled. "I hate you! Just you wait now!"

Louis wandered from room to room, horrified by the destructive anger of the crowd, unable to check the frenzy.

"He was a collaborator, too!" Joseph shouted.

"He had German soldiers here in the hotel."

They grabbed Louis and roughly bundled him out into the street. The table was still there outside the Town Hall and they kicked and punched and stood him before his judges.

"He's a collaborator!" they shouted.

"No. No." Louis denied the charge.

"Did you have German soldiers in the hotel?"

"Not by choice. Nobody asked me whether I wanted to take them."

"What about the British soldier," Joseph called. "The one at Luxat. Who betrayed him?"

The crowd roared their anger.

"Go on! Who betrayed us?" Joseph taunted him.

"Please, no. I didn't betray him. I didn't say anything."

Joseph shook his head. Of course he'd bloody well betrayed them. He'd always known it was Monsieur Monnier who'd betrayed Robert. Anyway, even if he hadn't said a word, he'd btrayed them. There were times when you had to speak up. And when had Monsieur Monnier ever spoken up for him?

"He's guilty," the judges declared.

The crowd roared their agreement and Joseph was swept up in the universal anger.

"Kill him!" they yelled.

"Kill him!" Joseph roared. "Kill the fucking bastard!"

They stood him up against the wall of the Town Hall, trembling with fear, pleading for mercy, calling to his friends to help him. Nobody tried to save him. They tied a dirty handkerchief round his eyes. Parents held up their children to watch.

Half a dozen men armed with hunting rifles lined up in front of the Town Hall. They raised their rifles: Fire! The shots rang out and Louis Monnier crumpled. His body twisted, shaken by the force of the bullets. He fell. One of the firing squad stepped forward. Dramatically he drew his revolver and fired one final bullet, to the head. It was for effect only. Louis Monnier was already dead.

The people of La Bastide, subjected for so long to Nazi tyranny, were delirious with joy. This was their doing. Power was now in their hands.

Joseph looked round. He caught sight of Marie Monnier, her thin features drawn rigid with terror. For a moment a hard smile touched his eyes, a malicious sense of sweet revenge. Then he recognised Janine: a little girl lost and bewildered, staring dry eyed at the body of her father. What had she done to deserve this?

EPILOGUE
August 1994: The 50th anniversary

The line of parked cars seemed endless. They were overwhelmingly local cars, from the Ariège or Aude departments, with 9 or 11 on the registration plate. There were a few from further afield, though even those were from no further than Toulouse or Montpellier.

Jean-Michel, Joseph's grandson, was making a survey of the cars, announcing his progress in a high, strident voice, but it meant nothing to the others, who had no idea what his survey involved. His younger sisters were playing horses, cantering with high, leaping steps, as they did in ballet classes. They had been practising through the house and the garden ever since they arrived. In Cherbourg they lived in a flat and they relished the space of their grandparents' home.

Other cars had already drawn up behind theirs and there was a steady stream of people moving along the forest track. How many were they expecting at the lunch? Two hundred was it Simone Vidal had said? There would be others, too, who had not booked for the lunch but would come for the opening of the museum.

At last they reached the path down to the cabin. Army engineers had done the work. The path was generously wide, the steep descent tailored into smart, wood-trimmed steps. The two elder children raced down, agile and excited, while Chantal held her mother's hand. It was a long, steep path twisting through the trees. Joseph walked slowly, unhappily aware that the walk back up would leave him breathless, with a pain in his chest.

He remembered when he had run along these paths, as his grandchildren were running now. How had the older men coped in those days? Men like Achille Cambon? Perhaps they had saved their strength and kept to the forest. But even within the forest, inside the camp, the paths between the cabins were unpleasantly steep for an older man. He caught Sophie, his wife, watching him. She was anxiously aware of his angina.

It was not his angina that worried him to-day. What had persuaded him to come to this circus? And why had be brought all the family? Elizabeth, his daughter, and the children had not minded but his son Robert had not been keen to come. Helen was there, his girl friend, and he would have would have liked to go off with her, the two of them on their own.

Joseph wondered if it was Helen who had persuaded Robert to come. She was interested in what had happened in the war. It was Helen who had noticed the avenue in La Bastide. Avenue Marius Peyrou. With the dates: 1932 - 1944. And the attribution: Hero of the Resistance. He would have liked that, Marius. Joseph remembered the day he had spent with his cousin, how he'd tried to impress the younger boy, how eager Marius had been to hear what they were doing in Luxat. Now Marius had an avenue named after him and a memorial at the roadside, above Festes, where the track led up to the farm. Children learned about him at school. They wrote essays, explaining what he had done.

At least he'd had that. They had taken his life. He'd had a brief childhood. When he died Marius had been not so much older than Jean-Michel was now. He had had no adult years. No experience of manhood, no maturity. He deserved his immortality, Joseph thought, with an angry shrug of his shoulders.

Helen had noticed the name plate on the avenue, the first time she went into La Bastide. She had read the name, quietly and curiously, then turned to him, a smile of pride and admiration hovering on her lips. "Peyrou? Was he one of your family?"

Why had Joseph not told her about Marius? He had shrugged, turned away, mumbled something incoherent. Helen had turned to Robert, who shook his head and grimaced. "Papa doesn't talk about his family. Goodness alone knows whether he was related to Marius Peyrou, Papa won't say. And Hero of the Resistance? Papa won't tell us what Marius did. He never talks about the war."

So why, after all these years, was he coming to this jamboree and dragging his family along?

They reached the end of the path. The old drop zone in front of the cabin had been cleared. The cabin itself, which six months ago had been no more than a pile of rubble overgrown with weeds and bushes, had been rebuilt. In the summer sunshine, the grey stone glowed with warmth, the roof tiles shone, brightly, red and cheerful. The old HQ was once more a hub of activity.

Old comrades, standard bearers with their flags, were directed to their appointed place, with hurried instruction. Cheerful greetings, anxious explanations, busy chatter, mingled with the music from loudspeakers.

Jean-Michel had his own concern. "There will be parachutes, won't there?"

They reassured him. "Yes. They're bringing the flag." Then spoilt it. "If the weather holds."

But they came. The colour party, led by their bugler, marched up to the cabin, left arm swinging smartly, right arm held across the chest, clutching a big black box of modern weaponry. They were fit, young, well-fed and smart, professionally trained for the job which Joseph and his friends had picked up as best they could, in constant fear of discovery.

The music ceased. The crowd quietened as they spotted the plane taking its bearings over the drop zone. They lit smoke flares to show them where to land.

"There! Look!" Sophie pointed into the sky. Joseph had been expecting the billowing silk umbrellas of fifty years ago. These parachutes fell, pencil-slim, and opened into a canopy like an inverted toboggan. They could see the men, walking through the air, coming in to land among the smoke. They touched down, somersaulted. Shrugging off the parachute harness, they delivered the flag. Jean-Michel watched, absorbed.

"Aux morts!" The standard bearers lowered their flags and the crowd stood in silence, heads bowed, as the bugler played the last post. "The Song of the Partisans!" The bugler played softly, trying not to drown the ragged efforts of the village choir.

"Ami! Si tu tombes
un ami sort de l'ombre
à ta place ..."

[Friend! If you fall, from the shadows will come a friend to take your place...]

A hymn of hope and determination, not a triumphant Te Deum of victory. Hesitantly, some of the older men joined in. Others began to hum quietly. Overwhelming the bugler and the little choir, the haunting melody echoed through the forest and across the open field.

Sophie put her arm round Joseph. Jean-Michel took his hand. He was weeping. Standing silent, immobile, tears streamed down his cheeks.

They listened quietly as Simone Vidal, Raoul's widow, thanked all those organisations and individuals who had helped to restore the cabin and establish the museum. She outlined the history of the Luxat maquis, remembering those who had not survived the war. She thanked everyone for coming, passed on news of those who were too ill to be with them. She outlined the current work of their organisation, including the schools' essay competition. Monsieur le Sous Préfet spoke briefly. Representatives of local and regional government had a few words to say but they were already setting up the tables, offering wine and soft drinks and the crowd was growing restless.

Inside the cabin, with surprisingly little formality, Jean-Paul Ramel distributed medals to the veterans of the war years. The Coste family was there. They exchanged news of retirement, of their children and grandchildren, slipping easily into an old intimacy.

The grandchildren enjoyed the day, playing in the forest. They understood also that this was something important for their grandfather. Helen was impressed. She spent a long time in the cabin, listening as old comrades pored over the photographs, recognising their friends, explaining who the people were and what they had done. She learnt that a young man had died in an ambush just below the camp, that the village had been burnt as the Germans left.

"I knew almost nothing about any of this," Robert exclaimed, bewildered. Why had his father not told them this history?

Joseph could see the admiration in their eyes, as they reappraised the man they knew and endowed his deeds with heroic stature. It was not what Joseph wanted. He had tried to play the hero once, with Marius. He had been young then and could smile now and forgive the boy he had been but he was a man, not a hero. They must not put him on a pedestal and expect too much of him.

It was Jean-Paul who touched him on the shoulder and took him quietly to one side.

"A problem," he said. "Auguste Monnier's turned up."

"Here?" Joseph was incredulous.

"No, not here. At the hotel in La Bastide. His mother's ill, old Marie Monnier. Dying. He's not there openly, under his own name. There's a chap staying at the hotel, apparently as an ordinary guest but the men in La Bastide are convinced it's Auguste. And they're out to get him."

For a moment Joseph closed his eyes. He rubbed his hand across his chin. He remembered the wooden coffin he had made. "You mean, they're going to kill him?"

Joseph avoided the hotel in La Bastide. If they wanted a meal out, he and Sophie would eat at the restaurant in Ste Agathe, or go to the lake, or drive into Mirepoix. If he was in La Bastide and wanted a drink he would go to the railway bar, still the favourite with veterans of the resistance. He had not set foot in the hotel since he returned to the south. But he knew the place was failing.

Marie Monnier had taken over when Louis's mother died, but she lacked the old woman's business sense and the family's war record was held against them. Janine had grown up with no men to temper the sourness of the two widows, her mother and her grandmother. She had succumbed, flattered, to the first man who paid her any attention, a philandering barman, who could not keep his hands off anything female and, when she fell pregnant, agreed to marry her in the hopes of inheriting a prosperous business. It was not in his scheme of things, though, to work to make the business prosper, or the marriage for that matter. It was not a happy family.

Joseph and Jean-Paul had met in the café Terminus. They were talking about Auguste's sister, Janine. "Her father had a roving eye, of course. And he was a weak man, got in with the wrong crowd during the war," the barman at the station café told Joseph. Then stopped, as he began to remember some story of Joseph's involvement with the family.

"Still, he was all right, was Louis," someone said, and they nodded, agreeing.

"Not this one, though. He's got a nasty streak."

"They say he's rough with his wife. Knocks her about."

"And the children. He's laid into them with a belt more than once when he's had too much to drink."

There was no great sympathy for the children, though. "Sylvie's a bit of a slut. The boy's a disaster. Spoilt by his mother and his grandmother. Stupid. Lazy. Befuddled with dope most of the time and probably takes the money for it from the hotel till."

It should have been music to Joseph's ears: the rout of his old enemies. Instead, he was disturbed by their misfortune. If they were prospering, he might have shrugged his shoulders and nursed his resentment but he had prospered while they had failed and he suffered qualms, wondered how far he might be responsible. Auguste was no loss to anyone but things would undoubtedly have been better for them if Louis had lived.

Jean-Paul's concern was more practical and immediate. "What are we going to do? If we do nothing, we shall simply wake up one morning and find a dead body in the street."

"Which might or might not be Auguste!" Joseph reminded him.

Joseph offered to check on the unknown guest. So next day Sophie, Robert and Helen were surprised to hear him suggest lunch at the Hotel du Commerce in La Bastide. As he ushered his family up the steps, he glanced with a wry smile at the plaque of the Avenue Marius Peyrou, so appropriately pinned to the wall of the hotel.

The entrance was gloomy. The tiles on the floor looked grubby. The reception desk, dark and poky, was thick with dust. The walls were covered with a dull, sepia design of bamboo shoots and leaves. In the bar the television was on but there were no customers and no-one waiting to serve them. They turned into the restaurant.

It was a big room, with space for fifty or more. Two clerks from the Credit Agricole, seated at a table near the window, were already well into their meal. At first Joseph thought they were the only customers. Then he saw someone else, in the gloom at the back of the restaurant, almost hidden behind the door where they were standing.

"Here!" Joseph stepped forward, pointing to the table next to the solitary guest. He held out a chair for Sophie and took the seat beside her, from which he could watch this man. Robert, showing Helen to her seat, shook his head in mute incomprehension. What was his father up to now?

A woman came, slow and unsmiling, to take their order. The cold meat was meagre, the salad tired, the dressing sweet and chemical. Paying no attention to his food, Joseph studied the man at the next table. Quite tall. Overweight. Scowling. It was difficult to distinguish his features in the dim light.

The waitress brought him a peach on a plate. That was when Joseph decided. As he watched this man sucking at that juicy peach, he remembered Auguste at the kitchen table, years ago, the way he sat, the way he ate. This man was Auguste. Without stopping to consider, Joseph got up from the table. At the door he paused. He spoke quietly.

"They know you're here, Auguste. They're going to get you. They're watching the hotel."

The man froze, every muscle tense. Joseph went out to the cloakroom. He was trembling. Had he threatened Auguste or warned him?

When he got back to his table, Auguste had gone. They waited a long time for their next course to arrive. It was cold and unappetising. The service was slow, incompetent, insultingly bad. They knew who he was and he was not welcome in the hotel.

"I can see why you haven't taken us there before," Sophie commented, dryly, as they left.

Joseph, who had hardly set foot inside a church since Maman died over forty years ago, was feeling the need for confession. Not the week-end confession of his childhood, mumuring half-imagined peccadilloes to a priest hidden in the confession box. He wanted to consider his life, to explain himself. To his family. If he was honest, he was perhaps seeking absolution, he thought.

He did not tell them where he was going. They got into the car and instead of driving back to Ste Agathe, he turned down beside the hotel, towards Festes, winding once more along the narrow road, coming out into the valley under the ruins of the square, medieval tower of the castle. He did not go into Festes, but circled round the village, passing the camp site and going out along the lane to Luxat.

Sophie was pleased. "So, we're going to Luxat," she said brightly, warning Robert to be gentle with his father.

It was a dismal, wet day, not raining, but with rain hanging in the air.

"A haar, they might call this in Scotland," said Joseph. "Almost." A haar is chilly though, and this day was wet and muggy.

He drove slowly through the tiny village and turned sharply up towards the hillside before stopping the car. "This was where I grew up," he said.

Helen got out of the car and the others followed. The house was small, neat, well-built. There was a woodpile to one side and a tent on the patch of ground beside the house, where the chickens used to roam. It looked like a summer holiday home now.

"The houses have all been rebuilt?" asked Helen.

Joseph nodded. "In the 1950s. After Maman died. She never saw the new place. After the war we just camped out here as best we could. Then when she died, I left. I never lived in this house."

He hurried back to the car. This was not his village. There were no children living here. All the permanent residents were old: in their seventies and eighties. The houses were occupied now, in August, but most of them were holiday homes. Joseph remembered the veillées, the evenings when the villagers gathered in each other's homes, to sing and tell stories and play games. He remembered the fun of Pig Day. It had all changed.

He set off again, up the steep, twisting lane, round the first bend. Then he stopped, as the lane twisted up once more, leaving the car on the broad sward at the edge of the cliff. They got out and looked down on the village at their feet, two rows of neat cubes, toy houses in a miniature village, on the edge of a fertile valley that stretched into the distance.

Joseph turned up, away from the village. The stone memorial was small, submerged by wreaths left by those who had come for the anniversary ceremonies.

The letter were roughly carved.
>
> Here died
> killed by German bullets,
> the "maquisard"
> Marcel Ferrie.

They read the inscription.

"This was the young man who was caught in the ambush?" asked Robert.

"He came from the village, didn't he?" Helen was quietly probing.

Joseph had brought them here to show them this. He wanted to tell them.

"Were you here with him?" Helen asked.

He shook his head. They waited. "I saw what happened, though. I was watching from the cliff top. From the look out point up there." Joseph gestured, vaguely, up to the left. It was difficult to talk now, after such a long silence.

"He came down to find out where the Germans were, when they began to encircle the camp."

It was Sophie who realised that Joseph had something more important to tell them.

"Who was this boy?" she asked.

"Marcel. My brother." They were stunned. Joseph had never mentioned a brother. He had told his family that he was fostered. He had spoken kindly of Maman and of Robert, the Scotsman who had helped him after Maman died.

"Marcel Ferrie." There was a question in Helen's reading of the name.

"My foster brother. We were both Public Assistance children. Madame Barthez, Maman, fostered us. She was very kind. She loved us. And we loved her,"

"Did you know who your natural parents were?" asked Helen.

Robert held his breath. He knew his father had been fostered. Anything beyond that had always been taboo.

"Yes. I knew," he said. "My mother came here once, during the war. She lived in Paris by then and when things got difficult there she came here, to the old family farm. She called in at Luxat to see me. Like a being from another world. So smart and polished." He smiled and his voice reflected remembered enthusiasm. "She gave me a bicycle." He turned to Helen. "She came from a farm near Festes. Marius Peyrou was her nephew. My cousin." As if excusing himself for not having claimed the relationship earlier, he added. "I only saw him once."

Joseph had worked in Paris. His family had grown up there.

"Did you ever see your mother, when you moved to Paris?" asked Helen.

"Yes." Joseph turned to his wife. "You knew her. We met at her house." She looked at him in surprise. "Madame Fournier."

Sophie was speechless. For her Madame Fournier had been simply an older woman, vaguely known to her husband because they came from the same part of France. She was smart, elegant. Prosperous. She seemed to like Joseph, the handsome young agent of a Scottish whisky company, who was a regular visitor at her house. Sophie thought back to those earlier days. Her father was a senior civil servant and she had always suspected that her parents had accepted her marriage to Joseph because he knew the Fourniers. But there had been no hint of a close relationship.

Joseph had called on Madame Fournier when he first went to Paris. So discreetly. As the son of some distant cousin from the south. They had never discussed their relationship. When he met Sophie and had children of his own, he had lost touch with his natural mother. She had never been close to him, like Maman.

"And your father?" asked Helen.

Joseph sighed. "That's enough, for now, I think. Later. Perhaps some other time I will tell you about my father."

That was the important part, of course. That was what he really wanted to explain. But he was exhausted. He had confessed enough for one day.

Auguste had disappeared. He was probably hiding somewhere inside the hotel, because Joseph had been right when he warned that they were watching the place and the watchers had not seen Auguste leave.

For the moment, though, Joseph wanted to forget the problems of Auguste and of the past. They took the children to Carcassonne and Joseph indulged Jean-Michel, buying him a set of medieval armour: sword, breastplate, helmet, made of hideous grey plastic. He put it all on and lunged happily, threatening with his horrid plastic sword. Sophie treated the girls to necklaces made of wooden beads that spelt out their names. They bought huge, delicious ice cream cones, smothered in whirling cream and chocolate sauce, and they left before the children had time to grow irritable. They put up the paddling pool in the garden and Elizabeth, the children's mother, provided plastic bottles and water guns and the children sat playing for hours. They even persuaded Uncle Robert and Helen to join them.

Sophie and Joseph liked Helen. "Just the right girl for Robert, much better than his previous girl friends," Sophie decided. "So I shan't say a word. It kills romance if his mother says she likes the girl." They laughed.

"Madame Fournier liked you," Joseph told her, glad that he could share this now with his wife.

"Well, I was special."

"Still are," he declared, loyally.

The Ste Agathe fête was that week-end. They watched huge lorries and trailers drive down towards the village square. On Saturday the sound system was being set up and all through the afternoon they could hear the music throbbing in the distance. In the evening they went down to see what was happening.

The children rode on the roundabouts and tried the games. The lights were garish, the things for sale were tawdry and over priced. Elizabeth let the children have burgers and chips for their supper, with coke to drink, and they all thoroughly enjoyed themselves. When the others left, Robert and Helen stayed on to join in the dancing.

It was hot. At home Sophie and Joseph sat outside for a long time, talking, watching the lightning in the distance, hoping that the storm would come to Ste Agathe and clear the air. They could hear the throbbing of the music and knew that sleep would not come easily.

They were asleep, though, when someone came to the door. The music had stopped. The knocking was insistent.

"Monsieur Peyrou?" the man asked, when Joseph answered the door. "Joseph Peyrou?"

He nodded.

The visitor spoke slowly and gently. He did not want to cause panic. "There's been an accident. Your son has been hurt. I was with him at the time and I thought you might like to come."

Sophie appeared, sleepy, rubbing her eyes, frowning at the brightness of the light. "What's the matter? Is something wrong?"

Joseph moved away from the door and found a chair. He did not answer her. Immediately practical, she thought of his angina, fetched a tablet. "Here. Take this." Joseph did as he was told and gestured to the stranger to explain.

It was the mayor of La Bastide. He offered to take them to see Robert at the clinic. Quickly they dressed, reassured Elizabeth and hurried out. Joseph tripped and stumbled, sprawling into the car.

As they went through the village they drove slowly through the thinning crowds. They crossed the narrow bridge. In the square the band was packing up, reeling in the electric wiring, dismantling the sound system. The party was over. The lights, no longer cheerful, cast eerie shadows. The night bleached all colour from the scene. It was like an old, silent film: black and white, the definition unclear, the movements simple but unfluent.

A few small groups, talking together, caught up by the drama, lingered uneasily and watched as they turned on to the road and picked up speed.

It was hot. The day had been relentlessly sunny and airless and night had brought no relief. Joseph fumbled for a handkerchief, took off his glasses and mopped his brow. He dabbed at his eyes. Beside him Sophie quietly took his hand. "Oh, God!" He fought off the image of Marcel, the memory of the dark room in the cottage, with Marcel lying on the table, covered with Maman's sheet. Panic overwhelmed him as, in his distraught imagination, the pale, thin body of Marcel was overlaid with images of Robert.

A crash of thunder drowned Joseph's choking sob. The storm, which had been rolling round the hills all night, finally reached them. Rain beat noisily on the roof of the car and cascaded down, swamping the windscreen wipers.

Already they were passing the hoardings, the supermarkets and petrol stations that announced the approaching town. They circled the market place and drew up outside the hospital.

Joseph stumbled from the car. As they pushed their way through the doors they saw Helen waiting in the foyer. She turned towards them, her face pale and strained. Sophie took her in her arms and they clung together, sharing a deep, silent dread.

The mayor of La Bastide shuffled uneasily. "I'll go now," he said, but stayed a moment before adding: "I'm sorry. I do hope he'll be all right."

"Did he come and call you?" asked Helen.

"Yes. We couldn't sleep ... the heat ... the music. He said Robert had been shot."

Helen tried to explain.

"Why Robert?" asked Sophie.

"I don't know. Robert didn't recognize him. He wasn't from Ste Agathe. From La Bastide someone said. He simply wouldn't leave us alone."

Joseph felt a moment of icy apprehension.

"Whenever we were dancing he would bump into us or try to kick Robert. Then when we sat down, he came up and made loud comments. Then he started shouting at us." Helen sighed. "Then he went away and we thought that was the end of it. That man ... the mayor from La Bastide came up and was very sympathetic and said he'd never been anything but trouble." Helen's voice fell to a whisper. "Then he came back. With a gun. And he just stood there and pointed it at Robert. And shot him." She flicked back her hair. "Why?" she cried. "What had Robert ever done to him?"

Joseph tried to speak but could find no words to say. He was angry. How dare anyone hurt his son! How dare they touch his family! He was frightened, too. Was Robert going to be all right?

They had not noticed the approach of the nurse who with professional kindness invited them to follow her. The consultant was ready to see them now.

The corridor was pale, insipid, modern. In the doctor's office there were bright red covers on the chairs and an African violet struggled to add colour to the window ledge. But the desk was covered with papers, a trolley laden with instruments filled the space between the desk and the window. The room was untidy and uncomfortable.

The doctor spoke quietly. "I'm sorry," he said. "He is not well. The injuries could be serious. He was shot in the thigh and has lost a lot of blood. We've ligated the blood vessel and we've stopped the blood loss but there's an abdominal wound also and we can't operate on that until his blood pressure is restored."

"May we see him?" Joseph asked.

"Of course. But he looks pretty bad at the moment. He's only just come from the operating theatre. He's still unconscious and he's tied up to tubes."

"Tubes?" Helen queried.

"Yes. He's lost a lot of blood. He's on a drip. And a naso-gastric tube. And a catheter."

Joseph was not sure that Helen understood the medical terms. She was English, though her French was fluent. Not that it mattered. The words were clinical, distanced from ordinary life and real meaning.

Softly they went in to see Robert. Pale, ghostly, surrounded by bottles, drips and tubes he lay unconscious and unmoving. Joseph touched his son's shoulder, hardly daring to lay the pressure of his hand upon this fragile body. He murmured words of comfort and reassurance. He was there. He would not leave him. His will, his love, must save his son. There had been too much death. This life must not be lost.

Helen bent and took his limp hand in hers, briefly brushed her lips against the pale, chill brow. "I love you," she said, speaking softly in English.

They stayed at Robert's bedside. Through the long hours before the sun brought the light of a new day and the birds began their morning chorus, they sat together. From time to time they spoke to each other or to Robert, trying to let him know that they were there with him. They heard the first movement of the day as cafés opened on the square.

As the town came to life Robert began to stir. Drifting in and out of consciousness, he shifted restlessly, muttered incoherently. The nurses checked his progress. The doctor returned. It seemed that Robert's blood pressure was restored. The doctor explained that they would take a look at the second, abdominal wound. They would do a laparotomy.

Sophie went home to get some rest and prepare food for their return. Promising to ring as soon as they had news, Joseph stayed with Helen. Throughout that long morning, as the heat of the day increased, their waiting seemed endless. They had nothing to say for they were too tired to talk and too concerned for the outcome of the operation to turn their minds to any other, more trivial subject.

At last the waiting was over. The bullet, it seemed, had gone through the bowel and lodged against the pancreas. The surgeon had joined the torn bowel. If the pancreas was damaged it would be serious but he had seen no evidence of such damage. They would be draining the area and keeping an eye on Robert's progress. They must wait and hope. Kindly, the young doctor advised them to go home. They could return later, in the evening. They all needed a few hours sleep. They would need strength and patience for the next few weeks as they waited and hoped that Robert might recover.

The police officer who called to interview Helen told them that Daniel Armand, who had attacked Robert, was the son of Janine Monnier from the Hotel du Commerce at La Bastide.

"He asked whether I knew of any reason for the attack. I said I didn't," Helen told his parents.

"But you think we might, don't you?" Sophie suggested.

"I think it might have something to do with what happened here during the war."

They both looked at Joseph. He had to tell them. He spoke slowly, choosing his words with care. He needed to explain, but to tell them simply how it had been, what had happened. He didn't want to flood them with emotion. He didn't want to rekindle those terrible emotions of his childhood and his youth.

"As a little boy, I loved Louis Monnier, the father of this boy's mother," he explained. "I didn't need a mother, I had one. I was looking for a father figure and I chose Louis Monnier. Who let me down. His son and his wife hated me and he did nothing to protect me from them.

"Then the war came and I found another father figure: Robert, the soldier from Scotland. When we took him in, we took sides, against the Germans and against the Vichy government. Louis Monnier welcomed German soldiers to the hotel. Worse, he betrayed Robert - and Maman and Marcel and me, by telling the police where he was hiding. At least ..." This was difficult for Joseph. "At least I thought he did." Joseph spoke so softly they had to strain to hear him. "I'm not so sure now. He tried to tell me that he hadn't betrayed Robert."

"I learnt that Louis Monnier was my natural father. And when the war ended I stood in the street outside the Town Hall, opposite the hotel and I was in the crowd that accused him of collaborating. I was part of the crowd. They couldn't find his son, so they took Louis Monnier. And shot him."

Joseph remembered the scene, only too well. "I hated him. I wanted him to suffer." It was too painful. Joseph wept. Not silently as he had wept at the anniversary celebrations but with loud, wracking sobs. Sophie brought him a glass of water.

"You don't have to explain," Helen told him.

"Yes I do. You see, I hated him but I loved him too. I didn't want to hurt him." He shook his head. He tried to explain what it had been like that day. Marcel had been killed in the ambush, the village had been burnt, there was constant news of German atrocities.

"And it was Auguste we were looking for. Auguste Monnier, Louis's son. He was a thug. It was he who tortured and killed Marius. That's why they chose that street to carry his name: to remind the Monnier family of what Auguste had done." Joseph took a sip of water. "If Auguste had been there, we would have killed him. Rightly. He deserved it. But Auguste wasn't there and we killed his father.

"When Monsieur Vidal heard what had happened at La Bastide he was furious. He said we had struggled for years against the Germans and the French collaborators because they were brutal, sadistic tyrants. Then we'd shaved the head of a helpless young woman and paraded her through the steets and we'd killed a prisoner of war and shot Louis Monnier without any trial. And I felt that I had betrayed what we had fought for."

They tried to comfort him, to reassure him that they understood, to remind him that everything had been confused at that time and he had suffered so much. "I know," he protested. "I know I didn't shoot Louis Monnier. Perhaps I couldn't have prevented it. But I didn't try. I shouted with the crowd and for a moment I wanted them to kill him. I know, we can understand why it happened, why I did it. But it's still a terrible thing to have done.

"And look at the consequences. I had Maman to look after me. She thought I'd been terribly wrong but she still loved me. When Maman died, Robert came over from Scotland, just to see me. Invited me to stay with his family in Scotland. After my military service I spent a year there with him and I worked for him. He got me a job in Paris.

"There were people around who cared for me and saved me from despair. Nobody bothered about Janine and her mother.

"They must have hated me. I was Louis Monnier's bastard, his son by a servant girl. When Marius died I made a miniature coffin and sent it to Auguste, to show that we meant to kill him when the Liberation came. And I signed it. I wanted them to know that this was personal. And when we couldn't find Auguste I shouted that Louis was a collaborator. That Louis had betrayed Robert, the British soldier. 'Kill him! Kill him!' I shouted. For all these years they must have hated me and blamed me for Louis's death and for their failures."

Sophie and Helen protested. "You aren't responsible for everything that went wrong for them."

"Things were not so very easy for you."

"That crowd in La Bastide didn't kill Auguste, though. We killed his father. And Daniel didn't shoot me. He shot Robert." Robert, his son, for whom he would willingly have died.

The veterans of Luxat wanted to hear what Joseph had to say about the man at the hotel. They respected Joseph. He had been in the resistance right from the start, from the 'première heure' as they said. And he was the cousin of Marius, whom Auguste had killed, the father of Robert, a man who had been shot by Auguste's nephew.

Jean-Paul came to ask Joseph what he thought they should do. First, though, he asked after Robert.

"He seems to be doing well. They've removed the tubes and he's awake. Weak, but improving. He's taking sips of water. We're hopeful." For a moment a flash of happiness appeared on Joseph's face. "He seems glad to have Helen around, too."

So, what should they do about Auguste? "We could hand him over to the law. There would be a long trial and he would be sent to jail. Or we do nothing. Eventually he leaves the hotel."

"We all know what happens then. Someone comes along with a gun and bumps him off. That's a death sentence," said Joseph.

"Well, there isn't any other alternative, is there?"

Joseph was not sure. "We could help him to get away. He's been hiding somewhere all these years. We help him get away to Toulouse or Montpellier or somewhere and then it's up to him."

Jean-Paul looked at him in amazement. "You must be joking!"

"No. I mean it."

"Why?"

"I'm not proud of the part I played in his father's death at the end of the war. Atonement, perhaps," said Joseph. "And Robert, of course. I've had enough of revenge. I'll opt for mercy. For charity."

Jean-Paul grinned. "When?"

"To-night?"

That night, Jean-Paul and Joseph drove into La Bastide. They went up the steps of the Hotel du Commerce and made their way to the bar. The place was empty but Jean-Paul went through to the back with a letter for Auguste.

Half an hour later the watchers opposite saw the two men get into the car and leave. They were surprised when Madame Peyrou went into the hotel next morning and left with her husband. They had not noticed him when she arrived. Still, it was not the Peyrou family they were watching.

It was some days before they realised Auguste had got away. They suspected that Joseph and Jean-Paul had something to do with the escape and in the weeks that followed when they'd had a few drinks, they would get angry and rage against two men, who called themselves leaders of the veterans but had helped a brutal war criminal escape from justice.

But Simone Vidal did not complain and everyone knew that Jean-Paul Ramel and Joseph Peyrou had played an honourable part in the French war against tyranny and injustice.

Revenge and Regret is dedicated

to all those who worked with the resistance in France,

particularly those of the Maquis de Picaussel

and to the memory of

Jean Carbou

Joseph Lebret

Auguste Cathala

The author wishes to acknowledge the help of

Françoise Maury, Marius Plantier and François Deloustal

and, though she did not meet him, Lucien Maury, who led the

Maquis de Picaussel and whose two volumes of

La Résistance audoise were

an invaluable source

of information and inspiration

THE MAQUIS DE PICAUSSEL

In Corsica a man who needs to hide disappears into the wild scrubland, 'takes to the maquis'.

So, in wartime France, 'the maquis' became a name for the resistance.

The origins of the Maquis de Picaussel sprang from a mistake in March 1943 when an RAF pilot dropped his parachutes in the wrong place. Four young men from the village of Lescale rescued as much as they could and Lucien Maury, the village schoolmaster, made contact with the Armée Secrète.

Forced into hiding, Lucien Maury and his colleague Marius Olive, found refuge in a cave near Lescale. By the summer of 1944 they had established a camp in the forest of Picaussel, above Lescale.

There were almost 400 maquisards living in the camp when the Germans moved in to attack on 6th August 1944.

Two young men from Lescale, Jean Carbou and Joseph Lebret, two of those who had rescued the first parachutes, went down to investigate. On the way back up to the camp they were caught in an ambush and killed.

That night five RAF planes dropped additional supplies and the next day the Maquis de Picaussel fought off an attack by the German army. The end of the battle and the fate of the maquisards and of the village of Lescale are described in the novel Revenge and Regret.

To celebrate the 50th anniversary of the German attack, the ruins of the old HQ were restored as a memorial to the Maquis de Picaussel.

LUXAT

Readers of the novel Revenge and Regret will recognise that the Maquis de Picaussel provided the inspiration for the Maquis de Luxat.

Some of the events are taken from the history of the Maquis de Picaussel. The end of the battle which this maquis fought against the Germans and the fate of the maquisards and of the village of Lescale happened as they are described in the novel.

But Revenge and Regret is a novel. Much of the action is fiction. The events following the German attack, described in the chapters about the Liberation and the Settling of Accounts, are entirely fictional.

The characters also are characters of fiction and bear no relation to any people who lived in Lescale or were part of the Maquis de Picaussel.

CHRONOLOGY

1939
1st September Germany invades Poland
3rd September France and Britain send an ultimatum to Germany

1940
10th May   Churchill becomes Prime Minister
               Germany invades Holland and Belgium
15th May   Dutch army surrenders
26th May   Evacuation from Dunkirk begins
28th May   Belgium surrenders
10th June   French government leaves Paris
14th June   German army enters Paris
16th June   Pétain calls for an end to fighting
18th June   BBC broadcasts de Gaulle's call for France to continue fighting
1st July   French government moves to Vichy
3rd July   Britain destroys the French fleet at Mers El Kébir
10th July   Pétain becomes Head of State under a new constitution

1941
22nd June   Germany invades Russia
7th December   Japan attacks Pearl Harbour
11th December Germany and Italy declare war on United States

1942
22nd June — Laval declares that he hopes for a German victory
30th June — Mgr Saliège, bishop of Toulouse, protests at the treatment of Jews
4th September — Conscription of French youths to work in Germany
23rd October — Battle of El Alamein
8th Novermber — Allied troops land in North Africa
11th November — German troops occupy southern France

1943
30th May — De Gaulle goes to Algeria
3rd September — British troops land in Italy
10th December — French troops engaged on the Italian front

1944
25th March — French maquis engaged at Glières
6th June — Allied landings in Normandy
21-23 July — Maquis de Vercors destroyed
12-16 August — FFI liberate 14 French departments
14th August — US and French troops land in Provence
20th August — FFI liberate Toulouse
Pétain leaves Vichy
25th August — De Gaulle arrives in Paris

1945
30th April — Hitler commits suicide
7th May — German army surrenders unconditionally at Reims
8th May — La Rochelle liberated
Victory is celebrated

"At last I understand what happened in France during the war."
Alison Borissow

"A good story."
Frank Carter

"I'd been an au pair in Biarritz and I'd travelled around the foothills of the Pyrenees. And I could see it. When I read the descriptions, I was there."
Sarah Brown

"When I read it again, I wasn't expecting to be so moved. I knew what was going to happen. And I still cried."
H C

Cover design by big squid, Bristol
Front cover: Liberation parade of the
Marquis de Picaussel
Back cover: The author, aged 11, in Belesta in 1947

ORDER FORM

Please send me ☐ copies of Revenge and Regret

☐   £14.95 a copy UK postage included

☐   £15.95 a copy including European postage

☐   £17.45 a copy including world wide postage

Name_____

Address _____

_____

Postcode_____ Tel: _____

I enclose a sterling cheque payable to

Camdale Press 4 Thorndale Bristol BS8 2HU   ☐

Please charge my credit card:
Type of card _____

Signature_____

Credit card number: Expiry date _____/_____

☐☐☐☐ ☐☐☐☐ ☐☐☐☐ ☐☐☐☐ ☐☐☐

Issue number (Switch only) ☐☐